Playing with my Heart Strings

also by h.k. green

The Road and The Rodeo

Standalones

Short Stories and Novellas

Playing with my Heart Strings

H.K. GREEN

Editing by Andrea Halland, Editing by Andrea

Cover Design by Sam Palencia, Ink & Laurel

Formatting by H.K. Green

Paperback ISBN: 979-8-9909156-4-0

To anyone who's been told their dreams aren't worthwhile.
Prove them wrong.

setlist

Hey Mr. Nashville | Charley Crockett

You Ain't Dolly (And You Ain't Porter) | Ashley Monroe

Cowboys on Music Row (ft. Carter Faith) | Lauren Watkins

(You're The) Devil in Disguise | Elvis Presley

Someone New | Hozier

Jackson | Johnny Cash and June Carter Cash

I Wish You Would (ft. Midland) | Mackenzie Carpenter

I'm Gonna Love You | Cody Johnson and Carrie Underwood

Over My Head | FLETCHER

Maybe It Was Memphis | Pam Tillis

I Know Places (Taylor's Version) | Taylor Swift

scared of my guitar | Olivia Rodrigo

Hell on Heels | Pistol Annies

A Life Where We Work Out | Flatland Cavalry and Kaitlin Butts

reckless driving | Lizzy McAlpine and Ben Kessler

Ain't Nothing 'Bout You | Brooks & Dunn

Supercut | Lorde

15 Minutes | Sabrina Carpenter

Burning House | Cam

Crazy | Patsy Cline and The Jordanaires

High | Stephen Sanchez

9 to 5 | Dolly Parton

Don't Mind If I Do (ft. Ella Langley) | Riley Green

Dancing With Our Hands Tied | Taylor Swift

Worst Way | Riley Green

The Devil You Know | X Ambassadors

The Chain | Fleetwood Mac

Slow Dancing in a Burning Room | John Mayer

Siren sounds (bonus) | Tate McRae

The Aftermath | Carter Faith

I Love You, I'm Sorry | Gracie Abrams

Only Love Can Hurt Like This | Paloma Faith

Linger | The Cranberries

If You're Gonna Break My Heart | LEW

Ghost Town | Benson Boone

She Knows (feat. Amber Coffman & Cults) | J. Cole

Suspicious Minds | Elvis Presley

Come A Little Closer | Dierks Bentley

All That Ever Mattered | HAIM

I Got A Problem | Drake Milligan

author's note

Playing With My Heart Strings is a romantic comedy, and though it is fairly lighthearted in nature compared to my other novels, the book contains mature themes, explicit language, and sexual content. If you wish to skip the spice, please refer to the closed door modifications in the back of the book. I've tried to provide page numbers and scenes for the best reading experience, but skipping some chapters will unfortunately cause you to miss important story elements.

Playing With My Heart Strings takes place on a reality dating competition show, and the male main character, Dusty, is dating multiple women at once. However, besides two occurrences of on-camera kissing, there is no explicit sexual content with anyone other than the female main character.

Additional contents include:
• Alcohol Consumption
• Manipulation

prologue

Heart Strings

dusty

one month ago

THE CONFERENCE ROOM in my record label's main office crackles with tension. I sit at one end of the long rosewood table, the president of the label sitting at the head, and various other men in suits lining the sides. A meeting with the entire board is rarely a positive thing, but I roll my shoulders and straighten my posture, hoping it gives me the confidence boost I desperately need.

"Gentlemen," I acknowledge them as my manager Craig follows closely behind, taking a seat at the corner of the table. "Let's get down to business, shall we?" I'm not keen to apologize for my impatience, even as mutters rise through the conference room.

Rob Acerra, president of Ace High Entertainment, stands, and if my tone phases him at all, he doesn't show it. "As I'm sure we all know, Dusty, your music isn't hitting the charts like we need it to. You've been stagnant, and it's been weeks since you've had a song in the top one hundred. We need you in a better position here." He stares at me with a steel expression.

"Rob, with all due respect—" Craig starts to protest, but Rob holds up a hand.

"The label has put a lot of thought into this. We don't believe a solo career is the best move for you."

I side-eye Craig, my eyebrows pinching in confusion. We assumed the meeting wouldn't be amazing, but we weren't expecting anything like this. "What are you suggesting?"

"We think the best move for you, and for the company, is a duo. Think Brooks & Dunn, Johnny Cash and June Carter, Faith Hill and Tim McGraw," Rob explains. He must see the puzzled look on my face when he mentions only one male duo, because he continues. "Listeners don't just want anyone in a duo. They want sparks, chemistry. *Love.*"

Love? What the hell does Rob know about love?

"That's not really my brand." I wrinkle my nose a bit. I'm not a *love* guy.

"That's not your brand *yet.*" Rob smirks. "This is a non-negotiable, Dusty. Either you do what we say, or you're out."

Nothing about this was outlined in my contract, and if I'm going to be making better music, the last thing I should be doing is worrying about someone else. Rob can be merciless, though. I'm not gambling with my future, so despite being unconvinced by this new strategy that will supposedly get me topping the charts, I ask, "All right, well, how do you suggest I find my so-called 'other half,' then?"

"I thought you'd never ask." He sits, leaning forward and resting his hands on the table. "We host a competition of sorts. We allow women to send in their demos then narrow it down to say, thirty, who you will get to listen to. Only you won't see their faces, just what they sound like. From those thirty, you'll choose ten who you'd like to get to know better and potentially perform with. See if you have chemistry, on stage *and* on camera."

"Hold your horses there, Rob. Cameras?" I interrupt.

"Well, yeah. It'd be televised, of course. Viewers *and listeners* will eat this shit up." He says it like I'm stupid, as though I'm a child being lectured.

"Hmph," I grumble. "All right, continue."

"There will be eliminations each week based on your connections. Viewers will also have voting power to save one woman at risk of elimination based on what they see. In the last four weeks, we'll host live concerts—a mini tour, you could say—and the final woman you choose will not only get a spot at the record label, but you'll perform together as a duo, record an album, and go on tour." He smiles as he crosses his arms, leaning back in his chair.

"So, what, you want me to be some kind of quasi-country-music Bachelor?" I scratch my head, trying to wrap my mind around this crazy idea.

"Exactly! Now you're getting it. Like I said earlier, Dusty, this is non-negotiable if you want to stay at Ace High Entertainment." He shifts forward again, resting his elbows on the table as his expression shifts away from his normally charming attitude to something more…tyrannic. "We've already got our thirty women chosen for the show. We start filming in a month."

1
baylor

Who Needs Twelve Cowboy Hats?

present day

"ALL RIGHT, EVERYONE, *LISTEN UP*!" Colette St. James, the executive producer of the new reality dating show I'm working for, calls out, her sharp demeanor all business. Camera crew members, sound techs, hair and makeup artists, public relations—which includes me—and interns all circle around her. "Our lead will be here this afternoon! We'll go over logistics and details to ensure filming goes smoothly, then tomorrow we'll start filming with all the women!"

"She's so loud," Daniella Marshall, my best friend and roommate, whispers in my ear, and I cover my mouth to keep quiet. "I'm not sure why she feels the need to scream when we're all right here."

"You think she was a drill sergeant in a past life?" I purse my lips to prevent a laugh from slipping out.

"Oh my God, Bay!" Daniella snorts, and all eyes shoot in our direction.

I exchange a panicked look with Daniella, and we both put our heads down in embarrassment.

Colette *is* loud, though, that's just the truth. There's no denying it. She commands every room she's in, although I'm not sure if it's because she's respected or feared. Most likely the latter.

"As I was saying…" Colette shoots us a glare that has everyone avoiding eye contact. "Dusty will be here this afternoon. We'll need to get some preliminary shots of him, he'll do some interviews with the PR team, and then we'll go from there."

No one says a word or dares to move until Colette barks out, "Dismissed!" Then everyone disperses to continue on with whatever task they were doing before Sergeant—I mean, Colette—called the meeting.

"So, Dusty Wilder." Daniella nudges me with her elbow as we walk through the studio. "I hear he's quite the heartthrob."

"I've heard he's quite an asshole." I shrug her off. I have no interest in a country singer, much less Dusty Wilder. I've seen all I've needed to in the media. Dusty Wilder is the type of man who thinks he's God's gift to the Earth.

As we pass by my desk, I grab a notepad and pen to prepare for interviews later this afternoon.

When I graduated with a public relations degree from Auburn, I never imagined I'd be working on reality dating shows. In fact, it was the *last* thing I was hoping to do. I imagined my path would be more aligned with politics on Capitol Hill, not rich influencers looking for their fifteen minutes of fame on prime-time TV.

I applied for the job with Sparks Studio Productions a few years ago because, let's face it, I was desperate. I'd spent months trying to get a job in Washington with no success. In my defense, I didn't know I would be working on reality TV. I assumed I would be doing public relations for movies or, I don't know, a show like *CSI* or *House of Cards*. Perhaps that was naive of me, but I needed a job and the company promised a competitive salary. Besides, maybe if I do good enough work here, I'll have credible references and the ability to move on quickly.

"What? You don't think he's even a bit attractive?" Daniella raises her brows.

"I mean, sure, he's easy on the eyes, but—"

She's smiling at me in this Cheshire Cat sort of way. "So you *would* date him!"

I scoff, shaking my head. "I definitely did not say that. Besides, I value my job way more than a date with some country singer whose music isn't even that good."

"If you say so, Baylor. Me, on the other hand? I'd totally snatch him up if I had any kind of musical talent." She winks as we get to the set where the crew will film the preliminary shots for the show.

Large windows stretch floor to ceiling in the studio, and although filming is closed to the public, it doesn't stop fans from crowding the glass to see whatever so-called heartthrob is in front of the camera.

Camera crew members are already walking around to set up equipment, and designers fly by with racks of clothing. Pearl snap shirts, suit jackets, racks and racks of… cowboy hats. Who the fuck needs *twelve* cowboy hats? Apparently, he's not only an asshole, he's a pretty boy, too. *Great.*

"Marshall! Sommerfeld! Get over here!" Nails on a chalkboard scrape through my ears. *Oh wait, no, it's just Colette's voice.*

Daniella rolls her eyes at me before we head in her direction.

"What's up, Colette?" Daniella asks. When Colette calls you over by name, she's either delivering fantastic or horrible news. There's no in-between.

"I need one of you to take the lead on interviews with Dusty. The other one will move over to the social media team for now," she instructs, thrusting binders into both of our arms. When we open our mouths to ask her who she wants to do what, she makes a gesture with her hand to cut us off. "I don't care who takes what, I just need it done!"

Fantastic news: neither of us are getting fired for our disruption during the meeting. Horrible news: there's a chance I'll have to work directly with Dusty. Translation: Daniella will try to make me take the lead on interviews with him as some kind of matchmaking scheme.

"I already know what you're going to say," I mutter as I look at her. She's practically beaming.

"Nope, actually. I think you should take social media on this one," she replies, and I'm immediately suspicious. Daniella is always trying to set me up with someone, and I wouldn't have thought this situation would be any different.

"Hmm…okay." I won't argue with her, as skeptical as I am.

"Listen, babe, you said it yourself. You wouldn't date Dusty, so why on Earth would I pass up the opportunity to spend time with him? Right?" She tries to justify why she volunteered to take the job I didn't want, when normally she would be metaphorically throwing me to the wolves. I love our friendship, cherish it more than any other friendship I've made here in Nashville, but she can be a lot sometimes.

"All right, Dani, whatever you say." I swap binders with her, taking the one that says *Heart Strings Social Media Guide*.

The job is easy enough. Write copy for socials, make sure the photos the photographers get to us are good, and take B-roll footage for stories. When I was in college, I was the social media manager for several different companies throughout Alabama. When I first moved to Nashville, my job was social media focused, and then a year ago, I took this job. Long story short, this is my bread and butter. It's what I'm good at, so maybe that's why Dani let me take the reins on this. But at the same time, she has the same, if not more, experience than I do with two additional years in the industry.

I'm sure she has some kind of ulterior motive—usually she's pushing me toward a celebrity who she deems "hot" in the hopes that sparks will fly between us—but I can't worry about that right now. Reality TV doesn't stop for skeptics like myself. Personally, I wouldn't attempt to find love in front of cameras with the entire country watching, but to each their own. And yes, I say *attempt*. Because, realistically, how many of these relationships actually work out? Not that many.

With a crew of over two hundred members, *Heart Strings* is no small production. Especially with how the show will be run, all hands are needed. Episodes air the same week they're filmed to allow for live viewer voting. If the team can pull this off, I'm sure the show could take off.

My thoughts are interrupted by squeals from some of the hair, makeup, and wardrobe girls followed by cheers and claps from the camera crew. I look to my left toward the hallway Daniella and I had just come through to find Dusty Wilder walking in our direction.

The fans aren't completely crazy for finding him

attractive with his tall stature, sable hair that sweeps under the brim of his cowboy hat, five o'clock shadow, and thick mustache. Hazel eyes meet mine, and a dimple appears as Dusty cracks a small grin toward me. I raise my eyebrows, and his smile falters before he moves on.

Yeah, buddy, that charm doesn't work on me, sorry. Move along.

Daniella, on the other hand, practically has hearts shooting from her eyes as he tips his hat then heads over to talk to Colette and the director of the show.

"What?" She looks at me with zero remorse for practically undressing *the lead of the show we work for* with her eyes.

"Nothing, Dani, it's just that maybe you should have put in an application based on the look on your face right now," I tease.

"Like I said, Bay. I would have jumped on that train so fast if I had a shred of musical talent. If I had half the voice you have."

Daniella is one of few people who have ever heard me sing. It's a rare occasion for me to sing around other people. And it's never anything original, just covers of old country songs.

"I'm not made to be a singer, really."

"What about those songs you've written, then?" she asks.

"What songs?"

"The ones in that journal you're always carrying around."

Oh. That.

"Those aren't songs. They're just poems or whatever. It's nothing special. Not compared to some of the girls who applied to be on the show, that's for sure."

I'm not even saying this to win pity points or anything.

It's a known fact. Several of the applications came from singer-songwriters whose careers aren't quite at the level they want them to be. Since the winner of the show not only gets a record deal, but also gets to go on tour with Dusty as a duo, it's a no-brainer for them to at least try.

"Baylor, you have talent. I swear, I'm not just saying this because I'm your friend."

"Well, now I definitely think you're just saying it because you're my friend. It's not like I could apply—we're about to start filming. Not to mention I *work* here. That's a huge conflict of interest, even if I *wanted* to go on the show."

"Yeah, I guess you're right." Her shoulders drop for a split second before she quickly composes herself. "It's too bad, though. You really are talented."

I know I have talent. But musical talent doesn't pay the bills unless you have the same kind of status that Dusty has. And even then, it's rare to make a living off just music. There's a reason they're called *starving artists*.

My parents were disappointed enough when I decided on a public relations degree. Coming from a family of doctors, it made sense, but I was never meant for that path. It was evident when I struggled through anatomy class in high school. I can't do blood. Or any kind of internal organs. That's why I need to get to Capitol Hill. I need to prove that my degree is worth something—that *I'm* worth something.

Would I try to pursue music if there was a guaranteed payoff? Maybe. Probably. But that's a dream that will never come true. I don't need it to.

Colette has Dusty set up in front of cameras, while Daniella is there to assist. She's not so much tasked with interviewing him as she is writing down his answers for press releases, and in some cases, coaching him with his answers. You'd think he'd be a pro at interviews, considering he's constantly in the public eye, but no. He's awkward in front of the camera, brash and pointed with his responses, and he keeps getting distracted by the fans crowding the windows outside.

"Dusty, what are your thoughts about finding not only a musical partner, but potentially a life partner, on the show?" one of the producers asks him.

"I, uh, I don't have high hopes, honestly," he grumbles with a frown. "I'm only here because my label forced me to be here."

"Cut!" the director shouts.

"Can you at least act a little excited about this?" Daniella squeezes the bridge of her nose as she, yet again, coaches him on how to provide a more TV-appropriate answer. Her head turns toward me as she shakes it, clearly regretting taking on this task.

I avoid eye contact with her as I walk away, pretending to be busy with something else. I know I'll have to deal with him eventually to get social media content, but I don't envy Daniella at this moment.

2
dusty

Can't Trust a Drunk Girl

I CROSS my arms over my chest as the producers ask me yet another question about why I wanted to be on the show. *I didn't.* But saying the only reason you're here is because someone forced you to be is apparently not reality TV worthy. Ironic, considering that *is* my reality right now.

"Maybe if we get some shots of you playing guitar, that'll be more natural for you?" the blonde woman who's been trying to tell me how to answer these ridiculous questions suggests.

"I think that's a great idea! Someone get him a guitar!" the obnoxiously loud executive producer orders one of the film crew members. Her hair is bleached far too light, and she's got on this cherry-red lipstick that makes her resting bitch face stand out even more.

Someone hands me my guitar as another person grabs a stool for me to sit on. I strap on the guitar and take a seat. "So, what? You just want me to play something?" I ask, only slightly annoyed by all of this.

"Yeah, play whatever is comfortable for you," the younger blonde tells me.

"Alrighty then." I sigh and start to play one of my newer, more popular songs.

Soon enough, a crowd gathers around behind the camera crew, including the brunette woman who I flashed a smile at when I walked in.

She has her phone held up, clearly recording me, which immediately makes me think she's a fan. It's odd that a fan would be on set, but then again, there were enough of them crowding the entrance to the studio when I got here that one easily could have snuck in. Not to mention, the droves of women and young girls pressed up against the studio windows trying to get a glimpse of what's going on. Some of them even have signs like it's *Good Morning America.*

Whatever, it's not important.

She doesn't stay for the whole song, only about twenty seconds of it, before she's on the move again. Fans don't usually leave partway through my performances, so I'll admit this is new for me if she even is one. My eyes track her as she leaves, but then they snap back at the cameras I forgot were there.

I finish my song, and clapping fills the set.

"That was great, Dusty. Can you tell us a little about that song? What's the meaning behind it?" a producer asks as the cameras continue to roll.

Meaning? Fuck if I know. That song is one of the popular ones. One I didn't write. The label shoved it in my face saying listeners would love it, so I put it on the album. I have no idea what the meaning behind it is. There's nothing particularly profound about the lyrics either.

"Uh…" I smack my forehead with my palm as the director once again yells, "Cut!"

Jesus. Why did I have to be the one to be subjected to this stupid TV show?

Another painful hour of interviews passes, and by the time we're done, I'm officially over it. I'm about ready to march into Ace High Entertainment and give Rob Acerra the middle finger. Fuck my contract; I can deal with the consequences later.

"Hey"—the blonde grabs my forearm as I'm trying to leave—"this is obviously hard for you, but the more you cooperate and actually try to answer the questions, the sooner we can all move on."

I stare at her, slightly in shock at her bite, a bit like a feral kitten, before looking down at my arm and back up at her.

"Sorry." She takes her hand off me and extends it for a handshake. "I'm Daniella. I do public relations for Sparks Studio Productions. I don't mean to be rude or harsh, I'm just trying to do my job."

"Well, Daniella. I should probably apologize. You see, I don't want to be here any more than I imagine you do." I stumble a little on my apology. "I'll try to do better. Interviews just aren't my thing."

"That's all we can ask for." She looks down at the ground and back up. "All right, you need to get headshots done." She dismisses me just like that.

All business, I guess.

An assistant leads me over to the backdrop where the photoshoot is taking place. *C'mon, Dusty. It's just a couple photos and then you can go home.*

It is in fact *not* just a couple photos. The photographer has me do every stupid pose on the planet, and just when I think it's over, they tell me to stay put because they have to make sure all of the shots look right. You would think I was going on the cover of *GQ* and not an ad for a reality show. They even made me put on makeup. *Makeup!* What kind of bullshit is this?

The knowledge that this show is crucial to me being able to keep my music career alive so I can support my family is the only thing keeping me from walking out. That and the small glimpses I get of the girl who was taking videos of me playing my guitar. She's still here, snapping photos, but every time I try to make eye contact with her, she disappears. I'm starting to believe it's possible she's not actually real and my brain has made her up.

We finally wrap up, and the producers give me the okay to leave the set. I'm ready to go home and forget this day ever happened, but a hand grasps my shoulder before I can get to the door.

"Where're you going, Dusty?" the staff member asks.

"Home?" I raise my eyebrows at him.

"No, we've got a hotel room set up for you tonight. The car is packed and ready for you to go."

I cross my arms, already annoyed with this contract. "I need to get some things from my house."

My hope of them understanding and letting me go home is demolished when he replies, "What do you need? We can have someone go get it for you."

"I—never mind. It's fine," I grumble as I roll my eyes.

He leads me in the opposite direction to the car that will take me away from my normal life, into this alternate reality where I'm the star of a TV dating show. I wish it were all a dream and that tomorrow I'd wake up in my bed, able to laugh about it with Craig.

baylor

We wrap up filming for the day after countless complaints from our leading guy. I have to bite my tongue several times to prevent myself from making a sarcastic comment under my breath. If he didn't want to be here, why did he allow the label to force him to? He seems like a bit of a pushover, but then again, I would probably do the same thing if Colette was at my throat telling me I had to.

"Are you regretting taking the lead on interviewing Dusty?" I tease Daniella as we walk out of the building.

"We both know it was for the best that I took the lead on it." She laughs, but from the tone, I can tell she's mentally exhausted. "I'm sure you'd be halfway home to Denver by now if I hadn't."

"That bad?" I cringe. I already know the answer. What would normally be quick shots took twice as long with Dusty, because apparently the man has zero emotion in real life. A stark contrast to the country superstar on stage.

Her eyes widen as though she's recalling the events of today. "Bad enough that I feel like I need to drown myself in margaritas tonight. You down?"

"I'd never say no to a marg." I link my arm with hers as we continue to the employee parking garage.

That evening, we find ourselves in a small bar on Music Row, and Daniella's already deep into her fourth margarita.

"Baylor, I don't think you realize how much I love you." Her words slur together as she giggles into her glass, no doubt an effect of the alcohol.

"Okie, I think that's enough margaritas for you." I gently pull her drink away from her as a singer gets on stage.

"Ooh, music!" she squeals, practically falling out of the booth as she gets up to move closer.

I follow her, grabbing my glass but abandoning hers. Miss Ma'am does not need any more alcohol.

The singer on stage is a young guy, probably in his mid-twenties like Daniella and me. He's playing an acoustic Johnny Cash cover, and I have to admit, he's good.

"Thanks, y'all. If you have any requests for songs you'd like to hear, let me know."

He flashes a smile as Daniella shouts, "MY FRIEND CAN SING!"

No, no, no, Daniella. God, no.

"Is that right?" He leans into the microphone. "Well, where is she?"

Daniella points right at me—*subtle, thanks*—and he beckons me to come up on stage. I start to shake my head no, but then Daniella is pushing me to the front and everyone is whistling and clapping, fueling the fire. The last thing I want is for them to start chanting, so I begrudgingly comply.

"What's your name?" the singer asks once I'm on stage.

"Baylor," I reply with a sigh.

"Well, Baylor, are you familiar with this song?" he asks as he nods and the band starts to play the starting notes to "You Ain't Dolly (And You Ain't Porter)."

I roll my eyes as he hands me a microphone. We start singing lyrics about how the other is nothing like Dolly Parton or Porter Wagoner, and how everyone will probably see me singing on that TV show with the blind auditions one day—*doubtful*—and then I notice Daniella holding her phone up.

Note to self: make sure that video doesn't see the light of day.

She's so drunk she probably won't even remember taking the video, and it's probably so shaky that no one would want to watch it anyway. She won't miss it when I delete it.

The song ends, and the singer tips his hat to me, while also slipping me a piece of paper that most likely has his phone number on it. I put it in my pocket with zero intentions of ever texting him. I don't have time for relationships, serious or casual.

"You owe me for that," I mumble to Daniella as I get off stage and the guy continues with his set.

"You were *so good*!" She takes my hand and *skips* out of the bar.

We bounce from bar to bar, Daniella sneaking shots when she doesn't think I'm watching. I'm absolutely keeping track, though, and occasionally I tell the bartender to give her a shot of water instead of whatever liquor she's craving. She doesn't notice the difference. Must be some kind of placebo effect.

We're waiting for an Uber to take us back home when I notice my phone has been vibrating non-stop, which is extremely odd given that it's eleven thirty on a Monday. I fumble through my purse to dig it out and look at the screen where hundreds of notifications for the *Heart Strings* social media await me.

Oh. No.

3
baylor

Damage Control

"SOMMERFELD!" Colette St. James releases her wrath on me the moment I step through the doors of the production building. Hell hath no fury like the executive producer of a TV show after seeing a drunkenly posted video on the company social media account. It's the cardinal rule of social media management. You *always* make sure you're on the right account before you post anything. Better yet, you log out of the company account before a night out in case you, or apparently your coworker, gets drunk.

The video has since been deleted, but not before hundreds of thousands of likes and shares. In other words, my singing voice is currently all over the internet.

I take a deep breath, trying to calm my pounding heart. *I will not lose my job today.*

"You called, Colette?" I try to sound as collected as possible in hopes that she doesn't notice the shake in my voice.

"What the *fuck* happened last night?" She's fuming,

frown lines cutting through her skin. I can practically see the smoke coming out of her ears.

"I-I have no idea. I guess something accidentally got posted." *Obviously.* I'm not going to throw Daniella under the bus, though, and get her fired too.

"No shit, Baylor. This type of thing is unacceptable."

Here it comes. I'm about to lose my job. My parents are going to be pissed, and then they're going to tell me *I told you so.* My pride is about to take a brutal hit, one I'm unsure I'll be able to recover from.

"Wait, Colette! You need to see this!" One of the marketing strategists runs over holding out her phone.

Colette snatches the device out of her hand and scrolls, her face pinched in a permanent frown. She scrolls for what feels like an eternity and then hands the phone to me.

"Well, well, well. It seems as though the internet has saved you today, Baylor."

I look at the phone, confused about what she means. And then I see *exactly* what she means.

There are thousands of comments on just one repost of the video.

OMG, she better be on the show!

I don't even know who this girl is, but I'm rooting for her so hard.

They posted this on the official social media. It has to mean something!

"Wait, you're not firing me?" I ask, blinking in shock.

"No, although I should," Colette mutters. "I'm not firing you, but only on one condition. You are going to clean up this little mess you made."

I raise an eyebrow. "And how exactly am I supposed to do that?" I mean, I can handle a social media crisis. I've done it before. It's just never involved *me* before.

"You saw those comments, didn't you?" She eyes the

phone in my hand. "You're going on the show, Baylor." She flips her hair over her shoulder and takes off.

What. The. Fuck.

"Wait, Colette." I'm speedwalking, trying to keep up after she dropped that absolute bomb on me. "What do you mean I'm going on the show?"

"Exactly what I said. You'll be joining the other girls on the show." She shrugs, barely paying me any attention.

"But—"

"Do you want to keep your job or not?" she snaps, to which I nod. "Okay, then you'll do what I ask. As of today, you're not part of Sparks Studio Productions, you're part of the cast. Which means you should probably stop following me around like a lost puppy."

I frown and stop in my tracks. *So callous*, I think.

Then, *I don't know what I'm supposed to do.*

"Baylor!" Daniella calls out to me. "Hey, I'm so sorry." She starts to apologize, but all I can think about is the fact that I have to go on the show now.

"What am I even supposed to do?" I mumble.

"I can't believe I did—huh? What do you mean? What happened?" Daniella snaps her head in my direction, no longer worried about what she did. "Oh my God, you got fired, didn't you? I need to go tell Colette it was my fault."

"No, no, I didn't get fired." I stop her before she does anything rash. "Although I'm not sure if that would be worse than the alternative."

"What do you mean?"

I let out an exasperated sigh. "Because of how popular the video has gotten, instead of firing me, she's putting me on the show."

"Wait, that's good! Isn't it?" Daniella asks, a little unsure of herself.

I purse my lips. "I mean, for someone who wants to go on the show, sure. But the fact is I'm only going on so I can keep my job." I don't want her to feel bad. It could have happened to anyone. And I was the one responsible for the social media accounts, so it's just as much on me as it is on her. "I have zero idea what I'm supposed to do now, though, as a contestant instead of an employee."

"I mean, I can ask?" she offers as she shuffles her feet, unable to maintain eye contact. "It's the least I can do, really."

I wave her off. "I'm sure someone will brief me."

No one briefed me, so when the call for contestants came and I showed up, you could probably imagine my confusion and frustration when I was told to leave. Not only was I told to leave, but a bunch of the actual contestants gave me the stink eye. They probably thought I was some poser trying to get on the show.

Don't worry, ladies, you have nothing to worry about. I don't actually want to be here, I think as I head from backstage through the tunnel that connects to the main building where a group of producers are congregating.

"Is anyone going to tell me what the hell is going on?" I roll my eyes, hoping to get at least *one* of them to help me. I know I probably sound like a diva, but my job is on the line.

One of my producer friends, Alex, pulls me aside. "Baylor, maybe you should just go home today. The thing is, we don't need you right this moment."

"I'm confused. Colette told me that I'm going on the show."

"Yes, well…you are. But we aren't going to have you sing in front of him. The world has already heard your voice. They already *know* they want you on the show." He ruffles his hair.

"Isn't Dusty supposed to choose the ones he wants?" I know sometimes shows are scripted—well, let's face it, *most* are scripted—but this makes it seem like Dusty isn't even going to have a choice. And I hate that.

"I mean, yeah, but we want a good show, too, Baylor. And the people want you. We can't risk him not choosing you on live television."

Wow, thanks for the confidence boost. I don't hesitate to tell him that either.

"Jeez, thanks for having faith in me, Alex. So, what does Colette expect me to do?" I'm officially annoyed—no, I'm *past* annoyance.

"Just hang tight until the first week of filming is over, okay? Trust me on this." Alex pats me on the shoulder before he heads to the set. "Think of it as getting paid to sit at home!" he calls over his shoulder.

"Think of it as getting paid to sit at home," I grumble as I pace around my living room for the fiftieth time this afternoon. This is *boring*. I wasn't made for sitting at home all day.

I don't want to be on the show, but I would rather sing in front of Dusty Wilder a thousand times than twiddle my thumbs wondering what to do for the next week.

I type in "Heart Strings" on social media. While the original video Daniella posted of me was taken down, it was reposted hundreds of times. The video quality isn't even good. It's shaky and blurry, like a four-year-old took it. You can even hear Daniella's *breathing* in the background.

"You're so lucky you didn't get fired." I curse Daniella even though she's not here. No one is here. Just me and all my thoughts. A scary combination, if you ask me.

Instead of dwelling on the consequences of our actions, which would most certainly send me into an even deeper spiral, I pull out my journal. The edges of the leather are worn, and small amounts of coffee stain the lined pages, but I'd never throw it out. Writing is my escape when the world gets a little too heavy. It's why I bring the journal with me everywhere, but I didn't think people actually paid attention to me writing in it.

Music, and especially lyrics, have always called to me. There's a certain type of beauty in pouring all your feelings and emotions into a song. How some of the most upbeat songs have the saddest meanings behind their lyrics, or how a melancholy tune can evoke hope if you listen closely enough.

Even though I don't want to be on the show—can't afford the setback in my career goals—maybe it will spark some inspiration in me. Deep down, though, my hope is that it'll allow me to muster up the courage to stand up to my parents, to tell them my passions are worthwhile, even if they don't make me millions of dollars. That I can have a successful career and, if I'm lucky, maybe pursue music, too.

I pull out a pen and open the journal to the very first page, running my finger over the faded inscription.

This journal belongs to Sylvie Mae. My mom.

Four hours later, Daniella walks through the door of our shared apartment and immediately starts apologizing again.

"Baylor, I'm so sorry. I had no idea the video was going to blow up. Hell, I didn't even know I posted it. I was so drunk, oh my God." She's rambling, and it takes everything in me not to smack some sense into her, if not just to get her to stop word vomiting all over the carpet.

"Daniella." I try to get her attention, but she keeps sputtering about how she ruined my career and she can't handle Colette on her own and what if I have to move back to Denver?

"I can't believe I did—"

"DANIELLA!" I shout at her.

"WHAT?" she shouts back.

"Chill the fuck out! It's fine."

She gives me a look that tells me she's not convinced it's fine.

"Seriously. I'm fine," I reassure her. "I'll just go on the show, make it past the first few eliminations, and then Colette will be happy enough that she won't fire me. It's not like I'm being forced to fall in love with the guy."

"I mean, isn't that the point of the show, though?" She grimaces.

"It's a dating show, yeah, but there's a thing called faking it, Daniella." I roll my eyes. "Besides, reality TV isn't *real*. I just have to give the viewers a good show. That's all."

"Hm, yeah, that's true. Are you sure about this,

though? Maybe we can talk to Colette and I can explain what happened."

"And risk both of us getting fired? No way." Even if Daniella technically did royally screw me over, I'd rather neither of us lose our job.

"I just feel terrible." She sits on the couch and places her head in her hands.

I sit next to her and try to comfort her by rubbing circles on her back. "Just keep your head down and work. It's not that big a deal. Two months tops, and then everything will be back to normal."

4
dusty

Ripping Off The Voice

"OKAY, so here's how this is going to work…" A producer explains the recording process to me as we walk down the tunnel to the area we'll be filming in.

The space has the appearance of an auditorium, with seats arranged in a semi-circle around the stage. However, a temporary wall divides the stage down the middle, so you can't see the other side. It gives off a similar atmosphere to *The Dating Game* or *Love is Blind*.

"You'll sit on one side of the wall, and the singers will be on the other. You won't be able to see the women, just hear their voices."

"So you're ripping off *The Voice*?" I deadpan as we walk onto the stage. All that's missing is a turning chair.

The producer starts sputtering over his words. "W-well…no. We're just taking inspiration from it, Mr. Wilder."

"I see. What exactly am I supposed to be doing?"

"Well, Mr. Wilder, we have thirty women here that will perform for you. You'll hear all of them, then at the end, you'll choose nine of them to compete for the spot as your music partner," he explains as we head toward the stage.

"Why nine? I thought I was choosing ten?" I ask, confused.

"Er, well, technically there are going to be ten women competing. But one has already been preselected." He fidgets with the sleeves of his shirt like he's hiding something.

"And how come I don't get to hear her sing? Shouldn't *I* be the judge of whether she's good enough? After all, it is my career that we're talking about. Right…" I look at his name tag. "Ezra?"

"I-I mean—"

Before he can continue stammering like an idiot who doesn't know how to do his job, the executive producer interrupts. "Ezra, I'll take over from here, thanks." She dismisses him, and relief flashes across his face.

"Y-yes, ma'am." He practically runs off stage.

The executive producer turns to me once he's gone. I hadn't bothered to ask her name, which was probably rude of me, but I also consider it rude to have been forced into this situation in the first place. Besides, that first day of interviews was so hectic, I never had the opportunity to get *anyone's* name besides Daniella.

"I'm sure you have a lot of questions. Here, let's take a seat and talk." She gestures to the stools on stage.

I sit, and she follows suit. She's still wearing the god-awful lipstick that makes her look more clownish than anything and also dons a matching bloodred pantsuit.

"I apologize, but I don't believe I ever got your name." I reach out my hand to shake hers, which she takes. Her handshake is firm. Much firmer than I expected, but I suppose when you work in this industry, commanding attention is a must.

"Colette St. James. I'm the executive producer of the show. Rob never bothered to tell you who I am, I'm gathering," she scoffs, and I get the impression she's not a fan of Rob.

Interesting. Maybe I can use this to my advantage.

"No, ma'am, he did not. I assure you, I'm…not like Rob Acerra. He's a bit—"

"Callous? Oh, I know," she cuts me off. "Anyway, enough about Rob. What questions do you have?"

How about what the fuck I'm supposed to do? And the girl who was "preselected?" What the fuck does that mean?

"I—" I try to get a word out, but she immediately starts talking over me.

"Here's what we'll do. I'll give you the rundown of everything that's going to happen, and then we can go from there." Colette proceeds to tell me *the exact same thing* Ezra told me about there being thirty women to listen to— *How many minutes is thirty songs?*—and that I'll narrow it down to nine, which solidifies the fact that *someone* was preselected.

She does not allow me to ask any questions.

"Wait, Colette—" I call out to her, but she's already gone, leaving me to marinate in my confusion.

"Welcome to *Heart Strings*, the brand new reality show brought to you by Sparks Studio Productions in partnership with Ace High Entertainment. I'm your host, Jarrod Stone."

I stand backstage with my arms crossed over my chest. All of this is so ridiculous.

"Let's meet the star of the show, folks. He's country music's rising star, and he's looking for a partner, in music and life…"

God, that's so bad.

"Please welcome Dusty Wilder!" Jarrod gestures toward the side of the stage, and I plaster on a fake smile, waving as I walk out on stage.

"Pleasure to be here, Jarrod, thank you." I tip my hat to the camera after shaking his hand.

"So, Dusty, the fans are dying to know. Why'd you come on *Heart Strings*? And how is a guy like you, a successful musician and heartthrob, still single?" Jarrod looks at me expectantly.

Just as you rehearsed, Wilder. Don't fuck this up. Remember what Daniella said.

"Well, Jarrod, like you said, I'm looking for a music partner. Someone to record an album and go on tour with. In regard to your other question, I guess I've just been waiting for the right one to come along." I look off stage to see Daniella giving me a thumbs-up.

"Well, buddy, I hope we can find you just that. Best of luck to you." He pats me on the shoulder. "All right, folks, the moment you've been waiting for. Let's bring out our first musician!"

The first few singers feel like a fever dream. One of them, Jacky or Jordan or something, was good? But shit, this is more difficult than I thought it would be.

Footsteps approach on the other side of the barrier as the next woman sets up to perform.

Here we go again. We're filming half today and half

tomorrow, so at least I won't have to listen to thirty people in a row. Truthfully, I'm more curious about the girl who was apparently good enough to make it past the auditions with me.

"Hi, I'm Aspen Barlowe," the girl on the other side of the wall introduces herself, and any thoughts I had about the mystery woman disappear when I hear her smooth, melodic voice.

Once she starts singing, I'm absolutely captivated. Her alto voice has an edge to it. It isn't quite gravelly, but it isn't like her delicate speaking voice either. No, her singing voice has power. *Soul.* I make a mental note to keep her around.

The song doesn't last nearly long enough for my liking. When someone can sing in such a way that makes you *feel*, that's how you know they're good. And that's exactly what listening to Aspen Barlowe was like.

Before I know it, fifteen singers have performed, and the day is over. There are a few singers who I know right away won't make it through the final cut and a few more who I want to keep.

Alex, my producer for the day, pulls me aside the moment I step off the stage. "Dusty, let's talk about who you're liking."

We walk to a lounge area and sit down to debrief. Alex goes through the list of the women who performed today. Honestly, a lot of them weren't memorable enough, but the ones that I do remember stick out to me.

I list off the names of the girls I know I want to keep. "I know I liked Aspen and Sage."

"That's great, Dusty. There will still be fifteen more performances tomorrow, but we've got at least two of the nine picked, so that's a great start."

Back at the hotel, I call my manager Craig. He's been like a father to me all of these years. He took me on when I was an eighteen-year-old kid trying to make it in a cutthroat industry and has stayed through everything. There have been plenty of times when I wanted to quit and Craig talked me down from the ledge.

"Hello?" He answers on the second ring. "Dusty, how's it going?" His voice washes over me, bringing me comfort I didn't know I needed today.

"Everything's going great, actually," I admit. "The first day on the set was rough. I didn't know how to answer their questions."

Craig laughs. He knows how terrible I am at interviews. It's been the one thing that hasn't changed in eleven years.

"Today went a lot better, though. The first fifteen women performed, and there were some really impressive singers. This process might actually work." I pause as I catch myself being optimistic about this show.

"Wow, only one day on the set, and they've already got your mind changed on this whole reality TV thing, huh?" he teases.

I roll my eyes, and all the while he's still chuckling. "If this is what it takes to keep my career on the rise, I'll do it, Craig. You know this."

"I know, Dusty. And I'm proud of you. You've come a long way since you rolled into Nashville that first day." If I'm not mistaken, Craig sniffs on the end of the other line.

Is he crying?

Craig has always been the more emotional one of the two of us. I know it's just because at the end of the day, all he wants is for me to succeed. I owe him a lot, if not everything, for what he's done to get me where I am today.

5
dusty

Give a Little to Get a Lot

THE SECOND DAY of auditions is in full swing. After listening to fifteen singers yesterday, I feel like I have a better idea of what I'm doing and what I'm looking for. It might be more difficult to choose seven more women at the end of today, if I keep Aspen and Sage in mind, but that's something I'll figure out when I get there.

"My name is Kelsie, and I'll be singing an original," the light, feminine voice on the other side of the barrier says before strumming a slow, melancholic tune on her guitar. Her voice is haunting, eerily beautiful. It's not my usual style, but I feel like we could make it work.

When her song ends, I don't say a word, much like how the auditions from yesterday went. She says a brief thanks, then they bring out the next girl.

I wish I could at least sing *with* them to see how our voices would fit, but I guess that's something that will happen later. It does seem odd that they have me choose singers based on their voices alone instead of how well they fit with mine, but it's too late to change anything now that we're halfway through the auditions. I'm not sure I'd have any choice in the matter anyway.

The next singer comes out, and I find myself instinctively tapping my foot along as she sings a cover of an old Trisha Yearwood song. This is the type of girl Nashville wants me with. Even though I don't have a single idea what she looks like, I'm already confident she fits the bill.

"Thank you, my name's Katherine."

I have ears on so producers can talk to me, if need be, since we're rolling live and they can't exactly come out on stage. They also take the opportunity to tell me when there's someone they think would be a good fit for the show and strongly recommend I listen carefully to them.

"Up next is Jade. She's high on our radar, just so you know," the producer says in a dry tone.

I roll my eyes, hopefully not obviously enough for the camera to pick it up. That's the last thing I need Rob Acerra seeing. I'm never in the mood for his nagging.

Heels click against the floor as Jade walks to where I assume is a stool. I've gotten into the rhythm and can predict whether someone is carrying an instrument or not based on the way they walk, and I don't think she has one.

I know my prediction for Jade is right when a backtrack of a song I've never heard once in my life begins playing. It's a country song, but it's one of the newer, poppier songs. Just because I'm considered a mainstream country artist doesn't mean I actually listen to mainstream country. I'd rather not be clumped in with those guys—the ones who probably wear their cowboy hats backward and have never touched a horse in their life. But realistically, am I that much better?

I may be from the country, but my dream was to always get out, get off the farm, and make something of myself.

Of course, the producers would say this girl is on their radar. Not that she's bad. It's the opposite, in fact. Even though I've never heard the song before, her rendition would no doubt make people want to get up and dance. Her energy alone would be great for an album and a tour, assuming her stage presence matches her voice.

When the song wraps up and the click of heels fades away, I take a deep breath, letting my lungs fill, and then exhale, pushing everything out.

"You doing all right, Dusty?" the producer babbles in my ear.

I subtly nod, an action small enough that his prying eyes can see but the camera won't pick up.

"Next singer is a go," someone else says in the background through my earpiece.

I sigh, trying my best not to let my emotions show.

None of this is real. I need to keep reminding myself that. This is all for show. It's no different than the media persona I've had to put on for the past eleven years.

After an hour or so, we're down to the last four singers of the day. Then comes the hard part: narrowing thirty women down to nine. I kind of wish I had a notepad so I could write down all of their names. Surely they'll have recordings that I can listen to, even though the auditions are airing live.

My thoughts are interrupted by a crash backstage. My head whips to the side as I try to figure out what the hell is going on.

"Act natural! You're on *live television*, Dusty!" the producer, whose name I still can't remember, screeches in my ear, and I resist the urge to flip him the bird. That definitely wouldn't look good on live TV.

I turn my head away from the camera and toward the crew off to the side of the stage and mouth, *What the fuck is going on?* I'm only met with a shrug and a gesture to turn back to the camera.

"What do you mean I'm not allowed on stage?!" A high-pitched shriek hits my ears, causing them to ring. "I'm *part* of the auditions! I deserve a fair shot!"

I hear a few mutterings of, "Ma'am, calm down," and, "We're going to need you to leave the premises."

"Bring out the next singer, we need to keep rolling," echoes in my ear.

I'm going to have a few words with the producers after this, even if just to figure out what the fuck is going on.

"I'm Abigail," a sweet country accent greets me.

Her song is short and sweet, much like her introduction. I enjoy it a lot, though. Her voice matches what the label is looking for, and I already have a feeling our voices would mesh well together on an album. If she ends up making it that far, that is.

Only three more left.

The last three singers' performances go by quicker than I anticipated. There's only one of them who I truly see myself performing with, though. The other two probably won't be on my final list.

"Cut! That's a wrap on the auditions." Once the cameras stop rolling, the lights on the stage dim and I immediately receive instructions from the producer who has been nagging in my ear all day.

"Dusty, we need to see you in the green room to

debrief, and then we'll need to get some confessional shots."

I turn my head over my shoulder to see the producer already impatiently gesturing for me to follow. I give him a nod and face forward again, if only so I can get my annoyance out while I'm still in private and not in front of more cameras or an audience of producers.

Especially that executive producer lady. She scares me.

I plop down in a dark-green chair in front of a larger couch where several producers are sitting, running my hands over the fabric as I wait for them to say something.

"I think that went well." The only female producer looks at her male counterparts.

"I agree," one of them says, as if I'm not right there in the room with them.

I clear my throat, hoping it will prompt them to talk to me, instead of just amongst each other.

Their heads all snap toward me at once.

"Ah, Dusty, yes. Let's debrief, shall we?"

I'm finally able to see the nametag of the producer who was talking to me through the headset. *George.* I frown. He looks too young to be a George. Wonder if it's a family name or something.

"We've got a lot of work to do tonight. We need to narrow thirty women down to nine right here, right now."

I nod slowly, trying to remember the singers, but it's hard to remember names when I can't place a face to them. "Are there…recordings or something that I can listen back to?" I ask.

"Sure, sure. But we'd much rather not have to listen to

thirty performances again, yeah?" the female producer, Leah, points out.

"Here. This will probably help?" George slides a piece of paper over the glass top coffee table that separates us. I pick it up, seeing the names of all thirty women who auditioned…minus one that's scratched out.

"Why is this name scratched out?" I furrow my brows, pointing out the name covered in black Sharpie.

"Oh, she's…she's not important," Leah stutters, clearly hiding something from me.

"With one woman already having been chosen, we unfortunately had to cut someone from the auditions," the second male producer, Tobias, cuts in.

"That hardly seems fair." I look up at them, raising an eyebrow. "She made it to the auditions, why didn't she get a chance?"

"The decision had already been made, Dusty, let's not get into it too much. Besides, this will help make your job easier, won't it?" George says impatiently.

So, this is how it's going to be?

I'm already annoyed that I have to be here. Now I come to find out singers are having their fair chances taken away from them because of a girl I didn't even choose?

Whether the producers like it or not, I will be taking hold of the reins for this show. On camera and off camera.

"All right," I concede, although the thoughts of someone unfairly being cut still wash through my brain. "Let's get into it, then."

"We already have Aspen and Sage down on the list from speaking to Alex yesterday. Are you still confident in those choices?" Leah asks, picking up a clipboard and a pen.

I nod.

"Great, we'll mark those as a go. Anyone else in particular you liked or disliked?"

"Abigail," I immediately answer, since her performance is fresh in my mind. "I liked Abigail."

Leah and George exchange a look while Tobias puckers his lips and nods slowly.

"Something wrong with her?" I ask, perhaps a bit too harshly, judging by the way Leah recoils slightly.

"Er, no, not necessarily. We just aren't confident about the way she looks on television," Tobias admits.

"That's not what this is about, though, is it?" I snap. "It's about finding a singer who matches my voice."

"Well, that's part of it, sure, but viewers want good television. They want sparks. Drama. Not…plain Jane from a podunk town in the middle of nowhere."

I roll my eyes. "I'll have you know, I'm from what you would probably call a 'podunk town' and I'm doing just fine." I earn myself shocked expressions, but I continue. "I want her on the list. And if not, I'm out."

"You can't—" George frantically tries to speak.

"Try me," I counter, already ready to get up from my seat and walk out.

"It's fine, George." Tobias raises a hand to get me to stop. In a low voice, one he probably assumes I can't hear, he says, "We can just eliminate her early. It's fine."

Not if I have any say in it, I think, even though it's been made abundantly clear I really don't have any say in things.

"Let's get back on track. What were your thoughts on Morgan?" Leah asks, scribbling down some notes on her clipboard.

Who the fuck was Morgan?

"I'm not sure I remember her," I admit.

The producers nod, and one of them picks up a remote to snap on the television. The camera angle cuts off Morgan so I can't see what she looks like even now, but I don't think I really need to. Her voice—the tone and pitch—doesn't appeal to me.

Before I can even open my mouth, George gets his two cents in. "Our team likes her. And from the interviews we've seen of her, we think she'll fit right in."

Gotta give a little to get a little, Dusty, I tell myself. There's clearly going to be no debate, especially after what just happened with Abigail, so I'm going to have to compromise. If that's what it takes to get them to loosen the reins on me, I'll do it, but I'm not exactly happy about it.

Too much time passes before our deliberations conclude and final decisions are made. I had to fight for some of the singers, and, unfortunately, I did lose some of those battles. At the end of the day, though, I won the most important ones. And I showed the producers I'm not some puppet they can control for entertainment. I'm still going to do this my way.

Now, as long as this mystery girl—the one chosen by America—doesn't ruin it all, everything should be smooth sailing.

the confessionals

Producer: How are you feeling after hearing thirty women perform?
Dusty: Honestly? Overwhelmed. But I think I have an idea of who I want to move forward.
Producer: Do you think this process is working so far?
Dusty: I mean, it's definitely working in the musical aspect. I can see myself working professionally with some of these women for sure.

Kelsie: I'm nervous. Relying solely on someone else's perception of my talent is terrifying. It's…humbling, for sure.

Producer: You're the mystery woman of the season. The

world knows who you are, but Dusty doesn't. How does that feel?

Baylor: Fine, I guess? It's not like I planned to be on the show. I didn't even know about the video until after it went viral.

Baylor hesitates.

Baylor: That's not going to be in the final cut is that?
Producer: No, you're fine.

6
baylor

Camera Shy

"BAYLOR, we'll need you on the set today," Alex says through the phone.

Fucking finally. It's been the longest week of my life. Who knew I was such a workaholic? I mean, I did, I always have been, but that's beside the point.

"Great. What time?"

"In about an hour. Dusty's making his final decisions for who he wants on the show, and then we'll do some quick filming with the girls who were chosen and do some clips of you, too. Tomorrow, the first episode will air for everyone who didn't get to watch the auditions live, and Thursday is when the fun will begin," he explains.

My heart hammers in my chest as the reality of my circumstances sinks in. It's all very overwhelming. I shut my eyes and try to steady my breathing.

"Baylor? Are you all right over there?" Alex's tone has a twinge of concern in it.

"Yeah, I'm fine. I'll be fine." I downplay my emotions as much as possible. No one needs to know I'm actually terrified of being *in front* of the camera.

"All right. Well, get to the set in an hour and go straight to hair and makeup," he instructs then hangs up.

I love Alex, truthfully. He, Daniella, and I have been friends since I started working at Sparks Studio Productions. But sometimes he can be blunt and *too* straight-to-the-point.

Maybe that's what I need right now, though. Someone who will cut the bullshit and get me through this.

I pull up to the studio and head straight to hair and makeup like Alex instructed.

"Oh good, Baylor, you're right on time." One of the makeup artists grabs my arm and pulls me over to a chair.

"How has everything been going?" I ask. I'm sure I'm not allowed to know, but what's the harm in asking?

"It's been busy. But everything seems to be going okay," she replies as she organizes her products.

"That's good to hear. No more social media scandals, then, I assume."

It's a poorly timed joke—I know it is, yet it still slips out of my mouth—and she gives me an awkward laugh, making me feel even worse about the whole situation.

It wasn't your fault. Just get through these next ten weeks to save your career and then you can move on.

"Let's get you ready for tonight." She starts dabbing foundation on my face, working mostly in silence, which I'm okay with. Less room to make things more awkward after my comment.

Once she finishes putting a full face of makeup on me, she starts working on my hair. I wonder if any of the other contestants get this treatment or if it's just because I'm part of the production company. I don't imagine they do. Colette wouldn't waste her time and resources on mere contestants who may not make it past the first week.

I let the question lingering in my mind slip out.

"The other contestants? No, they have to do their own. After today, you will, too, just so there's no favoritism, but since you weren't part of the auditions, Colette wants you to look your best. Can't have America regretting their decision." She shrugs in the mirror.

I do my best to ignore the backhanded comment but fail.

"Yeah, I guess they wouldn't have seen me with the quality of that video." I snort. "The only way I knew it was me was because I was the one on stage. Hopefully America doesn't see my face and immediately hate me. I mean, would it be that bad to get eliminated early, though? Would put me out of my misery." I can't stop the self-deprecating jokes from flowing out of my mouth. Word vomit, if you will.

"Yeah…" She draws out the word, and we're back to the awkward silence we were in before.

I swear she works even faster, but I can't really blame her.

"Okay. All good to go." She brushes a curl out of my face and dusts on a tiny bit of powder. "Go with Alex, and he'll direct you to where you need to head next."

I nod, standing from the stylist's chair then walking over to the door where Alex is waiting.

"Dang, Sommerfeld, you sure clean up nice." He teasingly nudges me with his elbow.

"We already knew this, Alexander." I roll my eyes, giving him shit back with his full government name. "I damn sure clean up nicer than you do."

"Can't argue with that." His tone shifts from playful to one of genuine concern. "Are you ready for all this?"

"Yep," I lie.

"Honesty, Bay."

I sigh, letting out all the air I've been holding hostage the past couple days. "If I'm being honest, no, I'm not ready for all of this. But I don't really have a choice if I want to keep my job. I hate being in front of the camera in general, but the idea of being in front of the camera with the whole country watching makes me want to throw up."

"Those are valid feelings. I know it's easier said than done, but just do your best and be yourself. You've got me and Dani in your corner. It's not like you have to win to keep your job, right?"

I shake my head, and he continues.

"Well, there you go, then. That should be a little less pressure on your back? Trust me, you'll be great."

At this point, we've arrived at the auditorium where auditions were held. Several women are chatting backstage with one another.

"They're going to be pissed," I mutter.

"They'll get over it," Alex answers. "Odds are if they didn't make it through with you here, they still wouldn't have made it without you here."

"I can't tell if that's a compliment or an insult."

"It's whatever you want it to be, Sommerfeld. Now play nice, all right?" He pats me on the back before all but shoving me toward the group of girls standing around. A few of them shoot me glares, but some of them give me soft smiles before continuing the conversations they were already having.

I continue walking, trying to find a place out of the way of everyone else to stand or sit. Although my head is on a swivel, I somehow still run directly into a girl with fiery red hair.

She spins around, shock plastered on her face. "Oh my goodness, I'm so sorry!" She's got a bit of a Southern accent, the kind that immediately comes to mind when you think of country music. If I had to guess, I'd say she's from Georgia or one of the surrounding states.

I raise an eyebrow. "No need to apologize. I was the one who ran into you."

"I know, it's a bad habit of mine." She extends a hand. "I'm Sage."

"Baylor." I take it and get a better look at her. She's beautiful, with lush, bouncy curls and full curves. She doesn't fit the typical image for reality TV—I hate that my mind immediately goes there, but it's not entirely false. Most of our competing reality shows cast max size-two women, so it's refreshing to see Sparks Studio Productions prioritizing diversity.

"I don't think I saw you earlier this week. But then again, there were so many people here that it's hard to keep track as it is." She laughs, her eyes gleaming.

"Yeah, there are a ton of people here. I'm not sure how the producers keep everyone straight." I chuckle nervously.

"Producers? I don't know how *Dusty* is able to keep everyone straight. But at least he only has to get to know ten of us, right? Actually, that's not very reassuring," she says, her mouth moving a mile a minute.

"I'm sure it'll be okay," I try to reassure her.

"Right, right. I'm getting ahead of myself. I need to not get so worked up over it. What's meant to be, will be, right?" She gives me a tight smile, but her nerves reflect in her eyes. Is this how I should be feeling? I mean, I'm nervous, but it's for an entirely different reason.

"Ladies, if I could get your attention please!" As Colette St. James walks through the sea of women, all eyes snap toward her. "We're about to start filming, so if everyone could please listen for a moment."

"Here we go." Sage gives me a nervous glance as the other women crowd around Colette, although the chattering doesn't completely stop.

Whispers of, "Will Dusty be here tonight?" and, "I hope I don't go home," can be heard from all sides of me.

I'm wedged between Sage and a dark-haired girl with a sharp stare and fox-like features. We make eye contact for a split second, and while I give her a soft smile, she looks me up and down, assessing me. Instead of acknowledging me, she lets out a puff of air, a tiny smirk creeping into her lips.

All right, then.

"Okay, ladies, here's how this is going to work. There are a lot of you tonight, so we want to make this as quick as possible so you can get settled and ready for a big day of filming tomorrow." Colette steps out onto center stage, her heels clicking against the laminate floor. "We'll be calling the names of only the contestants that made it through. Ten of you will advance. Twenty of you will be going home."

Whispers intensify as the reality of what is going to happen sets in. It finally feels like an actual competition.

"If your name is announced, you'll walk out on center stage then line up on the risers. Got it?"

Heads bob up and down around me.

"Great. Let's roll." Colette gestures to the cameramen before the host of the show steps out onto the stage as the space floods with lights and music starts playing.

"Welcome back to *Heart Strings*! I'm your host Jarrod Stone. You've seen women from around the country sing their hearts out for the chance to win over Dusty Wilder's heart. Tonight, ten of those women will move forward.

"Every week, there will be eliminations, and every week you, the viewers, will have the opportunity to vote and save one of the bottom contestants to give them another shot at winning Dusty's heart and a record deal.

"Now, without further ado, let's meet the women!"

Jarrod announces the first couple women, and even though I know I'm making it through, my heart still races.

"Next up, we've got Aspen!"

The fox-faced girl next to me gives me the side-eye as she plasters on a smile and steps forward, heading to center stage.

Great. Of course, she made the cut.

Six of the ten names are called, and they still haven't announced me yet. I wouldn't put it past Colette to do some dramatic reveal, but it's also my understanding that they want to keep my real identity a secret. After all, it wouldn't be a great look for the production company if everyone knew that they had planted someone on the show.

Then again, it was pretty obvious by the looks I was getting from the other girls here that I wasn't at the auditions. If they do some dramatic reveal, they'll probably be able to say I was "America's choice" or some shit like that.

"Sage, you are going through!" Jarrod calls out.

Sage's shoulders drop in relief, and she can't seem to hide her smile as she walks out on stage.

As the number of spots dwindles down, the tension in the room steadily increases. I know that's part of what Colette wants. The camera captures everything. I may not be a producer with the company, but I've seen a lot working in the communications department. I know from experience that drama makes for good television.

"For all you folks back home, we're down to the final three spots, and the tension on this stage is palpable. Let's meet the rest of the women, shall we?"

Two women who aren't me are announced, and I roll my eyes at the fact they chose to introduce me last.

"Ladies and gentlemen, our last contestant is a very special young lady. Those of you at home may recognize her voice from a video that went viral recently. This was something not even our producers saw coming, but we always want to give you, the people, a voice of your own. So, without further ado, our last contestant, America's choice, is…Baylor!"

I shake my head, knowing Colette would pull something like this, but plaster a smile onto my face as I walk out on stage. I squint to adjust to the spotlights, wave to the camera, then take my place next to the rest of the girls, some of whom have understandably shocked expressions on their faces.

"And with that, here are the ten women who will be vying for a record deal and Dusty's heart!"

"Cut! That's a wrap on that, everyone. Take ten, and we'll do some individual filming next," the director calls, and the stage, which once had an air of tension, is now a scene of bustling producers and camera crewmen.

7

dusty

Great Value Chris Harrison

LAST NIGHT, I was told the recording of the *Heart Strings* live auditions and contestant selection aired and I wasn't allowed to watch. The only person I could talk to was my manager, and I had to use the hotel landline to contact him. The producers took my cell phone after the second day of filming the auditions and have kept it.

It's not like I'm going to look up anything related to the show, but whatever. I get it. They don't want us on social media or reading anything *Heart Strings* related. It's been an adjustment not being so connected to the outside world and my fans, but I've never really been a huge fan of social media anyway.

I was given the rundown about how filming will work going forward. A few days a week will be for the bulk of filming, where I'll spend time with all the women and "test out our chemistry." Then we'll have a day for interviews, followed by free days that the production company will use for editing the footage. Although, I'm not quite sure what kind of freedom I'll have. From my understanding, I'll basically have someone with me at all times except when

I'm shitting, showering, or sleeping. I'm twenty-nine, for God's sake. I don't need a babysitter. I can behave.

Today, I'm meeting all ten of the women I—and the producers—chose.

"Dusty, are you ready?" the staff member assigned to babysit me today calls from outside my room, breaking me out of my thoughts.

Ready as I'll ever be. I sigh as I pull a tan cowboy hat off one of the racks I had the styling team bring in. They tried to get me to fit into their specific image, but I told them it was either what I normally wear or nothing at all.

Today, I put on starched Wranglers, a white button-down, and a tan suit jacket with gator skin boots. I skip the tie, ignoring what the stylist told me to wear, and undo a couple of the snaps near the top of the shirt. If this is the way for me to keep a shred of control and possibly rebel against the label, I'll take it.

After combing through my mustache with my fingers, I open the door and step out, looking my personal babysitter —Brent?—in the eyes. He opens his mouth to say something, probably about my appearance, but I raise my eyebrows at him and he quickly shuts it.

"Hello, Bryan." I nod at him.

"It's Brett," he sighs. "Come on, we're going to be late."

He leads me to the car that's going to take us to where we'll be filming for the day. It's a sleek, black Range Rover with tinted windows. I open the door and slip inside, the scent of leather filling my nostrils. Brody follows, and we sit in silence for the twenty-minute drive.

While the auditions were filmed in the production building, the rest of the show will be filmed in different locations around Nashville. The filming schedule obviously isn't released to the public—they don't want fans showing up and leaking information—but I have a hard time believing fans won't find a way to show up regardless.

We pull up to a gated traditional European-style house —well, mansion may be a better way to put it—near Brentwood. Security opens the gate once they verify who we are, and we head down the long drive.

"How rich is Sparks Studio Productions?" I gawk at the scenery around us.

"*Heart Strings* may be new, Dusty, but SSP is not," Brandon replies simply.

I'll say. I can't believe they can afford to buy these properties, but I guess if they're filming several of these types of shows a year, it makes sense.

"We don't own these properties, but the owners let us rent out the spaces we need." He answers the question floating around in my head. "Here's the deal. Today is when you'll meet all of the women chosen to compete. It'll kind of be like speed dating. You'll have five minutes with each of them to get to know a bit about them. Then at the end, you'll choose one woman you'd like to spend a little more time with one-on-one."

"What happens with the rest of them?"

"You'll have more time with everyone in a group setting. Then on Wednesday, based on how your interactions go, you'll choose seven women to continue on. At the end of the episode, viewers will get to save one of the bottom three women during live voting."

Damn, so they're cutting two people right off the bat. They don't mess around here.

"How will I know who to keep?" This whole thing suddenly feels a bit overwhelming. Sure, I've had fans showing their affection for me, but I've never *dated* ten people at the same time.

"You'll have your favorites, of course. But the production team can help you make your decisions. After all, we want a good show, right?" He winks at me, and then the car comes to a halt.

I step out of the Range Rover, and production staff instantly flock to me, guiding me into the massive property.

Immediately upon walking into the house, I notice a chandelier overhead and a checkered tile entryway opening to a massive sitting area with a fireplace. I walk across the living area to double doors that open to a huge deck. It overlooks a pool that looks like it came straight out of a scene from ancient Rome, with its marble columns and sculptures.

"There'll be time for a tour later." A voice over my shoulder startles me. "But it's stunning, isn't it?"

I look back, and it's just Jarrod, the show host. I assume we'll become best buds by the end of this experience if he's anything like the old host of the *Bachelor* franchise shows, Chris Harrison, was.

"Yeah, it's definitely way out of my budget." I laugh.

"Well, get used to it, because you'll be staying here for the next few weeks." He claps me on the shoulder as he walks away and stylists take over. They lead me to the master suite bathroom where the entire hair and makeup department is set up.

By the time late afternoon rolls around, I'm already exhausted and ready to call it a day and we haven't even started filming anything. I can already tell it's going to be a long night.

"Dusty, over here." Film crew members direct me to the spot I'm supposed to stand.

"Let's get a shot of Jarrod and Dusty together!" the director yells. "Action!"

Jarrod puts a hand on my shoulder. "How're you feeling, man? You ready for this?"

I put on an artificial smile for the cameras, although the pit in my stomach isn't fake. "I'm a little nervous, to be honest. I've never dated this many women at once."

"Man, I would've thought a big country music star like you would have women falling at his feet." Jarrod chuckles.

I suppress the urge to roll my eyes. Sure, they do tend to fall at my feet, but that doesn't mean I date several of them at once. Musicians may have the reputation of getting around and having fun, but some of us are just trying to put food on the table and get by.

I give him a playful nudge instead and say, "You'd be surprised, Jarrod." *God, this is so cheesy. This isn't me.*

"Cut!" the director calls. "That was great, guys. The women will be here soon, and then we'll start filming again."

About twenty minutes later, a touring bus pulls up in front of the house. Not quite what I was expecting, considering the house we were filming at, but maybe they didn't want to use a limo for fear of really ripping off other dating shows. I'll never understand reality TV.

One by one, women file off the bus. They're all ushered inside, but that doesn't stop some of them from waving or trying to steal glances at me.

"Dusty, we're going to have you stand here." A

producer directs me to the small courtyard next to the house.

Another fifteen excruciatingly slow minutes pass, and nothing happens. My mind starts to wander a bit, and my stomach growls. *I'm hungry. Is there going to be any food here?*

After a little while longer, the director *finally* comes back, as well as the executive producer.

"All right, everybody, the moment we've been waiting for." She claps her hands together. "Let's get this show on the road."

The cameras start rolling, and Jarrod dramatically walks toward me. It all feels so scripted, except I have no idea what to do.

"Hello, Jarrod," I say, wanting to break this awkward silence.

"Dusty. We've got ten amazing women here to meet you. Are you ready?" he asks as if we didn't already have this conversation.

"I am." Is it hot out here? Maybe a suit jacket was a bad idea for early summer in Nashville. At my side, my hands are slick and clammy. Am I nervous? There's no way I'm nervous; this isn't real. It's all just for show, right?

"Best of luck to you, Dusty." He gestures to the house as the doors open and the first woman walks out.

She's stunning, and I shield my eyes to make sure I'm seeing her clearly. *Why the fuck would they have me facing the sun?* I take in her long legs and suntanned skin. She's wearing a denim skirt and a flowy white top, and her caramel-colored hair falls just below her shoulders.

"Hi, Dusty." She smiles as she takes my hands. "I'm Katherine. It's so nice to meet you."

I remember her voice from the second day of auditions. "You look stunning." I'm not even sure what comes out of my mouth next, but I do know I need to get a grip, otherwise I'm not going to remember anything from these conversations besides how gorgeous they are. That's not what I'm here for.

Our five minutes feel like thirty seconds, and I'm not convinced that I didn't black out for half of the conversation. All I remember is her saying she's not from Tennessee, but she was so glad that she made the trip out here for the show.

"I'm so glad we got to talk. I'll see you later?"

I nod, and she smiles as she says goodbye then walks back into the house.

Jarrod comes out of nowhere. "So, first lady of the day? What's going through your head right now?"

"Honestly, I don't know. I may have blacked out for those five minutes," I reply, to which he laughs.

"How about we move so you can sit for your next conversations. Maybe that'll take some of the pressure off?" he suggests, and I nod.

We walk to a shaded area where benches are already set up. Thank God, because if I had to stand out in the sun any longer, I'd start sweating through my clothes. *That* would not look good on television.

"All right, man, I'll check back in with you later." With that, he's gone, and the next contestant, a tall, fair-skinned blonde, is walking out.

"Hi! I'm Jordan." Instead of taking my hands like Katherine did, she pulls me in for a hug.

It takes me a moment to gather myself, but I hug her back, getting a whiff of her perfume. It smells like peaches and florals. I blink to prevent myself from sneezing.

"How are you, Jordan?" I ask as she releases me from the hug and I gesture for us to sit.

"I'm great! Super excited for this opportunity." Her bubbly voice reminds me of sunshine. *She* reminds me of sunshine with her bright hair and big, expressive eyes.

"Where are you from?"

"I'm originally from Knoxville, but I made my way out to Nashville a few years ago to try to pursue music. Now I'm here."

I know a lot of the women who came on the show are musicians, but it has me curious about how many of them are here just to move their music career forward. Not that it really matters to me, because at the end of the day, that's all I'm trying to do, too.

"How has that gone so far?" I'm hoping she'll give me an idea of her intentions, if not for myself, then for the show. People love speculating whether contestants are "here for the right reasons" or not. At least, that's what I've heard from my cousin who watches a lot of dating shows.

"You know, it hasn't exactly been successful, hence why I'm here and not doing my own concerts or recording albums. But I truly came here to meet you, the record deal was just an extra benefit."

She seems sincere, but I feel like they always do. Then, once the experience gets more stressful, you learn their true motives.

"Well, it was great to meet you, Jordan, but I think our time is up." I stand, giving her a quick hug. Our conversation was pleasant, and now that the nerves have started to dissipate, I'm finding myself eager to meet the rest of the women.

Six conversations later, and I'm exhausted. My social battery is starting to deplete, and it's like I ran five miles instead of simply talking for a couple hours.

"Only two more. You can do this." I take a deep breath, trying to calm the pounding in my chest. We changed locations a couple more times, and the last place they have me sitting is in a lounge chair by the pool.

"Rolling," the director calls out as the next woman starts walking, no *gliding*, down the stairs.

"Hello."

I instantly recognize her voice. How could I forget it? *Aspen.* I thought her voice was captivating, but it doesn't even compare to her looks.

"H-hi." *Get yourself together, man.* I can't stop staring at her whirlpool eyes.

"How are you?" She walks over to me and pulls me in for a hug, which I welcome, wrapping myself in her scent —lavender and vanilla.

"I'm great. Do you want to sit?" I hope she doesn't see I'm nervous, even as sticky sweat soaks through my shirt. She has this effect on me that I can't explain.

"I'd love to sit." She sits, crosses her legs, and gives me an amused look.

"What's that look for?" Heat rushes to my face. I'm not normally like this. Women are usually the ones falling at my feet, not the other way around.

"You're just…different than I expected you to be," she admits, tucking a strand of hair behind her ear.

"How so?"

"I don't know. I guess I just expected you to be full of yourself. I never expected a country superstar like you to turn beet red at the sight of a pretty woman." She winks, and I wish this conversation wasn't going to be broadcasted on television for the world to see. Maybe fans will find it endearing, but I find it slightly humiliating.

I let out a shaky laugh. "I guess I'm just full of surprises, Aspen."

"I guess so. I can't wait to see what else you have up your sleeve, Dusty Wilder." She pauses then calls me out. "So, are you going to ask me any questions or what?"

This woman. She's going to keep me on my toes this season. "Right. Where are you from, Aspen?"

"I'm originally from Oklahoma, but I moved here to Nashville when I was eighteen. I've been here for eight years now."

Similar to me, then.

"That's a lot like how I ended up here, too. I grew up in Oklahoma, but came out here after graduating high school in pursuit of a music career. It took me some time, but eventually Ace High Entertainment took a chance on me and signed me." I can admit I owe Rob Acerra for signing a twenty-year-old kid with a dream.

It's somewhat emotional to think about what it took to get here. And it's slightly embarrassing to think about how much I could lose if this reality show stuff doesn't work out. I've worked hard to make a name for myself, and as much as I hate the mainstream box they're trying to shove me in, this is how I'm able to help support my family. I need to do this for them as much as I need to do it for myself.

But if it were up to me, I'd write the songs I want to sing, ditch the heartthrob character the label has assigned me, and sing real, authentic country music. Not this autotuned, over-produced shit.

"That's incredible. You should be really proud of

yourself. Nashville is lucky to have you. Hopefully, this will lead to prosperous music careers for both of us."

I dip my chin in acknowledgment. "I hope you find what you're looking for here in Nashville, Aspen. I'm excited to see more of you."

The tone that signals our time is up goes off in my earpiece, and I stand, taking off my hat and taking her hand. "It was a pleasure."

She stands, and I take a moment to kiss her hand in farewell.

"I'll see you around."

I watch her disappear into the house, and my eyes linger on the door longer than I'd like to admit. So much so that I don't even realize the last woman walked out of the house until she's directly in front of my face.

Her.

8
baylor

America's Sweetheart

THE PRODUCERS INSISTED I went last. Unfortunate, considering Aspen, the girl who went right before me, practically has Dusty drooling over her like a lovesick puppy.

I'm standing in front of him when he finally snaps out of her trance. His eyes meet mine, and his brows furrow in confusion.

"What are *you* doing—" Recognition flashes in his eyes, but I cut him off, giving him a sweet smile.

I am *not* losing my job today. "I'm Baylor."

Suspicion is written all over his face, but he reluctantly introduces himself. "Dusty… I know you. You were at—"

"I don't think so," I interrupt, not letting him finish his sentence on camera. "You must have confused me with someone else."

Come on, you idiot. Help me out here.

"Right, no, you're right. I apologize. It's very nice to meet you, Baylor." He takes my hand and presses his lips to the top of it, sending a shockwave through me.

Get it together, Baylor. This is fake. *You are not going to fall for his phony charm. Play the game.*

My experience working in public relations and my education have prepared me for these things. Interviews are all just acting, after all, how hard is it going to be with this?

It's just an act.

A performance.

No feelings involved, just a way for me to keep my job then advance my career.

I've spent the past couple hours in the house with the rest of the women waiting for our respective "speed dating" rounds with Dusty. Most of them seemed sincere, genuine. But I've been around women my entire life, and I know it's only a matter of time until the claws come out and some of the "nice girl" facades start to fade.

"So, what brings you to the show?" he asks, causing my focus to snap back to the present.

"I've always loved music," I reply, going through my rehearsed speech in my head. That was the truth. Music has always been my outlet, a way for me to release whatever I'm feeling. "The opportunity to have a musical career alongside someone I've fallen in love with is very appealing to me." *Lie.*

I'm sure several other women had similar answers, so I'm just hoping that Dusty doesn't see right through the act.

Neither of us say a word, the pause hanging in the air between us. I'm hyperaware of the cameras as Dusty flicks his eyes to the side where the producers are gesturing for him to continue, to do something.

He clears his throat. "Music definitely has that effect. When I was growing up, there was no better stress relief than turning my music up as loud as possible, lying on the floor, and just letting myself *feel*." He pauses, like the confession feels a bit too vulnerable, too deep for reality TV, but then throws in what I assume is a quick joke. "Definitely also helps when your music gets you millions of fans."

I give him a quizzical look, trying to figure him out, but snap out of it quickly. "Yeah, it must be nice having a passion that people see value in. Anyway, I'm *very* excited to be here, meeting you in person."

"Oh, yeah? You seem absolutely *thrilled* to be here." His lips quirk up in a cocky smirk as though a girl like me being excited to meet him strokes his ego.

I playfully roll my eyes. "What gave it away? Wait, don't tell me, was it my *undeniable charm*?" Sarcasm drips from the latter part of my comment, but it doesn't seem to phase him. Instead, when a strand of hair falls in front of my eyes, he simply tucks the traitorous lock behind my ear.

My gaze darts to his hand brushing my cheek as he pulls it back. Even with the absence of his touch, it's as though flames lick at my skin, and I hope to God my face isn't showing how flustered I am.

"Something like that." A small glint of amusement shines in his expression as he studies my face.

"Well, I'm glad you think it's endearing." I smile, forgetting about the cameras for a moment. But one glance over my shoulder is all it takes to bring me back to reality.

dusty

Baylor smiles, continuing to joke with me, but I can't control the muscles in my face as they contort into confusion. Before she can ask me what's wrong, I quickly fix my expression and blurt, "I don't remember seeing your name or hearing your voice during the auditions."

"Yeah, that's because I didn't audition." She breaks eye contact with me for a moment. "I was the lucky girl chosen by America to be on the show."

"America's Sweetheart, are you?" I tease, willing her to look back up at me. "Well, I can't blame them. From first impressions alone, I'd say America has pretty good taste."

"T-thanks." Her brows pull together, and for a moment, I wonder if I've said something wrong. But I'm not given an opportunity to find out, because the producers cut us off, pulling her away. I'm not sure why, the signal that our time had come to an end hadn't gone off yet, but I don't fight them. If anything, it just deepens my level of intrigue.

"I'll talk to you soon, Baylor," I call after her, cementing the look she gives me over her shoulder in my mind.

"So, after meeting the ten women and finally putting faces to their voices, how are you feeling, my man?" Jarrod and I stand in the courtyard where filming first took place.

I think back to the conversations I had today, mainly with Katherine, Aspen, and Baylor, and the smile that pulls at my cheeks is a genuine one. "Optimistic, Jarrod. I think

I've got a great group of women here, both in personalities and musical talent."

"That's amazing to hear. The fun isn't over yet. In a few minutes, you'll have the opportunity to choose one woman who really captured your attention today to go on a solo date with. You'll spend a romantic day together to get to know each other better. This date will hopefully help you determine if you see the potential in spending your career and life together."

The pressure of his words weigh heavy on me as the reality of how big the decisions I will be making on this show are. This isn't just my career at stake. It's the rest of my life, or at least until this contract is over.

I try my best not to trip over my words. "Jarrod, I don't think reality has set in until now. These are big decisions I'm making."

"Sure are, buddy. But I have complete faith in you that you'll make the best decision at the end of the day. Just listen to your heart."

Said heart drums in my chest, and I take a deep breath as the cameras cut.

"Who are you thinking of taking on the first solo date?" Brett asks as we walk to our next location.

I think for a moment. "Baylor, Aspen, and Katherine were my favorites from the conversations today."

What looks like a mix of surprise and confusion flashes across Brett's face as he flushes a rosy shade of pink. "B-Baylor?"

"Is there a problem with her?" I narrow my eyes.

I remember how she answered my questions regarding why she came on the show, and while I believe half of her answer—the part about loving music—the other half seemed rehearsed. It felt a bit like the answers I've been giving to the producers, but it only made my interest in her grow. It made me wonder what her story actually is. I also didn't miss how her eyes darkened a bit when she mentioned people seeing value in my passion for music, like shadows settling in.

"N-no, there's no problem with her, I'm just surprised," he mumbles, his words slurring together as he races through the sentence. "I'd say Katherine is your safest bet, though. From everything we've seen so far."

I slowly nod at his suggestion. Our pace never slows through the entire conversation until we come to a stop at the double front doors of the house. "So, you're telling me I should pick Katherine?"

He confirms, nodding. "Yes, you should pick her."

"All right, then." I agree, because I'm confident that my time with Aspen and Baylor will come. It just has to be the right time.

When the producers open the doors, ushering me into the house, the chatter that once filled the living room comes to a halt, silence embracing the space before a burst of cheers.

"Dusty!"

"He's here!"

A collective of cheers and greetings welcome me, and warmth spreads through my chest. It reminds me of the cheers from the crowd when I walk on stage during a tour. It's electrifying. Exhilarating.

"Hello, ladies." I tip my hat as I walk to the center of the living room, the expectant eyes of the women glued to me the entire time. "It's been an absolute honor and joy getting to speak with you all today. I'm very excited for this opportunity, and I'm doing my best to embrace it all. I'm not much for interviews, much less being on national television, so we're all in this together."

A few giggles arise in response to my miniature speech.

"I'm not sure if you've been informed of what's next"—I sneak a quick glance at the producers off to the side, who give me a thumbs-up—"but we're jumping right into this process. I have the pleasure of taking one of you lovely ladies on a solo date tomorrow."

My eyes scan over the room. I can't help but notice that while some of the girls look anxious, a couple of them look almost bored, America's Sweetheart being one of them. Normally, the disinterest would be a turn off, but all it does it make me want to know the truth of why she's here.

I dismiss the thoughts of my mystery girl and focus on the one who I'll be taking on a date tomorrow. "Katherine?" I think it shocks her a bit, as she startles in her seat, eyes blinking rapidly. "Would you like to go on a date with me tomorrow?"

"It would be my honor." She beams, and I let out a breath of relief.

"Well, ladies, it was great to see you. I look forward to this journey together." I clasp my hands, and they all wave as they're ushered out of the house, toward the bus that will take them back to their hotel for the night.

9
dusty

The First Solo Date

WHEN I WOKE up this morning, a wave of excitement and nerves washed over me as I prepared for my solo date with Katherine. Not only will it be my first date with her, but it will be my first date on the show and the first solo date of the season. I have no idea what's in store for us today, but I have a feeling whatever it is will set the tone for the coming weeks.

A few producers and crew members show up to get me camera ready for the day, a bit to my dismay. I was hoping we were done with the makeup. The fancy clothes, although not my personal taste, I can get used to, even if it's a bit like playing dress-up, but the makeup? I'm not sure I'll ever get used to that.

I'll be meeting Katherine at a trailhead by the Cumberland River this morning, and then in the afternoon, I'll be meeting the rest of the women to spend time with them in a group setting. Even before the producers told me I would be meeting her at a trailhead, I was dressed pretty casually—a pair of cargo shorts and an athletic T-shirt—so I have enough reason to assume we're doing something active and not just sitting down for a meal. Which I'm completely okay with. Eating at a romantic restaurant in front of cameras for the very first date seems like a lot of pressure.

The entire car ride to the trailhead is uncomfortably silent, with Brett driving and me sitting in the passenger seat. The camera crew is coming in a separate vehicle, a detail I'm grateful for, but it makes the drive with Brett a bit painful. Not even Chris Stapleton crooning "Broken Halos" over the radio can provide me any relief or distraction, so I resort to looking out the window.

"All right, we're here," Brett announces as he pulls into the parking lot and cuts the engine. "We'll get out of the car together, but you'll walk ahead on the path and the camera crew will follow behind you. Katherine's already here."

I nod before getting out of the car. Brett falls behind as the camera crew hooks me up to a microphone and sends me on my way. I walk on the path as instructed until a flash of brown hair catches my attention up ahead. In a matching lilac workout set and her hair pulled back in a high ponytail, Katherine stands by one of those self-service bike rental kiosks.

"Katherine, hey!" I call, prompting her to whirl around with a wide smile on her face.

She meets me in the middle, pulling me into a hug as she greets me, "Hi, Dusty!"

I pull back for a moment to look at her. "You look beautiful."

Her eyes sparkle as a rosy tint creeps into the apples of her cheeks. "Thank you, you also look incredible."

"Let's rent some bikes, shall we?" I gesture to the bike

racks. "I haven't ridden a bike in years, so we'll see how this goes."

She laughs at my admission but lightly squeezes my arm. "It's been a long time for me, too, so we'll struggle together."

"Sounds great." I chuckle as we each unlock a bike and grab a helmet. I secure the strap under my chin before Katherine is able to buckle hers, so I face her and tilt her chin upward before grabbing the straps. "Here," I murmur as the buckle clicks together.

"Thanks," she whispers.

I try to ignore the camera crew and the fact that we're currently mic'd up, trying to treat this like any other date. But the knowledge that someone is watching us crawls up my spine.

I shake off the discomfort as I walk my bike backward. "Shall we?"

We start off slow, and a bit shaky, on our bikes. Well, *I* start off shaky, but we get into a rhythm pretty quick where we can pedal side by side and have a conversation.

"So, I'm pretty sure I blacked out during the entire speed dating process," I admit with a laugh. "Where did you say you were from?"

"I'm from South Carolina," she replies, not giving me any sort of impression that she's upset I didn't remember. "My goal is to move out here permanently, but I do still live in South Carolina right now. Music was a hobby, until it wasn't."

"You said you're a nurse, right?" I ask, remembering at least one detail about her from the whirlwind of a day I had yesterday.

"Yeah, I work in pediatrics. I love it wholeheartedly, and as much as I would love to stay, I tell those kids to follow their dreams. If I'm not following mine, then who am I to give them advice? I owe it to them—especially the ones who won't get to follow their dreams—to chase mine." Her face falls slightly, but there's still a glint of passion in her eyes. I can tell she really loves what she does.

"That's admirable, truly. The kids you work with are probably so proud that you're here." I reach out my arm to touch her shoulder, attempting to ride one-handed. The moment is fast, though, a bit too fast, as I start to lose balance and have to return my attention to the handlebars.

"I miss them, I really do, but I wouldn't trade this opportunity for the world." She looks over at me, a seriousness in her eyes. There's no way I'll send her home after this. She's so…genuine. As much as this process is for me, I also want this for her.

"What's one thing you want to do before you die?" The question pops in my head out of nowhere, falling out of my mouth.

"Like a bucket list item? Hmm…I really want to run a marathon."

Damn, so she's pretty, has musical talent, and is athletic? I think to myself.

"How about you?" she asks, after a few moments of quiet.

"Definitely not run a marathon." I laugh. "I can hardly ride a bike, as you can probably tell. I'm not much of a runner either, so unless walking the marathon is an option, I unfortunately won't be joining you on that venture. But in all seriousness, I've always wanted to play a big music festival like Stagecoach. Or during CMA Fest."

"You haven't done that before?" Her eyes widen. "But you're a big country star?"

I shake my head. "I almost played CMA Fest, but

something came up and I wasn't able to anymore. That was when I was a newer artist, too, and the opportunity just hasn't arisen again."

"I hope you get to cross that off your bucket list one day, Dusty Wilder."

We ride around for about an hour, chatting about things like favorite movies and musical idols. I learn that we have similar tastes in music, both preferring classic country over mainstream Nashville country, a bit ironic considering my label is trying to push me into the mainstream pool of music.

"Katherine, I'm so glad we had this time together." I take her hand after we return our bikes to the rental kiosk.

"Me too. I feel like I learned a lot about you. And I think you're a pretty great guy."

My date with Katherine leaves my body warm and my heart thundering like wild horses in my chest. But I'm only given a couple hours to change and get ready for my next date—axe throwing with five of the other nine women—so I can't dwell on it for too long.

When I walk in the doors of the axe throwing building, the girls chosen by production—Kelsie, Jade, Sage, Aspen, and America's Sweetheart herself—are already waiting.

"Hey, handsome." Aspen immediately walks over, looping her arm underneath mine to rest her hand on my bicep.

"Hi, ladies." I glance down to the spot where her hand rests. "I'm excited to spend time with you tonight, have a little bit of fun, and hopefully get to know you all on a deeper level."

Aspen's hand is still on my arm, despite the other girls awkwardly shifting on their feet at the sight. I debate pulling away, but then an employee gets our attention, directing us to the three stalls we'll be using, separating Aspen from me anyway.

Kelsie and Sage are put in the stall to my left, and Baylor and Aspen to the one on my right, leaving me and Jade next to each other in the middle stall. Each stall only has one small hatchet.

"Oh, God, I'm probably going to be horrible at this." A laugh erupts from my left side as Kelsie picks up one of the axes and stands in front of the target.

Sage leans away from her, a grimace on her face. "I'm going to stay away from you, then. I don't really feel like getting hit by an axe today." She backs up slightly, ensuring that she's out of any potential line of fire. I don't blame her, because with the way Kelsie is holding the axe, there's no telling what direction it could go.

Still giggling, Kelsie throws the axe, or at least attempts to throw it. Just like she predicted, she misses horribly. She half-skips over to the hatchet lying on the floor. I'm glad she's having fun, though, more than I can say about the grumpy girls to my right. Neither Baylor or Aspen look particularly interested in the activity.

Baylor reluctantly picks up an axe while Aspen picks at her nails.

"Show me what you've got, America's Sweetheart." I wink at Baylor.

The look she gives me sends a chill down my spine, and I can't explain why. There's something about her that draws me in.

She huffs out a breath as she lines up and raises the axe over her head. The muscles in her arms contract as she pulls the tool back then throws it at the target, the blade soaring through the air before sticking in the middle ring.

The other girls turned their heads, looking at Baylor's target.

"Not too bad." Jarrod approaches from behind me, clapping his hands. "I hope you girls are warmed up, because this isn't just any date. It's a competition."

I can't tell who it is, but one of the girls lets out a quiet groan as they circle around Jarrod.

"Just a friendly competition, but whoever wins may or may not get an advantage." He raises his eyebrows. "The winner of tonight's challenge will secure themselves a solo date next week."

One of the girls gasps, but Jarrod continues, unphased. "Yes, that means that if you win tonight's challenge, you are granted immunity from the elimination later this week."

"Well, this isn't fair," Aspen grumbles.

Kelsie snorts. "Guess we already know I'm not winning."

"Ladies, you'll be given five axes to throw. If you hit a bullseye, that's five points. The middle ring is worth three points, and the outer ring is one point. Now, there's also those small green circles on the outside. If you can stick one of those, it's seven points. Your axe must stay in the target for the points to count. Whoever has the highest score at the end will win the challenge."

Once Jarrod finishes explaining the rules, a few employees bring out a couple more axes.

"All right, let's get started, shall we?"

Each of the girls line up about twelve feet away from their targets. Speed isn't a factor, so there's no need to rush, but when the buzzer sounds, it's as though a spark of competitiveness flares within all of them.

Aspen throws her axe first. It rotates through the air before sticking in the middle ring. One employee stands by each station to keep track of the scores.

"How are you doing over there, Kelsie?" I call out to her, amusement in my voice. There's no way she's going to win this competition. Almost every single axe she's thrown has either been a horrible miss or has hit the target then fallen to the ground.

"Great! I suck at this!" She laughs, and I wonder how she could be so carefree knowing the stakes of the competition.

Sage has racked up nine points, Jade has five, and Baylor and Aspen are leading with twelve points each. The rest of the girls are too far behind to catch up, so it's down to these two. Competitive energy radiates off them as they side-eye each other after every throw. Even the cameramen are focusing on the two of them, a rivalry seeming to form between the girls.

"I'm going to get that solo date," Aspen grits through her teeth, her voice barely audible over the clattering of axes on the floor, likely from Kelsie's end.

She's down to her last one, and sweat beads on her forehead as she raises the hatchet. A hushed silence falls over the group as she throws it. It floats right into the bullseye, adding five points to her tally and securing the win, unless Baylor can hit the small green targets.

"Ooh, we've got a competition on our hands." Jarrod claps from the side of us. "It's down to the wire here."

I'm secretly hoping Baylor wins, because I want to spend more time with her. Figure her out. Even though it's up to me who makes it through, Baylor winning the challenge secures her spot, so the producers can't try to convince me to cut her.

Baylor tucks a strand of hair that fell in her face behind her ear then grabs an axe, walking slowly to the line. Her shoulders rise and fall as she takes a deep breath, and then in a moment's time, the axe is floating through the air. It spins once before it hits her target: the green circle worth seven points.

Yes! I mentally pump my fist.

Jarrod walks over to her, taking her wrist and holding it up in the air like she just won a boxing match. "Congratulations, Baylor. You're the winner of the first ever *Heart Strings* axe-throwing competition. You'll be going on a solo date with Dusty first thing next week, which also means you're safe from elimination. How does it feel?"

She shrugs. "Good? I guess?" She doesn't sound too convinced, and the corner of my lip lifts in a slight grin.

I like this girl.

"Now that the competition is over, I'll leave you all to it. Ladies—other than Baylor—you're at risk of elimination, so use this time wisely," Jarrod warns before he walks away.

The girls at risk of elimination waste no time trying to get to me, but Jade is able to steal me away before anyone else—namely Aspen—is able to. As we walk toward a seating area, a few of the other girls look over their shoulders to watch us go. Before we turn a corner, Aspen chucks a hatchet, hitting a bullseye and splitting the target right down the middle.

"That was quite the competition, wasn't it?" I laugh as we take a seat on a plush couch tucked in a quiet area away from the action.

Jade smiles as she wraps a long strand of ink-black,

pin-straight hair around her index finger. It's so silky that it immediately slides off, and I resist the urge to brush it behind her ear. "Yeah, I didn't expect the competition to be so cutthroat right away, but I should have known better."

"Well, I think you did amazing." We're sitting close enough together that our legs touch, and I notice her bare skin is covered in gooseflesh. "Are you cold?"

"Me?" She points to herself as she shivers a bit. "I guess, a little."

"Here." I grab a shag blanket folded on the arm of the couch and lay it over our laps as she scoots closer into me.

"Thank you. I just wanted to say I'm really grateful to be here and that it's *you* who we're here for," she admits. "I have a lot of hope for this process."

"I do, too," I confess. "I never pictured myself on a reality TV show, much less a dating show, but there's a first for everything, right?"

"I'm honestly surprised that you're here. How is a guy like you single?"

"I could ask the same thing about you." I bump my elbow against hers.

I look into her onyx eyes as she sighs. "I used to be in a long-term relationship. We were really great together, playing music and performing at small shows. But I guess we just grew apart."

Her confession hits me like a knife to the chest.

"I can't imagine what that was like." I'd been in relationships before, although most of them were PR relationships set up by the label to keep up the image they'd created for me. They'd never been deep. I don't know if I've ever been in love before.

"I honestly believed it was love and we were meant to

be together. But if that's what loving the wrong person felt like, then I can't wait for what loving the right person is like."

"Thank you for sharing that with me. I know it can't be easy, with me basically being a stranger and all."

Footsteps approach, cutting our conversation short, as Aspen comes over to the couch.

"Hey…" She shifts on her feet. "Can I talk to Dusty?"

Jade blinks as she grabs the blanket, moving it off her legs, and stands. She's so much shorter than Aspen, probably standing at five feet max. "Yeah, yeah, of course. Thanks for chatting with me, Dusty."

Aspen replaces her, sitting a bit too close to me and covering herself with the blanket, although she's wearing jeans, unlike Jade in her shorts.

"How are you holding up after the competition?" I ask, knowing she was close to securing a spot next week.

"I'm doing all right. It was obviously a bit disappointing to lose, but I'm determined. I want to be here, and I'm willing to prove that however I need to."

We talk for a few more minutes before I end the conversation to talk to some of the other women here. The disappointment on Aspen's face is evident, but she quickly hides it.

By the end of the night, I've gotten to talk to everyone except for Baylor. It makes sense in my head because she's guaranteed to make it to the next week, but a heaviness still settles in my stomach.

When Sage—the last person I'd been talking to—and I return back to the main area, Jarrod is waiting for us with the rest of the group.

10
baylor

Drama, Drama, Drama

DUSTY AND SAGE walk back from their conversation as the rest of us stand around waiting with Jarrod.

"Dusty, it looks like that's all the time we have for tonight," Jarrod announces.

Dusty's face falls a little, but in the blink of an eye, his expression reverts back to normal. He takes a deep breath. "Ladies, thank you for such a fun evening. I will see you all tomorrow night." He gives Sage a hug then moves down the line. When he finally makes it to me, I sigh, letting my shoulders drop as I sink into the warmth of his chest, a gentle woodsy scent enveloping my senses.

I didn't intend for that reaction—I didn't *want* that reaction—but there's something about him that causes me to drop my defenses.

"Thanks, Baylor," he whispers in my ear as a tingling sensation drops down my spine. "I'll see you tomorrow."

"See you," I murmur back.

Any intimacy is cut short, though, as Jarrod whisks Dusty away, and we're escorted to the vans to head back to the hotel that production has us staying at. It doesn't make a lot of sense for *us* to be staying at one, but Dusty is already staying at the house we filmed in, and they want to limit our interactions with him off camera.

Sage, Aspen—unfortunately—and I are riding in the same car, and Sage sidles up next to me as we exit the axe throwing building.

"So, what do you think of Dusty?" she asks, quiet enough that Aspen can't hear.

I shrug. "I think he's okay." I'm still skeptical of him, but I'm here for a reason, and as much as I want to trust the other girls, I have to play the part.

"Just okay?" She laughs, pulling me out of my thoughts.

"He's different than I expected," I admit. "I don't know, I've only ever seen what the media portrays."

She ponders what I say for a moment. "That makes sense. I feel like he's got a deeper side to him, though. I had some really great conversations with him, and I think he's really leaning into this whole process. It's gotta be hard dating multiple people at once, so I'm trying to give him the benefit of the doubt."

"What are you guys talking about?" Aspen's voice is monotonous and disinterested, like she's only talking to us because she has no one else to talk to.

"We're talking about Dusty," Sage offers. "I think he's got a deeper side than the country star persona he puts on."

She scoffs a little. "I mean, he's a celebrity, though. Sure, everyone's going to have a deeper side, but at the end of the day, he's still a famous musician. How different is he really to the rest of us?"

I'm not sure, but I want to find out, I think as she continues.

"We're all just trying to make it, otherwise, we wouldn't be here."

I hate to admit Aspen has a point, but she does—everyone here is trying to get their big break. But at the same time, I have the insider info that Dusty never wanted to be here. If he was just like the rest of Nashville, like the rest of Music Row, then would he have complained so much about the exposure?

Sage and I both shrug, and the rest of the walk to the car is silent. Luckily, it's only a short distance, and soon enough, Aspen is climbing into the passenger side and Sage and I take the backseats. It's been a long day and I'm ready to flop down on my bed for a deep slumber, so I find myself zoning out the entire car ride back to the hotel.

The next morning, the rest of the girls—Valerie, Morgan, Jordan, and Abigail—leave for their group date with Dusty, but Katherine, the other girls who went on the group date last night, and I are driven to the property where the speed dating took place.

I personally would rather stay at the hotel, but we were told we can't spend all day in our rooms. Probably so the crew can get footage of any drama that happens between the girls who aren't on the date.

We are fortunate enough that we don't have roommates, because with my luck I'd get stuck with Aspen. I take it as a small blessing that once the day is over, I can at least have a little bit of privacy.

When we arrive, I get out of the car and reach my arms toward the sky, stretching out my limbs. Aspen shoots me a glare as she exits the vehicle she was in and walks toward the house without giving me a second glance.

I shake my head, rolling my eyes, as the rest of the girls and I follow.

We all plop down on the sectional couch in the living room, and silence overtakes the room. There's no TV or music—although, I'm sure we could listen to Dusty's music on a loop if we really wanted to. Just the company of five of Dusty's other girlfriends and the hidden cameras placed around the house. Kind of weird if I think about it too much, but reality TV has always stretched boundaries and norms.

"How was your date with Dusty, Katherine?" Sage asks.

The smile that spreads across Katherine's face tells us everything we need to know. The girl is practically glowing just from the mention of his name.

"It was amazing. We went for a bike ride, which doesn't sound romantic at all, but it really was. He's so understanding and engaging in conversations. I knew he was charismatic, obviously, but it really felt like he listened to what I was saying. I don't know, I just feel really good about where we're at so far in our relationship."

A few of the other girls squeal and blush, swooning over the details of Katherine's date, but Aspen rolls her eyes, scrunching her nose. No one makes any comments about her apparent distaste toward Katherine, but I make a mental note about her attitude. It was clear to me from the beginning that Aspen thinks she's better than all of us, but she doesn't have to make it so obvious to everyone else.

"That's so cute!" Kelsie bats her eyelashes as she rests her head in her hands, and Sage nods in agreement.

"It was a bike ride," Aspen mutters. "What's so special about that?"

I don't think any of the other girls heard her—at least Katherine didn't, luckily—but it's enough for me to decide that the next time she runs her mouth I'll pull her aside and ask what the fuck her problem is.

"What do you think they're doing today?" Jade asks, changing the subject.

"I'm not sure, but they were all dressed pretty nice when they left this morning," Katherine replies.

"Hopefully it's not something super romantic." Kelsie lets out a nervous laugh.

"Honestly, anything would be more romantic than axe throwing." Aspen has the guts to open her mouth, but it's not as snarky of a comment as I expected. To be fair, axe throwing wasn't the most romantic way to spend a day, but it was kind of fun once I got into it.

"Oh, is that what you guys did last night? I guess I didn't even ask how that went!" Katherine places a hand on her chest apologetically.

A chorus of, "It was fun," and, "It went really well," floats around between Jade, Sage, and Kelsie.

"I was horrible at the axe-throwing part, though." Kelsie giggles, making the rest of us laugh with her.

"She was *so* bad, Katherine. I was genuinely scared for my life," Sage teases. "But Baylor was so good at it. You should have seen her win."

Warmth creeps into my cheeks as I shrug. "It wasn't a big deal, really."

"It was, though! You get a solo date next week because of it!" Sage adds, and I can't help but recoil at the disclosure. I wasn't going to advertise that me winning the challenge meant I'd get an automatic pass from the elimination and make it to the next week.

"Oh…wow." It seems like Katherine is at a loss for words, and I can't say I blame her. It's a huge advantage in a competition like this. Every minute counts, because it could mean the difference between a record deal and going home.

"If anything, this should just prove that everyone needs to be on their A-game. No messing around." Aspen's lips curl up slightly as her eyes narrow, gaze hardening. "Besides, she got lucky and just barely beat me."

"It may not have been by much, but I still won." I just couldn't bite my tongue on this one, letting the comment slip. "It wasn't luck, though."

"Excuse me?" She crosses her arms, her tone a bit accusatory. "What are you trying to say?"

I decide that if I'm going to open my mouth, I might as well go all out and tell her what's really on my mind. "All I'm saying is that maybe if your axe-throwing skills were as big as your attitude and ego, you'd be the one getting the solo date."

Sage's eyes widen, and Aspen's mouth gapes a little, as if she can't believe what I said. I was trying to keep a low profile, be one of those contestants who is easily forgotten, outshined by someone else, but that clearly backfired on me.

"Hmm. Well, if that's how you really feel, I guess we'll see if Dusty keeps you around after your solo date." Her retort is nicer than I expected, but the fire in her eyes practically burns through me. Then she leaves the room without another word.

That was both awkward and better than I expected.

The only thing on my mind when I walk down the hallway of the production building toward my interview is the conversation from earlier today. I shake my head as I look down at my shoes, watching my feet pass each large tile on the floor.

So much for keeping a low profile. *Why* did I do that?

"I can't believe I—" I don't even realize I'm muttering out loud to myself until I hear, "Can't believe you what?"

My head snaps up right before I collide with the solid chest of the person who the voice belongs to…Dusty Wilder. I jump backward, putting a couple feet between us, as my heart pounds.

"I-I can't believe I actually won the axe-throwing competition." I make something up as I throw my arms up in the air to add to the pretend shock.

He lets out a chuckle. "You're not a very good liar, Baylor."

Panic rises in my chest. *Does he already know?*

Before I can protest, he takes a step forward, closing the distance between us. As if to drive the point further, he leans in to whisper in my ear. "I think you knew *exactly* what you were doing on that axe-throwing date."

When he backs away, I tilt my head so I'm looking him square in the face and force my shoulders back so I stand a little bit taller. "I guess I'm just good at pretending."

"You don't have to pretend with me."

"You'd be surprised," I scoff then widen my eyes. "Did I say that out loud? I just meant I'm full of surprises."

"I don't doubt it for a second. I'm looking forward to

being surprised by you, sweetheart." He looks me up and down then steps out of the way so I can continue walking.

I try to resist the urge to look back over my shoulder to see if he's watching me as I leave, but my heart gets the better of me. As though he was waiting for me to turn, he's facing me with a wide grin on his face.

I'm absolutely fucked.

the confessionals

Producer: Who do you think your biggest competition is?
Aspen: Competition? I would hardly call these other girls competition.
Producer: You're not worried about any of the other contestants?
Aspen: No. Frankly, none of them are worth my time. And they're going to have to do a whole lot better than winning a stupid axe-throwing contest to win over Dusty Wilder.

Producer: What's the dynamic with the other girls been like so far?
Sage: So far, so good, I think. Besides the drama with Aspen today.
Producer: What drama?

Katherine: Baylor totally told off Aspen today. It was kind of badass.

Sage: Aspen was making snide comments the whole morning, and Baylor just snapped. I know we just met, but I didn't know she had that in her.

Aspen: Baylor's a [bleep].

Baylor: Aspen's a [bleep].

11
baylor

Ruthless

THE SECOND EPISODE AIRS TODAY, which also means the first elimination happens tonight.

We don't get to watch the episode, but earlier this morning, we were told that all the girls will wait together in a briefing room, and once it's over, we'll learn who is at risk of elimination. Those who are will head out to the stage, and viewers will get to vote for the girl they want to save.

I shouldn't care or even be nervous about the elimination, considering I have immunity for this week, but I am. It was never explicitly said that my performance on the show determines my fate at my job, but it's been implied by the looks Colette gives me every so often when no one else is paying attention. Ideally, I'll get eliminated at week five or six and can put all of this behind me.

It's the opposite of what most of these girls want, but it's what's best for *me*. I'm sure Colette and I have different ideas of "what's best," though.

"Who do you think is going to get eliminated?" Sage asks as she wrings her hands together.

Before I'm able to answer, the door swings open and a producer comes in.

"I guess we're about to find out," I mutter as we all turn our attention to him.

He clears his throat. "Ladies. If I call your name, please come with me to the stage." Stress radiates off some of the girls in the palpable silence. "Jordan."

Her jaw drops and her shoulders fall as she prepares herself to go. I hadn't interacted with her at all in the past week, so I wouldn't know what her connection is like, but clearly it wasn't as strong as some of the others here.

"Kelsie. Morgan." The producer rattles off the remaining names, and after they leave, several girls let out a collective sigh.

"What do you think they'll have to do to try to get saved?" Abigail, a petite girl with mousy hair and a sweet Southern accent, asks, her voice hardly above a whisper.

"No idea," Valerie answers.

Although the rest of us are guaranteed the next week in the competition, the anxious energy in the room doesn't disappear. Some of the women here became friends with a couple of the girls who are at risk, even in the short time we've had together so far.

I try not to think about what's going on or who's leaving as I close my eyes and take deep breaths, in and out.

The twenty or so minutes that we spend waiting feel like hours. But then the door opens and one girl returns. Jordan.

Jade squeals and runs over to hug her.

"What did you have to do?"

"Was Dusty there?"

"Did you get any explanations for why you were at risk of being eliminated?"

Jordan recoils as questions are fired at her, everyone crowding her more and more. Her face pales into a ghastly white, and that's when I realize she's about to pass out.

"Move!" I push one of the girls aside, trying to get to Jordan.

"Oh my God!" The others realize what's happening and back up to give her space.

"Someone go get a producer," I order, and Abigail slips out. "Hey, Jordan, can you hear me?" I ask, and she nods. "Okay, we need to get you sitting somewhere. Can you walk over to the couch?"

She nods again, and I help her walk over to the sectional just a few feet away. The rest of the group disperses and goes back to what they were doing before Jordan came in.

"I don't know what happened there. I think there was just too much excitement and everyone crowded around me at once." She gives me an embarrassed look.

"It happens. And you just went through what was probably a stressful experience."

She huffs and then lets out a harsh laugh. "Yeah. It wasn't terrible, but it wasn't great either, you know? We were really just being judged based on how the producers edited the show. They didn't have us do anything out there, we basically just had to watch as the votes came in."

Interesting.

"It was really hard on the other girls. I mean, I was lucky. I don't know if they just did that because it was week one. I at least thought it would be based on our musical talent and how strong we felt our connection was, not just what was broadcasted on television. I mean, I don't know about you guys, but our group date had absolutely nothing to do with music."

"Ours didn't either, and neither did Katherine's solo date. But you're right, that does seem odd. I also thought they'd have you sing or do *something*." I try to wrap my head around the idea that the producers are only letting people vote based on what they see on a fabricated TV show. I make a mental note to ask Daniella about it.

"I hope it's different moving forward. It was hard having to watch votes come in and see how much viewers disliked you." She cradles her head in her hands.

"Just try to relax," I encourage. "I know it's easier said than done, but you made it this week. That's a good thing."

"Thanks…" she trails off, like she can't remember my name. I don't discredit her for that; it's been a whirlwind of a week, and even though there's only ten—well, eight, now —girls here, we didn't have a lot of interaction with each other if we weren't on the same dates.

"Baylor," I offer, and she gives me a look of gratitude.

Abigail comes back with a producer, and they start asking Jordan questions to see if she needs medical attention so I get up to stay out of their way.

About thirty minutes later, we're given the okay to leave the briefing room and head back to the hotel.

The sound of knuckles rapping against my hotel door wakes me from the short nap I was taking. The elimination mentally and emotionally drained me, even though I knew I was safe. I pad over to the door, looking through the peephole instead of blindly opening it for whoever awaits me on the other side.

A flash of curled blonde hair and Daniella's face reassures me, and I swing the door open.

"Hey, babe. How's everything going so far?" She makes herself at home, walking right over to my bed to flop onto it. This is the first time in a while that I haven't either seen her in person—since we live together—or at least texted her. But as contestants, we all had our phones taken away and have had to rely on each other for social interaction, a fact that makes my stomach churn slightly, knowing that Aspen may very well be the only person I get to talk to in the coming weeks. If I'm still here, that is.

"I swear Colette is some kind of sociopath, because what the hell was that elimination process?" I rant, letting out an exasperated sigh as I lie down next to her.

"Trust me, I had no idea until Alex told me what happened." She rolls on to her side to face me. "But you have to admit, it makes for good television. They're projecting that the ratings will skyrocket. I mean, it's already looking really good for SSP."

"I felt bad for the girls who got eliminated. And Jordan for having to go through it. I know I'm only here for a short time, but I wish I could do something about it without giving away my identity, you know?"

Daniella takes my hand, lightly squeezing it, a signal that she understands. "Just focus on getting as far as possible. You don't have to win the whole thing, but if that's something you want, Baylor, then I say go for it."

"I'm not a country singer, Daniella." I snort. "I don't know if touring and being part of a record label is what I should be doing with my life. I mean, what would my parents think? They'd probably lose their minds right now if they knew I was on a dating show."

"Okay, but are you saying that because that's what *you* want, or because that's what your parents want?"

I freeze, my eyebrows pulling together as I quickly reply, "Me. Definitely because of what I want." It's the truth. At least I think it is. I shouldn't be running around trying to be a famous singer.

"Well, you know if you change your mind, I'm always in your corner. It doesn't matter what anyone else wants. You have to follow your heart and think about what you want, okay?" If she sees through my lies, she doesn't say it outright. But the heart-to-heart she's trying to have with me makes me suspect that she does.

"I know, Dani. Don't worry about me. How's everything been going on the production side?" Even though she's not a producer, she still sees most of what's happening on the show. She knows how things are going for me.

"I will admit, I'd rather be working with you than Emily. She practically drools over Alex every time we're near him. You should see her, Baylor, it's ridiculous. I'm surprised Colette hasn't fired her already, even though Alex brushes off her advances every single time." She rolls her eyes, and I'm trying to figure out if she's annoyed because she's jealous, or if she's annoyed because of the rules.

Sparks Studio Productions has a zero-fraternization policy. Relationships with coworkers aren't allowed, and relationships with contestants are definitely not allowed. Except for my case, apparently, but then again, no one knows I work for SSP.

"She's digging her own grave if she keeps it up. Everyone knows the policy, and she's dumb if she thinks she's the exception to the rule." Daniella's face darkens for a split second, but then she rolls off the bed, hopping down onto the floor. She smooths out her pants before saying, "Anyway, I'm not supposed to be here, so I better get going. I just missed you."

"I missed you too. But listen, give it a couple more weeks and then everything will be back to normal."

"Right. I'll see you around." She heads toward the door, but as her phone chimes, she swings her head over her shoulder before reaching the door handle. "Oh, and Baylor? Enjoy your date with Dusty tomorrow. Rumor has it he had a long conversation with the producers about what he wants the date to be like and it's completely different from what was originally planned. In fact, Alex just texted me, and I'm needed to help with the planning of all that, so I've gotta run." With a wink and laugh, she walks out the door.

Oh, right. The solo date is tomorrow.

But wait. Why would Dusty want to change the plans for *me*?

12

baylor

Like Johnny and June

DUSTY AND I walk down 16th Avenue with enough space between us that you wouldn't be able to guess we're on a date.

"Are you going to tell me where we're going?" I ask, trying to ignore the camera crew following us.

"That would ruin the surprise, now wouldn't it?" He glances over at me and, after noticing the gap between us, takes a step closer so our shoulders brush every time we take a step.

My tongue ties itself up in knots as I try to figure out what to say. I'm stuck between knowing this is all fake and wanting to get to know the real Dusty Wilder.

"You're quiet. What's on your mind?"

"I'm just following your lead. And wondering where we're going," I mutter the last part slightly, although I'm sure the microphone still picked it up.

"Relax, Baylor, we're almost there." He reaches his arm around me, resting it on my waist. "Besides, I think you're going to like where we're going."

We turn around the corner, and a few paces later, he stops. The sign above my head reads *Casanova Records*.

"Come on." He grabs my hand and, to my surprise, I let him link our fingers together. He pushes open the door, and the bells hanging on the handle jingle as we step inside.

Checkered tile spans throughout the store, and vinyls hang from the ceiling like disco balls with fairy lights weaving between them. Record jackets with album covers plaster the walls that don't have shelves, and smaller stands create aisles leading to the back.

"Welcome in! Let me know if you need help finding anything," the employee behind the counter greets us.

Dusty gives him a nod of acknowledgment as he thanks him.

At this point, the camera crew has moved in front of us, recording our faces as we browse the vinyls. I've never loved being on camera, but I'm starting to get used to it. I have a feeling I probably need to tone down my facial expressions, though. I've been told, by my parents and Daniella, that I let all my emotions show.

A record catches my eye as we pass the country music section, and I slow my stride, causing my arm to yank slightly on Dusty's.

He slows as I pull out the Johnny Cash album from the late sixties.

"Johnny Cash and June Carter," Dusty murmurs as he looks at the record with me.

"My parents always used to listen to them when I was younger. I remember sitting at the kitchen counter while they sang 'Jackson' together." I recall those moments like it was yesterday. That was back when they encouraged music and would have been happy for me if I pursued a career in it. I'm not really sure what changed that.

I'm nine years old, and the twang of guitar strings fills the kitchen as the intro to "Jackson" starts playing. Mom stops what she's doing, spinning so her back is to the stovetop, as Dad rushes into the kitchen.

I rock back and forth on my stool set up by the kitchen counter as Dad grabs Mom's hands, and they spin in circles on the linoleum tile.

They're laughing more than they're singing, mostly due to the fact Dad can't carry a tune to save his life. But Mom makes up for it with her melodic voice.

"Come here, Baylor!" Mom calls for me, and I hop down from the stool before making my way over to them, my socks sliding across the floor.

Dad picks me up and holds me in one arm as his other wraps around Mom.

The memory fades as Dusty walks away, leaving me a bit confused. I shrug it off, continuing to flip through the albums. A couple minutes later, he comes back with a vinyl in hand.

"This was my favorite album growing up." He flips up the record to show Elvis Presley's face.

"I never would have pegged you as an Elvis fan." I grin, taking the opportunity to play around with him. "I didn't think country music stars these days listened to anything older than the nineties."

He rolls his eyes at the joke, but there's no malice behind the gesture.

"I'm not like those other country singers, darlin'." He winks, and I roll my eyes. "Come on, let's see how else I can surprise you with my music taste."

We spend a good hour or so looking at records, and I realize Dusty was right about me liking this place. I've really enjoyed the time we've spent together so far. Today feels like just another day, not a date being recorded on camera to be televised to the whole country. And I can't decide whether I'm happy about that, or if I hate it.

By the time we walk out of Casanova Records, he's got three new vinyls in his hand and I have two.

"Where to now, Romeo?" I smirk.

"Romeo?" He gives me a quizzical look, and I shrug. "No, no, no, you've got to choose a better name than that. I'm not going to have my nickname be a dude whose whole love story ends with them both dying."

"What if I come up with something entirely worse?"

"Then we'll keep trying until something sticks. Come on, I've got somewhere else to take you." He takes my hand, and we continue a bit further down the street until we reach a small dive bar. The place is admittedly cute, with outdoor patio seating and lights strung up everywhere. Music filters out through the open doors, inviting us in.

We step into the bar, and a blonde woman who looks to be around Dusty's age is up on stage, singing with her band. When she sees Dusty, however, she pauses the song. "Everybody, give it up for my friend Dusty Wilder!"

Everyone in the bar swings their heads to look at us. I swear Dusty's face turns three shades redder as he lifts his hand in an awkward wave, the expression on his face looking more embarrassed than egotistical.

"Dusty and I go way back, occasionally singing together in bars just like this one. But now he's a big-time singer!" the girl on stage carries on. "Why don't y'all come on up here? It'd be just like old times."

Dusty shakes his head as he gives a *no* type gesture.

"Aw, come on, Dusty. What do y'all think? Do you want to hear Dusty Wilder?"

The bar patrons cheer, encouraging him to move toward the stage. I follow, taking a seat at one of the tables as he hops up on stage.

"You haven't changed one bit, Brooke." He chuckles as she hands him a microphone.

I recognize her then, when he says her name. Brooklyn James was at one point an up-and-coming artist just like Dusty, but she fell out of the spotlight a couple years ago. No one really knew if it was on her own terms or not, but she clearly never gave up music since she's still playing small venues. I can't help but wonder why she didn't try to come on the show when they start performing together. They have a connection, that's for sure, but part of me thinks it's purely platonic when she invites me up on the stage after their song is over.

"Why don't you play a song with your lady now, Dusty?" She elbows him in the ribs.

"Oh, I don't know about that," I protest. The last time I performed in a bar it went viral.

"I think that's a great idea." Mischief shines in Dusty's eyes as he extends a hand to pull me up on stage. "Come on, Baylor, darlin'. Y'all, she's America's Sweetheart, and you're about to find out why."

I roll my eyes as I take his hand, climbing up next to him.

"This one's a classic." He turns around and whispers something to the band. The guitarist nods, and the familiar intro starts, just like it did all those years ago.

Dusty starts singing the first verse of "Jackson," and a few whistles ring through the crowd that's now gathered. The cameras are still rolling, and it takes everything in me not to shrink back. This is what I'm here for. I have to perform. Play the part and pretend I want this as much as the other girls.

And I play the part well.

When June Carter's verse of the song begins, I sing like I did back in that small kitchen with my parents. Dusty doesn't take his eyes off me the entire time, and a rush flows through my veins. It's natural, like I was meant to be on this stage singing this song. Our harmonies blend seamlessly, and before I know it, the dance floor is hopping with people.

When the song ends, he leans over and whispers in my ear, "Just like Johnny and June, eh?"

Heat rises to my cheeks, and I find myself thinking that if this is how performing with Dusty could always be, I'll gladly get burned.

"So, how long have you and Dusty known each other?" I ask Brooke. After her performance ended, we stuck around so we could hang out longer with her and get some drinks.

"Oh, gosh, how long has it been?" She looks at Dusty, and he shakes his head, a twinge of amusement in his expression. Brooke taps her fingers against her lips a couple times as she thinks. "It's been at least ten years, hasn't it?"

"Sounds about right." His voice is gruff, similar to how it was when I first met him.

"It has to be. I met you when you were just starting as one of Craig's artists. I was eighteen at the time, I'm pretty sure." She says it so matter-of-factly, and even if she's wrong, Dusty doesn't correct her.

"I feel like 'met' is an overstatement." He chuckles. "I

would call it more 'Brooke followed me around like a lost puppy until I finally acknowledged her.'"

Brooke elbows him in the ribs, a small, "Ouch!" escaping from Dusty's lips at the contact. She rolls her eyes before she retorts, "I was *not* a lost puppy."

The question clawing in my chest finally pries its way out, something that takes me by surprise. "Why didn't you audition for *Heart Strings*?"

She looks at me for a second, then at Dusty, then back to me, before letting out a snort of laughter.

"What?" I'm not in on the joke.

"No offense, but I wouldn't date Dusty Wilder if he was the last person on Earth."

Dusty grumbles, "Ouch."

"It'd be like dating my brother," Brooke clarifies before teasingly looking at Dusty in mock shock. "You wouldn't date your sister if you had one, would you?"

Dusty mutters something under his breath, but whatever it was is inaudible to me. He surveys our drinks and slides his stool back from the table. "I'll get us some more drinks?" He says it like a question before giving a slight nod and heading over to the bar.

Brooke sets her elbows on the table and leans forward. "So...what do you think of him?"

I pause, not wanting to say anything without thinking about it first, especially with the cameras still around.

She must sense my hesitation, because she interjects before I can say a word. "Don't worry, you don't have to lie and say he's amazing. He was a jackass when I first met him." She laughs. "I've seen the best and worst of Dusty Wilder. Nothing you could say would shock me."

I huff out a half-breath, half-laugh as my shoulders relax. "Honestly, I thought he was an asshole when I first met him. I don't know, I think I had this preconceived notion about him."

She nods, but doesn't say anything, so I continue. "The only impression I had about Dusty was what the media portrayed him as—this womanizing country singer who got everything he wanted easily."

"Dusty is a lot of things." She briefly looks down, but then her eyes snap back up to mine. "But one thing's for certain, and it's that he didn't have everything handed to him. He's a hard worker, and the more you get to know him, the more I think you can break down his walls and see the true Dusty."

I nod, my gaze trained on the wood grain running across the table. If today's date—especially the time we spent at the record store—has proven anything, it's that I don't know Dusty as well as I thought I did.

13
dusty

Come to My Senses

IT'S hard to focus my attention on Valerie, my second solo date of the week, and guilt rises in my knotted belly over it. She's beautiful, with tawny skin, deep-brown eyes, and ebony hair that falls past her collarbones in loose, bouncy curls, but I can't take my mind off Baylor.

Earlier this morning, I went on a group date with the six women who didn't get a solo date this week and it wasn't as difficult to keep my focus. My mind occasionally drifted, but then someone would start talking and bring me back to the present.

Right now, I don't have that luxury.

Valerie and I are walking around Centennial Park, and it's a beautiful day; the sun is shining and people are out enjoying the weather, but all I can think about is walking around the vinyl record store and performing at the dive bar with Baylor. Everything was so effortless with her. Maybe that's weird to say, considering we haven't known each other for that long and I'm supposed to be getting to know the other women as well, but there's something special about her.

I'm brought out of my thoughts when I look over at Valerie and realize she's looking at me like she's waiting for me to say something.

"What was that? I'm sorry." I run a hand through my hair as I mentally kick myself. I should be more present in the moment with her.

"I just asked how the whole process is going for you. I imagine there must be a lot of pressure on you from your label and fans."

"Oh." *Damn, does she have to be so observant and caring?* "Yeah, it's definitely taken some getting used to. I've never dated multiple people at once."

She laughs, and the sound—like the tinkling of wind chimes—relaxes me a little.

"How has everything been for you so far?" I'm genuinely curious. I have no idea what the position the women are in is like, and I want to hear her take on this whole show.

"It's been fine so far. Most of the girls are great. I haven't had the chance to get to know them too well, but from the conversations I have had, they all seem nice and like they're truly here to find their person, not just advance their music career."

My mind wanders back to Baylor when Valerie mentions the other girls. I wonder what she's doing right now and if she's making connections. There's a slight fear in me that maybe she's not here to truly find love, that maybe this is all just a means to an end for her. We didn't really talk about that yesterday on our date, and maybe that was something I should have asked.

"I'm glad to hear that." I take Valerie's hand in mine, trying my best to devote my attention to her.

She takes my hand, and we continue walking through

the park, looking for a place to sit. We eventually come up to a plaid blanket and wicker basket that's been laid out by the producers.

"Oh, this is cute!" Valerie places a hand on her cheek when she sees the set up for today.

"Brad really outdid himself today," I mutter to myself.

"Hmm?" She looks at me, a confused look on her face.

My eyes widen when I realize she heard me. "Nothing, nothing. Come on." I gesture for her to sit. She sits cross legged on the blanket, and I lower myself to the ground, sliding closer to her. There's another small blanket in the basket, and I drape it over us before checking out what else is inside.

"What do we have?" Valerie cranes her neck toward the basket, her chin close enough to rest on my shoulder.

"Looks like we've got some cold cuts, cheese, fruit, and bread," I reply as I pull out each item. There's also a wooden charcuterie board and a small container of what looks like melted chocolate.

"Mmm, this looks delicious." She places the board in front of us and starts unpacking all of the food, spreading it out on the board. I let her do her thing, because the arrangement won't look half as pretty if I'm the one setting it up.

"You're good at this." I turn my head toward hers as a wide smile spreads across her face.

"I used to do this in college as a side business, it's nothing." Pink streaks across her cheeks as she looks at me, and a loose strand of hair falls into her face.

I brush the curl out of her eyes and tuck it behind her ear.

"Dusty?" Her big doe eyes flick up to mine.

"Yeah?"

"Can I kiss you?" she whispers, the sound almost getting carried away on the light breeze.

I nod, moving in as I wrap my hand around the back of her neck. Our lips brush before the kiss deepens and the taste of cherries fills my mouth.

Baylor got cherries in her drink at the bar.

Fuck. Why am I thinking about Baylor?

I squeeze my eyes, trying to dispel my wandering thoughts, but as Valerie kisses me, the only thing I can think of is what Baylor's lips might feel like. How she would kiss. If she'd be shy and take things slow, or if she would confidently swipe her tongue between my—

Fuck.

I pull back from Valerie before the fantasy can go any further.

"Everything okay?" Her brows pinch together and the pit in my stomach grows.

"Yeah, Valerie, everything's great." I give her as convincing a smile as I can muster, because what else am I supposed to say? *No, Valerie, I was thinking about another girl while I was kissing you. A kiss that, I might add, is going to be aired on national television.*

Yeah, probably best if I don't say that.

She continues putting together the snacks, and I try my absolute best to push Baylor to the furthest depths of my mind.

I peer over my shoulder to make sure no one is following me. The producers said I could do whatever I wish with my time off. While I'm sure they don't want me visiting the women off camera, they never explicitly said I couldn't, and I'm more of an ask for forgiveness rather than permission type of guy.

I somehow manage to ditch the producer who's been following me around like a lost puppy the last few days to take an Uber to the hotel I heard the girls were staying at. After confirming the coast is clear, I walk up to the front desk.

"Can you tell me what room Baylor is in? She's a contestant on *Heart Strings*," I ask as I tap my fingers nervously against the counter. I don't know her last name, but realistically, how many Baylors would be staying here?

"Sorry, I can't give out that information." The girl doesn't even look up at me from behind her computer screen as she rejects my request.

"Please? It's an emergency." I turn on the charm, willing her to just look up. I hope she doesn't hear the desperation, but if I'm being honest, I *am* a desperate man.

"I'm sorry—" She looks at me, and her mouth gapes into an O shape. "Y-you're—"

"Dusty Wilder, yes." I flash her a smile, and she tells me Baylor's room number without any more hesitation. "Thanks." I tip my hat to her and rush over to the elevators.

I punch the level four button in the elevator when I see a producer walk through the sliding doors.

"Fuck, fuck, fuck," I mutter as I repeatedly smash the close button on the elevator doors and hide my face from view.

"Wait! Hold the elevator!" he yells, but the door has already closed, and I let out a sigh of relief.

That was way too close.

Peeking around the corners again to make sure no one is coming, I exit the elevator and speed walk to her door.

When I reach her door, I take a deep breath in an attempt to calm my nerves. I only need to knock twice before the lock clicks and the door opens to a shocked Baylor.

Maybe this was a bad idea.

You're going to get caught.

"Dusty?" She raises an eyebrow. "What are you—"

Fuck it.

My hands cup both sides of her face, and our lips crash together. For a split second, I think maybe she doesn't want this as much as I do, but then she kisses me back. Her mouth seems to fit perfectly with mine, and when she takes a small breath and I slide my tongue past the small gap in her lips, she opens up to me, entangling us in a slow but sensual dance.

Her hands slide up my jaw around the back of my neck as mine travel down her body to her waist. A soft moan leaves her, and I can't lie and say it doesn't give me a bit more confidence.

When we finally break apart, I look into her eyes, hoping to find a glimpse of something to further reassure me. Instead I'm met with what seems like uncertainty.

"Maybe that—" she whispers, but I place a finger against her lips. I don't want to ruin the moment with a conversation about why we shouldn't have done that.

"Shh..." I whisper and then kiss her again before disappearing down the hall into the elevator. I wish I could stay longer, but from now on, if I have any say in things, Baylor and I won't have to rush. We'll have all the time we need.

the confessionals

Dusty: Holy [bleep].

Valerie: We—

Dusty: —kissed.
Producer: On your date with Valerie?

Baylor: He kissed me.
Producer: Pardon?
Baylor: I mean, I wanted him to kiss me. We didn't kiss on our date, you guys know that. You were following us with the cameras the whole time. But…I-I wanted him to.

Producer: How is that making you feel about the whole process?

Dusty: I—man. There were sparks. She's—she's incredible, in more ways than just the kiss.
Producer: Valerie is?
Dusty: Erm, yeah. Yeah, Valerie.

Baylor: I feel…good. I'm confident in whatever we have going on…I think.

14
baylor

Sworn to Secrecy

THE PRODUCTION COMPANY reserves two days between the last date of the week and airing day for editing, which means I have two days to ruminate over the kiss with Dusty.

When I heard the knock at my door, I wasn't sure who to expect. Daniella had already been at my hotel room earlier that night, so I thought it would be weird for her to be back, especially since the hotel isn't exactly close to our apartment. But the *last* person I expected to see was Dusty. And I definitely wasn't expecting him to kiss me. Or for me to like it.

I don't really want to spend time with the other girls right now, even though I'm probably supposed to. I just need this time to decompress by myself. Besides, the producers did say we could spend our days off however we want to, within reason. Which really means we can do whatever we want in our hotel rooms or at the property SSP is renting, since we aren't allowed to go anywhere offsite without the whole group—and a slew of producers to watch our every move. I'm almost confident there are loopholes to that, though, especially if Dusty was able to sneak into the hotel to kiss me.

I pace the carpeted floor of my hotel room a few times before flopping backward onto my bed, the mattress immediately sinking beneath me as I stare up at the ceiling.

I can't believe Dusty kissed me.

God, I wish I could tell someone about the kiss. But we weren't even *supposed* to be kissing. Not off camera at least. As far as production is concerned, the kiss—the spine-tingling, stomach tangling, butterfly-inducing kiss—never happened.

My brain doesn't comprehend that, though, and the entire interaction replays through my mind like a film reel. The softness of his lips, and the sensation of his mustache tickling my skin, still lingers, even hours later.

If I thought I could confide in any of the other girls, I would tell them. The only one who I think I may be able to trust with this is Sage, but even then I'm hesitant. She's still a contestant on the show, and the girls are all here for the same reason—to win. Even though I'm not expected to win, I can't give anyone a reason to stab me in the back. Not with my job on the line.

This will just have to be a secret I keep to myself. At least until we kiss *on camera*.

A knock at my door interrupts my thoughts. I reluctantly roll off the bed and pad over to the door, looking through the peephole before opening it.

I'm greeted by an impatient-looking producer. "We're taking everyone to the house today. There's no reason for you all to stay in your rooms."

"O-okay. Let me just get ready," I say quickly before shutting the door in her face.

I take my time getting dressed, but after the producer raps her knuckles on my door again, I pick up the pace a little. With a few quick swipes of mascara and a couple passes through my hair with a brush, I'm ready to go. I open the door, strutting past her with a smile, despite the glare she shoots at me.

The producers herd us to the cars with an uncharacteristic urgency. I'm not sure what's going on for them to want us to leave the hotel in such a rush, but no one bothers to explain anything further.

I'm riding in a car with Abigail and Katherine this time, and conversation flows naturally. I'm sure they were going just as stir-crazy as I was this morning.

As if she can read my mind, Katherine jokes, "How are you guys doing? Going crazy yet?" as she lets out a small chuckle.

It's pretty boring when we aren't filming. Without access to our phones or the Internet, it's easy to get restless and go a bit stir-crazy. I know from working behind-the-scenes of plenty of reality TV shows that the rules for this one aren't as strict as others, but there are still rules in place that keep us disconnected from the world.

Abigail chuckles, and I respond, "I'm doing as well as I can be."

My stomach chooses to rumble at that moment, and Katherine turns around from the passenger seat. "Did you not eat breakfast?"

I shake my head.

"Baylor!" She looks at Abigail, who also shrugs. "You guys! When we get to the house, I'm going to make breakfast for everyone. I'm not going to let you all starve. Besides, we don't need any hangry drama."

It turns out the rest of the girls also hadn't eaten

breakfast. Apparently, Katherine was the only one who had this morning. I'm not sure where she got it. We aren't allowed to eat in the hotel's restaurant because of the TVs; maybe she asked the producers to bring her something.

She's a natural cook, something I lack. Unless Dusty wants to eat burnt toast and extremely crispy bacon for the rest of his life, I most likely won't be doing the cooking. But, then again, he's famous enough that he probably has his own private chef.

Katherine plates us all French toast, eggs, and sausage before she joins us in the dining room. For a while, we're all silent, savoring the meal. Either that or no one knows what to say.

Aspen, of course, is the first to break the silence as she pushes her food around with her fork. "Who do you think will get eliminated this week?"

A couple girls shrug, and Sage and I exchange a look that says, *Here we go again*.

"I personally think that it could be *anyone*. Especially since no one has immunity this week." She gives me a pointed glare. "Maybe 'America's Sweetheart,' as our leading man loves to call you, will go home."

"Who's to say, Aspen?" I scoff. "Maybe it'll be you, and then we can all be rid of the shitty attitude no one likes." I shouldn't be feeding into her mind games, but she pisses me off. I don't know what she has against me—besides maybe throwing an axe better—but I don't see her targeting anyone else.

"I'm not here to braid your hair or make friendship bracelets with you, Baylor. If I wanted friends, I would join a sorority," Aspen sneers. "I'm not here to play *nice*. I'm here to win."

"It doesn't hurt to have a good reputation, though," I

say under my breath. "Especially since viewer voting is a big part of the competition you want to win so badly."

"They want good television, too. Haven't you watched other reality TV shows? There's *always* a villain. It makes for great ratings." She tilts her head to the side and bats her eyelashes, an incongruous smile on her face.

I've seen more reality TV than you'd probably expect, I think. I *know* how this stuff works. There are things I'm aware of that I'll never be able to bring up. Things only people who work on a television set would know.

Also, I don't think Aspen is acting like a bitch to be the season's "villain." I think she just *is* a bitch, so being the villain comes naturally to her. But I just hum in agreement, not wanting to throw more gas on the fire. I know this is exactly what she wants. She wants me to slip up on camera, or better yet, in front of Dusty.

Katherine clears her throat, getting everyone's attention off me and Aspen. "I can't believe all the free time we have." She changes the subject, and I give her a grateful look.

"I really wasn't expecting it," Valerie adds. "I thought for sure we'd be filming 24-7. Or at least not have two full days of nothing. But then again, when we aren't on dates, we're kind of just hanging around."

"They definitely make reality TV look more glamorous than it actually is." Jordan laughs. "They could've at least provided us with a list of things to do in our free time, or I don't know, board games or something."

We're driven back to the production studio for the airing

of the third episode. Two people will be eliminated tonight, dwindling our numbers down to six.

Producers escort us to the briefing room where we waited during the first episode. We all split into groups once we enter the room, huddling with the people we've become closest with. Aspen seems to have become friends with Jade, and Katherine and Valerie immediately engage in conversation with Jordan and Abigail.

The episodes span about two hours with commercial breaks, but we have to be here early so we're ready when they get to eliminations. It also helps keep the tensions high, but that's not something the producers would ever admit.

"So, what's the deal between you and Aspen?" Sage asks me, her voice a hushed tone.

I shrug. "*I* didn't have an issue with her until she started running her mouth."

"She probably sees you as a threat," Sage points out, and I can't help but laugh. "What?"

"Nothing." I shake my head. "I just don't know why she would see *me* as a threat. Or why she would really see anyone as a threat."

"Everyone is technically a threat when you're all competing for the same thing."

"That's true," I mumble.

I guess I never thought about it because I didn't care that much. When the competition started, I'd been in it just to keep my job and stay out of hot water with Colette. I never thought too hard about the possibility of actually falling in love.

But then my solo date with Dusty happened. I can't deny the pull between us in the record store. It was like we reached some mutual understanding that day.

The kiss was another thing.

"Earth to Baylor?" Sage waves a hand in front of my face, breaking me out of my trance.

"Hmm?" I blink a few times. "Sorry, what did you say?"

"You've been so distracted the past couple days. What's going on?" Her eyebrows furrow before she lowers her voice. "Did something happen with you and Dusty?"

"W-what?" I stammer, unable to control my reaction.

"Something *did*!" she exclaims. "Baylor! How long were you going to keep this a secret?"

I shush her, subtly eyeing the other girls in the room. For a moment, I hesitate, wondering if telling Sage the truth is the best idea, but it's already too late and my reaction gave me away. "We kissed." My voice is barely above a whisper. I'm very aware of the fact that there are producers everywhere, and microphones and cameras could be hidden anywhere in this room.

"Oh. My. God." She gasps, her voice a bit too loud for comfort. "I need all of the details!"

"Sage!" I hiss. "I'm trying to keep it on the down low. I don't need more of a target on my back." I come up with an excuse. There's no way she would know that we didn't kiss on camera, but I can't risk anyone else overhearing our conversation.

"Shit, sorry, Baylor. I didn't even think about that. You'll tell me later, though, right?"

I let out a breath before nodding slowly. "You have to promise me you won't say anything."

She holds out a pinky. "I swear. You can trust me, I promise."

Interlacing my pinky finger with hers, I give her a small

smile. But the moment is cut short when a producer bursts into the room.

"Ladies, we're nearing the end of the episode. If I call your name, please follow me." Whatever energy was in the air before is immediately sucked out with his announcement and the room falls silent. "Jordan."

Jordan's head drops, and her eyes glisten. I feel sorry for her; being at risk two weeks in a row must be tanking her confidence. And I have a feeling she won't be getting saved this time as the producer calls out Abigail's name.

"Finally, Sage."

My head whips toward Sage, and my mouth gapes. She bites her lip as her chest rises and falls.

"See you, Baylor." She gives me a look of apprehensiveness before she gets up and follows the producer and the other girls out of the room.

Once the door shuts, the room stays silent for a few moments before someone starts clapping in a slow rhythm, the sound echoing in the room.

"Well, well, well. America's Sweetheart lives to see another day."

I roll my eyes. "I'm not sure why you're so surprised. Contrary to what you think, I do have a connection with Dusty."

Katherine opens her mouth like she wants to cut in and break up whatever is going on, but Aspen beats her to it.

"I'm just surprised, is all. Last week, you hardly seemed interested in being here, much less being in a relationship with him. I find it hard to believe that the producers would want someone with such a…detachment to continue every week."

There's an insinuation behind her voice, one I'm afraid to address. If any of the girls were about to defend me, they aren't jumping to do it now, all of them pausing like they're waiting to hear what my response is.

"So, why is it you're still here, Baylor?" Aspen crosses her arms, tapping her foot in impatience as she waits for me to answer.

The silence and tension in the room is so thick it could be cut with a butterknife as everyone waits for what I'm about to say. I could defend myself—*should* defend myself—but what good would it realistically do? If Aspen has her suspicions about me, then she has her suspicions. I doubt anything I could say would change her mind. In fact, I think biting back would make her more suspicious, like I'm trying to cover something up.

I settle for repeating the same thing I told her earlier. "I'm still here because, like I said, I *have a connection* with Dusty. He obviously wouldn't send someone who he has a connection with home."

"Wouldn't he, though?" she challenges. "Isn't that the point? He's forming connections with everyone here. I wouldn't go so far as to say he doesn't have a connection with Abigail or Jordan or Sage, would you?"

"I mean, yeah, but it's about the strength of the connection. I could ask you the same thing about why you're still here. If I recall correctly, you didn't seem very interested in the axe-throwing date either."

"Yeah, because I wasn't interested in axe-throwing. It wasn't because I'm not interested in him." She rolls her eyes but quickly gets back to her interrogation. "So, you do think your connection with Dusty is strong and genuine. You're not here because of, say, favoritism?" Her eyes narrow.

"That's a big accusation," Valerie cuts in.

"Yeah, but I need to hear her say it. Tell us you're not only here because the producers *want* you to be here."

I'm saved by the metaphorical bell as the door to the briefing room swings open and Sage enters the room. Her eyes are rimmed with red, but she gives us a small smile as Valerie, Katherine, and I rush over to her, like the heated conversation between me and Aspen never happened.

"I knew you'd be okay," I reassure her as we all hug.

She lets out a small laugh. "I've never been so stressed in my life."

"What happened this time? Was it the same as the first elimination?" Jade asks from behind me.

"It was similar, yeah. We had to answer a question about our relationship, but otherwise it was the same. Had to watch as the votes came in and everything," Sage explains. "I was honestly so scared I was going home. It was really close between me and Abigail. I'm sad to see both her and Jordan go. I wish we could all stay."

We nod, silence filling the room before there's another knock on the door. We weren't expecting the producers to come back so soon, since—besides giving Jordan medical attention—they didn't come back after the first elimination for about thirty minutes.

My head snaps toward the door as it swings open, revealing Dusty.

"Hi, ladies," he greets. "I know you probably weren't expecting me, but I just wanted to say hello and check in with you. I know these eliminations aren't easy, but I hope being here is still worth it." He stares at me while he says it, and heat rushes into my cheeks.

"That's really sweet of you, Dusty," Aspen chimes in, her voice sickeningly sweet compared to how she talks to us.

He lets out some kind of grunt as he nods. Then he clears his throat. "Um, Baylor, can I talk to you?"

I point to myself. "Me?" I know I sound shocked, but I'm unsure why he would want to talk to me in private, especially after an elimination. Has he found out? Am I being sent home, too?

He nods, but his expression isn't stern or giving the impression of a serious conversation. He actually looks calm and collected, at peace almost.

I stand, smoothing my pants as I follow, feeling Aspen's eyes burning into my back with each step.

Once we exit the room and the door slams shut, Dusty looks around then grabs my arm, yanking me into a darker hallway.

"What are you—" I stutter, but my question is cut short as he pushes me against the wall and his mouth collides with mine.

Butterflies rush into my stomach as I kiss him back, electricity teeming in my body.

"I needed to get you alone," he mumbles against my mouth. "The other night wasn't enough for me."

"The other girls, though," I whisper, turning my head to look down the hallway and make sure no one is around to catch us. Surely the consequences of someone seeing us together wouldn't be worth a quick makeout session, as much as I love having his mouth against mine.

He grabs my chin, forcing me to turn my head back to face him. "No one's around, Baylor. And I'm not worried about them, the other girls. You shouldn't be either."

What the hell does that *mean?*

My thoughts are interrupted as he presses his lips to mine again, and my senses overload with sandalwood and amber.

"Hey!" the voice of a producer booms from the other hallway, and we break apart. "Has anyone seen Dusty?"

"Go," I hiss, practically shoving him away from me. But before he goes, he takes a long look at me. The sound of footsteps approaching finally encourages him to turn and rush away, leaving my heart pounding in my chest and my mind swarming.

What the fuck is happening?

15
dusty

Get to the Bottom of This

LAST WEEK'S elimination was rough. Even though I've only had two weeks with the girls, genuine connections have been formed. The realization takes me by surprise, but I'm trying to lean into the process. Losing Abigail and Jordan was tough. I would've preferred to have Jade in the bottom three to save Sage or Abigail from being at risk, but the producers pushed me to keep her.

Now that we're down to six contestants, though, I've come to the conclusion that I'm going to have to be more firm and really fight for who I want. At the end of the day, this is about me and the person I want standing next to me when the season ends and the cameras turn off.

This week, I have dates with Sage and Aspen. I'm looking forward to deepening my connection with both of them, and also hearing their thoughts on the other girls. I've sensed a bit of hostility between Baylor and Aspen, and I want to get to the bottom of it.

I obviously don't see everything that happens between the girls, only what happens during group outings. But I've noticed Aspen's face contort with distaste whenever

Baylor's name is brought up. She tries to be subtle about it, but she's not very good at hiding her emotions. Then again, neither is Baylor. However, while I see determination and maybe a bit of ego in Aspen's expressions, sometimes the look in Baylor's eyes is one of nervous tension, trepidation. I don't think she has anything to hide, but I want to ease my own worries. I know she's closer with Sage than Aspen, so I plan to briefly bring her up during our date.

The producers don't give me much information about what the dates will entail, just that I'm to meet them at the front gates of the property once I'm ready. So I pull on a pair of denim jeans and a baby-blue pearl snap shirt before topping it off with a granite cowboy hat.

During the two days off from filming, the girls were brought to the house while I was sent to the production building for interviews. So. Many. Interviews. I can't lie and say I wasn't disappointed that I didn't get to spend more time with them, but I also haven't really had a moment to myself since filming began.

Normally, during really busy weeks, Craig would make sure I had some time to myself. To decompress. Sparks Studio Production clearly gives zero shits about that, because I feel like I've been pushed under water without a chance to come back up for air.

Man, I wish Craig were here to give me advice on how to handle all of this.

When I walk outside, there's a car and camera crew waiting for me.

"Good morning, Mr. Wilder," Brett greets me. I like to think we've reached a mutual respect, or at least an understanding between each other. He's only here to do his job, as am I. He stays out of my way, and I don't make his life difficult. "Are you ready for your date with Sage?"

"Yep," I pop the P. "This is one I've been looking forward to, Brett."

"Great to hear that. Let's get on the road, then, shall we?"

I nod and climb in the backseat of the vehicle. It doesn't take us very long to get to our destination, a bar known for its large dance floor.

Sage is waiting in front of the doors, wearing denim cutoff shorts and a blouse with bell sleeves. The outfit is complete with a pair of cowboy boots.

"Damn, you look good," I greet her.

She does a little spin for me, smiling the entire time. "Thank you. You also look great."

"Have you ever been line dancing before?" I ask as I look up at the neon bar sign.

"Have I ever been line dancing?" She raises her brows in amusement. "Of course, I have, silly."

"Don't judge me too much if I mess up the steps, then." I nudge her with my elbow before opening the door and holding it for her.

Sage enters the bar, and I follow closely behind. The bar is located near the back, and high-top tables surround the dance floor, where people have already gathered, although it's not so busy that we can't find a spot for ourselves. The cover band is playing a two-step, and without hesitation, Sage pulls me out onto the dance floor. We fall into the steps naturally.

"Have you been enjoying your time on the show so far?" I ask, not wanting to waste any time.

"Absolutely." She nods. "I'm so grateful to still be here.

That elimination was stressful, but I'm glad that the viewers saw enough in me that they wanted to save me."

"I'm glad they saved you, too," I say as I spin her around.

We spend the next couple minutes moving with the rhythm of the music. Sage even starts singing along to the cover band, and I remember why I liked her so much at the auditions.

As the second song begins, I decide to pick up the conversation. "How is the, er, environment of the house? With the other girls?"

She tilts her head to the side, eyeing the cameras, but quickly recovers. "It's been good so far. There's definitely an air of competitiveness, but for the most part, everyone has been respectful toward each other." She hesitates a little when she talks about the competitive energy between the girls, which only makes me want to push further.

"What do you mean by that?"

"I, uh, I guess some people have just butted heads a bit." She races through her sentence. When I don't answer, she continues. "Aspen's been a bit…harsh at times. She doesn't like Baylor very much."

Heat rises in my gut at the mention of Baylor, followed by annoyance toward Aspen. I *knew* there was something going on with her. Luckily, I'll have the opportunity to talk to her about it on our date tomorrow, but for now, I want to hear Sage out.

"Are you comfortable telling me more about it?" I ask as we move around the dance floor. "I won't mention your name to anyone, but if there's an issue among the other girls, I want to be able to address it."

Her face flushes a bit, and for a moment, I think I've maybe overstepped. Maybe she doesn't want the show to portray her in a negative light when the episode airs. But then she sighs. "We may want to sit down for this conversation."

My heart rate accelerates with a tinge of panic. I didn't expect the conversation to be that serious, but still I nod, leading her toward a booth in the corner as the song ends. I need to know what's going on.

"I don't want to make the entire date about Aspen, but I just…" she trails off. "I think she's a bit malicious. I don't know if that's her intention, but she kind of comes off as thinking she's superior to everyone else. I don't want to diminish the connection you have with her, but she's really targeted Baylor the last couple weeks."

Defensiveness tugs in my chest—not for Aspen, but for Baylor—without even knowing the whole situation. I had a connection, an attraction, to Aspen in the beginning, but over time, the feeling seemed to fade as I've gotten closer to Baylor. I can't say I would've broken the rules to go kiss Aspen off camera.

"What's she done to Baylor?" I demand, perhaps a bit too forcefully.

Something flashes in Sage's eyes, and they shift down toward the table. "It started out as small little jabs, but I guess last night, during the elimination, she accused her of only still being here because of favoritism from the producers."

Her words are a suckerpunch to my gut, and anger replaces my annoyance.

"Baylor wouldn't be here if I didn't want her here," I grit out, my jaw tense.

Sage shrinks back like she did something wrong, and I force myself to relax.

"Sage, I'm not mad at you. The opposite, in fact. I

really appreciate you telling me, and I swear your name won't be mentioned."

"Thank you," she whispers.

I didn't mean to make her upset. I've been distracted, despite my best efforts to focus on her, and guilt for the lost time claws at me. We still have plenty of time before the date ends, so I'll make it up to her somehow.

My date with Aspen is at Ace High Entertainment's recording studio. I think back to what Sage said yesterday about Aspen's claim that Baylor is only here because the producers favor her.

Based on today's date, I'd say the opposite. Baylor didn't get a recording studio date, Aspen did. If that doesn't scream favoritism, then I'm not sure what would, aside from scheduling us to elope. I let out a small snort at the thought.

"Well, if it isn't my favorite country singer." Aspen's sultry voice greets me as I step into the control room. She's sitting on a stool, leaning forward so her cleavage is visible in her tank top.

"Hello, Aspen." I try to hide my frustration with her. I have to hear her side of the story, but I trust Sage. And maybe it's foolish, but I feel like I can trust Baylor too.

Her expression falls, and she opens her mouth to say something, but a recording engineer interrupts by walking into the room. She sits up straight, transforming her pose from seductive to proper and professional.

"It's good to see you back in the recording studio, Dusty." He claps me on the back as he walks over to Aspen. "You must be Aspen."

"That's me." She gives him a bright smile.

"It's very nice to meet you. You've got a unique opportunity today, getting to record something with Dusty. Why don't you two head on in and we'll lay down a few tracks? See how your voices mesh together and go from there."

Aspen practically leaps up from her stool to enter the live room. She puts on her headphones like she's done this a million times before. Our microphones are set up so we're facing each other. It's a more intimate setup than standing side-by-side, and I can tell she's eating up every moment of it.

I, however, can't help but wish it was Baylor in front of me. Or literally anyone else, after knowing what I know about Aspen.

"Can you two hear me?" the engineer asks.

I give him a thumbs-up as Aspen nods.

"Great. Let's start with some warm-up exercises." He leads us through a few standard vocal warm-ups, and I hate to admit how well Aspen's voice fits with mine.

I'm trying my best to keep an open mind about her, but it's proving to be difficult. My mind keeps wandering back to the idea that Aspen was intimidating Baylor, probably trying to get her to break down or slip up or something. Anything that would cause her to go home.

I won't have it. She deserves a conversation about it, but depending on how it goes will determine whether or not Aspen makes it to next week.

My thoughts are interrupted by the sound engineer. "You guys sound great together! Wow."

Aspen blushes in front of me from the compliment.

"Should we record a song? Do y'all have anything in mind that you might want to try? This is just for fun and to see how your musical chemistry is, so we can do pretty much anything."

We brainstorm for a few minutes but eventually decide on a cover of "I'm Gonna Love You," a duet performed by Cody Johnson and Carrie Underwood.

It's a passionate love song, and if an outsider didn't know any better, they would probably assume Aspen and I are in a relationship. I have to give her credit—she has talent and she's determined. She possesses a fire reminiscent of myself when I first came to Nashville.

When the song ends and we step back into the control room, the engineer pulls me aside.

"I'm going to send this up to Rob," he whispers. "That was *fantastic*, Dusty. Even if you don't choose her at the end —though personally, I don't think you can go wrong—she would be a great candidate for Ace High Entertainment as a new artist. I know at the end of the day I don't have much of a say," he rambles on, "but I know talent when I see it. And that girl right there has it tenfold."

I cough slightly, the words I want to say catching in my throat, unable to surface. I simply nod then follow Aspen out of the recording studio. We need to have a conversation before I make a decision I might regret.

"Being in the recording studio was so much fun." She beams as we walk down the hallways of Ace High Entertainment. "I've always wanted to do that."

I remember that she's been in Nashville for eight years now, and curiosity about why she hasn't been picked up by a label piques my interest. "I can't believe you haven't before." My statement is leading. I'm hoping she'll take the hint, or maybe bait, and give me some insights on her own music journey.

"I've tried, believe me. I've had my eyes set on several

record labels in Nashville, but I just haven't had much luck." She pouts as she looks down at the ground. "I've been trying to catch the eye of Six-String Entertainment for a while now and Ace High Entertainment, too. I guess they just don't want me."

I find that hard to believe, but the music industry is cutthroat. Part of me wants to tell her about the engineer's intentions to send what we recorded to Rob, but I don't want to get her hopes too high or add fuel to the metaphorical fire that's apparently burning between her and Baylor.

"I'm sure it'll all work out." I rub the back of my neck then clear my throat. "Um, I wanted to talk to you about something."

She perks up at that, stopping in her tracks. "What's up?" Her voice has an air of uncertainty to it.

"I've spoken to a few of the girls"—I lie, so as to not expose Sage—"and I've heard there's some animosity between you and Baylor."

Aspen sucks in a breath as her demeanor immediately shifts. "I—" she starts.

"I just want to hear your side," I add.

She stares at me through thick lashes like she's trying to figure me out. Suddenly, her face falls, like she's been hit with a wave of sadness. "I didn't want to cause any rifts, or plant any seeds of doubt in your mind, that's why I haven't said anything. I'm not sure what you heard, but—"

I cut her off, wanting to get straight to the point. "Did you accuse her of only being here because of favoritism from the producers?"

Her face blanches, confirming what Sage said was true. "Dusty, I-I…" I've never seen her so at a loss for words during the several interactions I've had with her the past few weeks. "I'm not saying it's true but, yes, I have my suspicions. She—"

"Baylor is here because I want her to be here. I want to make it clear that this last week she stayed because *I* wanted her to stay, not the producers." I don't mean to be as harsh as I'm probably coming across, but I want to set the record straight that I'm the one making the decisions here. "My advice to you would be to worry about *our* relationship and less about Baylor."

She blinks like she's surprised I jumped so quickly to defend Baylor. Then she narrows her eyes, looking like she's about to say something, but instead of firing back a retort, she purses her lips and nods.

"What are you here for, Aspen?" I ask.

"What do you mean?" Her question is slow, wary.

"Exactly what I asked. What are you here for? The record deal with Ace High? Recognition?" I throw out some ideas of why I think she might be on the show.

An emotion that looks a lot like betrayal clouds her expression. "I-I mean those are a plus, but that's obviously not why I'm here. I'm here for you. Other people might be here to go viral or to jumpstart their career, but I'm here because of you."

I thought asking her what her intentions are would ease my mind, but it only leaves me more confused than I was going into this whole conversation.

"I think it's probably best if you head back to the hotel." I'm probably not supposed to cut our date short, but I'm annoyed and I need time to think. I also desperately want to talk to Baylor, but I'm not sure when my next opportunity to do that will be. "I like you, Aspen, I do. I think you have an incredible voice and we'd have a great partnership. But it hurts me to hear about a potentially hostile environment here."

"You know what, you're right. I'm sorry this made you want to cut our time short, but I understand. I do think you need to talk to Baylor. You may not believe me, and the other girls may not see it, but there's something off about her." With that, she walks away, not even giving me a second glance as she heads to the elevators, the camera crew trailing behind her.

Fuck. I forgot about the cameras.

I rap my knuckles against the wood grain of Baylor's hotel room door. When she opens it, she doesn't even look surprised to see me.

Instead, she crosses her arms and raises an eyebrow at me. "What do you want, Dusty?"

"What's wrong, sweetheart?" I smirk, ignoring her question. "Are you going to let me in, or are you going to risk me getting caught by our lovely producers?"

She lets out an exasperated sigh and opens the door wider, gesturing for me to come in. "You know, you're going to get us both in trouble if you keep doing this."

I walk past her, heading straight for the king-size bed. "That's a bridge I'll cross when I get there. Besides, seeing you is worth it. Gives me an adrenaline rush knowing any moment I could get caught." I wink, and she rolls her eyes.

"So funny. Seriously, why are you here?"

I sigh, letting my guard and media persona fall. "Truthfully, I just wanted to spend time with you. Away from the cameras. Away from the producers. I can't even say hi to you and the other girls without someone being in my face. I just want a break from all the noise."

Her expression softens at my admission, like she understands. She walks over to the bed and sits next to me. "And you came to me?"

"Yeah, of course, I came to you. I like spending time with you, believe it or not." I chuckle. "I want to get to know you. Our date was a start, but I want to know *more*. I want to know who Baylor is."

"I'm not sure you do." She snorts.

"Sure, I do. I want to know the real reason you came here. Your hopes and dreams. Your darkest secrets." I nudge her playfully to let her know the last part is only a joke.

"It's only fair if I get to know the *real Dusty Wilder* then, too," she fires back.

"Ask away, darlin'. I'm an open book."

"Okay, did you always know you wanted to come to Nashville and be a *famous country star*?" She's teasing, but her question hits hard.

"Not always, no." I shake my head. "But music has always been a part of my life, and when the opportunity arose, my parents encouraged me to take it. I don't have any siblings, so I've been supporting them—giving back what they gave to me—ever since." My music career has been a big reason my family is able to live a comfortable life. If they wanted to, they could sell the farm and be completely fine. I know they never will, and they insist on me keeping the money I've earned for myself, but I still want them to have options.

"What's your family like?"

"They're some of the most hardworking people I know." The admission comes easily, and the words start to flow out of me. "Everything I am, everything I've come to be, is because of the sacrifices they made. I was able to leave home at eighteen to pursue my dream because of them." I owe them everything, and that's why I've been working my ass off here in Nashville. Why I've allowed myself to fall into the persona Rob Acerra created for me. It's all for them.

"Wow, that's amazing. I'm glad you have such supportive parents. I'm sure they're really proud of you."

"They are." I nod. "I owe them everything."

"Your parents sound like incredible people. They clearly raised you to be an incredible person, too."

"The media may portray me as someone who only cares about himself, but they don't know the real me," I reply softly.

"I can see that," she murmurs back.

In the time we've spent talking, we've naturally gravitated closer to each other, and our legs brush.

"What about yours?" I ask gently.

Her eyes darken again, like they did during that first conversation we had. "I…I love my parents. I really do. But we have different ideas of what's worthwhile."

I want to pry, get her to divulge more than just a vague answer, but I can tell that's not what she needs at this moment, so I let it go, despite my desire for her to let me in.

"I remember you talking about them on our solo date at the record store. How they used to sing together." I'm hoping I'm not pushing too hard, but to my relief, she relaxes and her shoulders drop as if she let go of all the tension in her body.

"Music was a staple in our household growing up. My parents taught me how to play guitar and my mom…" she trails off. "My mom had this journal that she passed down to me. It's filled with songs she wrote. She's why I fell in love with songwriting. Lyrics have always…called to me, though. Songwriting is like poetry, there's something so beautiful about it. Even the most haunting lyrics have beauty." When she speaks, her eyes brighten, and I feel like I'm seeing Baylor in an entirely new light.

My fingertips wander from my thigh until they come to rest on her leg. She looks down then back up at me.

"Is this okay?" I ask, ready to pull back if needed, but she nods.

"Yeah, that's okay."

"I'm really glad you shared that with me, about the songwriting and lyrics. Thank you for trusting me with that."

"You trusted me with your story about your parents," she murmurs. We're close enough that if I were to lean forward slightly, our noses would touch. "You showed me a new side of you tonight, Dusty Wilder. I know the media portrays you in a certain light, but I hope everyone sees the person I can see—the hardworking, generous one—after all this is over."

We talk a while longer, at some point moving so we're lying above the covers next to each other on the bed.

I'm staring up at the ceiling when I hear a soft snore next to me. I roll over, and sure enough, Baylor has fallen asleep.

Careful not to wake her, I get up from the bed and walk over to her side. As I lean down, I plant a delicate, lingering kiss on her forehead. She doesn't wake, but I swear there's a hint of a smile as I whisper, "Good night, Baylor," and quietly sneak out.

16
baylor

Locked In

"TONIGHT, you'll all be competing in a team challenge." Jarrod walks into the briefing room at the production studio where we're all waiting for Dusty—who I haven't been able to get off my mind since last night. "You'll be divided into teams of three. The winning team will earn immunity from this week's elimination. Only one person from the losing team will be eliminated based on viewer voting, instead of being saved. If you're all ready, we'll head out and meet Dusty there."

After a few nods, we gather our belongings and follow Jarrod out to the sleek, black vans waiting for us.

I climb into the front car, and Valerie and Aspen—unfortunately—follow.

Lord help me if I have to be on a team with her. We will definitely not be winning the challenge if that's the case.

Valerie sits in the front seat, which leaves me and Aspen sitting next to each other in the back.

Lovely.

The drive is silent, however, which half puts me at

ease and half makes me more anxious for this team challenge we're participating in. I'm not quite sure what to expect.

About thirty minutes later, the car pulls to a slow stop in front of a large, dilapidated warehouse-looking building.

"What the fuck are we doing?" Aspen murmurs.

We move to get out of the car, but the driver stops us.

"Ladies, before you go, I was instructed to give you these to put on." He extends his hand, and in it are three small, black blindfolds.

I give Valerie a sidelong glance as I reluctantly take the blindfold and tie it around my head. The fabric is opaque, and there's no chance that I'll be seeing anything, unlike some blindfolds that give you a bit of leeway and allow you to see through the fabric or shift your eyes downward to see the floor.

When we exit the vehicle, footsteps approach and a hand firmly grasps my arm before a producer identifies themselves. There's mumbling coming from beside me, through a radio it seems, but the sound is too muffled for me to hear.

We walk for what feels like a long time, moving down long stretches only to take a sharp turn and go straight again. There are a few sets of stairs that we climb, but thankfully, the producer guiding me warns me about them so I don't trip over my own feet. After a few more turns and long hallways, we stop. Keys jingle next to me, and then I'm walking a few more feet before being sat in a chair.

My heart pounds in my chest as handcuffs bind my wrists behind my back and the metal clicks into place.

Did we get in the wrong vehicle? Did we get kidnapped? Is this some sick joke?

Someone takes off my blindfold, but it doesn't matter anyway. We're surrounded by darkness.

They get close enough to my face, though, that I can see it's Alex and not some random kidnapper.

"Good luck, Baylor," he says softly, his voice barely a whisper, before his footsteps retreat until a heavy door slams.

"Ladies, today's team challenge is an escape room. You've been split into teams of three and you'll have one hour to work together and find your way out," Jarrod's voice echoes in the dark room. "Remember, the winning team will have immunity from the elimination, so work quickly. Best of luck, your time starts now."

The lights don't flicker on like I expected they would, so I'm still in total darkness.

"Hello?" I yell out, hoping one of my teammates can hear.

No response.

"Hello!?" I yell a bit louder. "Is anyone there?"

"Baylor?" a voice calls back. Sage, I think.

"Yes! It's me!"

"Where are you?" she asks, a bit uncertain.

"I'm not sure. It's completely dark in here, and I'm cuffed," I respond, hoping that she's in a better situation.

"Shit. Well, it's not dark here, but I'm locked in this cage thing."

"Guys! Are you there?" I immediately recognize Valerie's voice.

"Valerie!" I yell and footsteps approach.

The door rattles but doesn't open.

"Dammit," Valerie curses. "It's locked. I didn't think it would be that easy, but I was hopeful. There's a window in this door, can you see me?"

"No, it's completely pitch black in here, Val. I didn't know there was a window in the door. Are there any switches on the wall out there?" I ask, trying to think of how I can get some light in this room.

Her feet shuffle around outside, so I know the door can't be too far away.

"I'm not seeing anything…" Her voice trails off for a few moments until she yelps.

"You good?"

"Yeah, I just tripped over something. Hold on, there's a toolbox here." She grunts, and I assume she's lifting it to carry it over to my room's door. "It's locked, but there's a padlock with three sets of numbers. Do you see anything that might help, Sage?"

"I'm looking! There's a bunch of shit in here, oh my God." She pauses for a few seconds. "There's a cabinet, a bunch of tools that probably won't help any…a whole wall of keys that will probably be useful in the future but maybe not for that…"

"Is there anything you can see with numbers?" Valerie asks.

"No…oh, wait! Yes! It's kind of hard to see, but it looks like there's a sequence of numbers on the wall. Three rows of nine numbers each. But there's nothing in the very middle and nothing on the bottom right. It looks like a puzzle. We might have to do some math," she explains.

"Oh, lovely. I'm not great at puzzles as it is, but throw in math and I'm hopeless," Valerie mutters, which makes me chuckle a little. From what I know about them, escape rooms are just one big puzzle. But then again, not all of them include math.

"We'll be fine. You have us to help you, and we just have to be faster than the other team," I point out.

To be fair, with Aspen on their team, I have little faith they'll be able to get out before us.

"Can you read out the numbers, Sage? The wall is dusty enough that I should be able to write on it," Valerie calls out. With the way we're all able to talk to each other, we must not be too far apart at least. That gives me some hope.

"Okay, the first row of numbers is five, nine, six, two, four, eight, three, one, seven." Sage recites the numbers, and Valerie lets her know when she's ready for the next row. "Okay, the middle row has four, seven, two, six, eight, and nine… And the last row has three, one, eight, six, seven, nine."

I'm the only one who can't see the numbers, so I'm trying to mentally picture the puzzle in my head.

Three rows with nine numbers in each. But the middle set is missing and the bottom right is also missing.

"What the fuck kind of puzzle is this?" Sage whines, and it breaks me out of my focus for a second.

"I don't know. It's confusing to me," Valerie sighs. "But we need to figure it out."

"Maybe we need to add the numbers up?" Sage suggests.

I'm still trying to think, but that's worth a try.

"Five plus four is nine, not three, so I don't know if that's what we need to do," Valerie says after a minute of silence.

"Yeah, you're probably right. Some of the middle digits add to double digit numbers," Sage replies with a disheartened tone.

Three rows of nine. Each column has three numbers.

What am I missing here?

"Maybe just try random number combinations. One

has to work eventually," Sage jokes, but her voice comes out flat.

Valerie laughs. "If that wouldn't take us thirty minutes, I'd go for it."

"Wait! Can you read the numbers again? Just the first row." I have an idea of what it is, but I need it confirmed.

"Yeah. Five, nine, six, two, four, eight, three, one, seven."

Five, nine, six, two, four, eight, three, one, seven.

Wait. One, two, three, four, five, six, seven, eight, nine.

"Sudoku!" I exclaim.

"Sudo-what?" I can tell Sage is confused.

"It's a sudoku puzzle. Or, part of one at least. Each row has to have numbers one through nine. And usually each column would, too, but they made it easy on us."

"Wait, Baylor, you're a genius!" Valerie cheers.

It only takes us a few minutes to come up with the missing numbers. Five, one, and three in the middle column, and two, four, and five, in the bottom right.

"Okay, now we just have to figure out what the combination is. Do we know how much time has gone by?" I ask, silently hoping that one of the producers is listening and will give us a time warning.

"No, but it probably took us longer than it should have, so we need to move fast. Five is repeated, which makes me think that's one of the numbers used. Now we just have to find the other two. Maybe just try five, one, three to see," Sage suggests.

Valerie fumbles with the padlock, the dials clicking into place. "Nope, that's not it."

"Maybe add the numbers up? Five plus one plus three is nine and two plus four plus five is eleven. Nine, one, one?" I throw out a wild guess with a laugh. If we don't make it out of here, they might *have* to call nine-one-one for us. The answer is probably so clear, though, and we're just not seeing it.

"That didn't work either," Valerie's voice is as dejected as I feel. To be honest, I don't want any of us to go home, so we need to figure this out. "Wait, guys. There's something written on the toolbox. I can't believe I didn't see this before."

"What does it say?" I ask before Sage can.

"It just says 'area.'"

"Guys, there are also some symbols on the wall here. A dash and two plus signs on top of a plus sign, dash, and a plus sign." Sage interrupts us.

"Interesting…" This was too much math for a reality dating show. "What were the six numbers again?"

"Five, one, three, and two, four, five."

"Okay, wait what if we matched the minus signs together and the plus signs together?" I do it mentally in my head. Five and four were the minus signs and one, three, two, and five had plus signs.

Five minus four is one… the box said "area."

Then it hits me. The padlock needs a code to unlock it, and the box says area. "It's an area code! Add the numbers up, and it's an area code."

"Val! Put in six, one, five! That's the area code for Nashville." Sage's words rattle out in a frantic tone, and I can hear Valerie trying to put the numbers in as quickly as possible.

"It worked! There's a flashlight in here. And… magnets? But there's no key," she explains the contents of her toolbox.

"Can you shine the flashlight into the window of my

door? Maybe there's something in here that I need to find."

A few moments later, a light beam shines through the window, providing the little bit of light that I've been needing.

"There's a small sliver under the door. I think these magnets might fit under it. Do you think that's what we need to do next?" Valerie asks.

I shrug. "It's worth a shot. I'll try to scoot my chair over to the door and see if I can grab them." I clumsily make my way over to the door, the legs of the chair painfully scraping the ground with every movement. "Okay, I'm here. Slide them under."

The light disappears and the clink of metal on concrete fills the room. Valerie pops back up and shines the light inside again.

"I don't think I can pick them up so I'm going to have to try to lean my chair back to grab them," I grumble, once again trying to maneuver my chair to a favorable position. God, I hope I don't fall over. That would be embarrassing. Not to mention, the last thing I need is a concussion.

I plant one leg on the ground to steady myself and lean my chair back as far as possible. I can't quite grab the magnets, but I don't need to. The attraction between the magnet and my cuffs is strong enough that one latches on. The cuff also clicks, releasing my arm.

"The cuffs were magnetic! Give me one second, and then I'll be free." I give the girls an update before grabbing the second magnet and attaching it to my other cuff. The metal slides off my wrist, and it's sweet, sweet bliss. I didn't realize how sore I was getting, even though the cuffs weren't heavy duty ones that police officers use, just prop handcuffs.

I stand, and Valerie just about blinds me with her flashlight. I grimace, but give her a wave. "Can you shine the flashlight around the room? Just so I can see if there's anything in here that might help me?"

She complies, shining the light along the walls and every corner. At first, there's nothing—to my dismay—but then a glint catches my eye.

"Wait! Go back to the corner you were just at."

Bingo.

Hanging from the ceiling is a key. I carry my chair over to the corner, because I already know I'm too short to grab it without a little bit of help, and then I stand on it.

"I have a key!" I exclaim, and I'm met with cheers from Sage and Valerie. I run over to the door to see if it unlocks my door, but no luck. "It's not for this door. It must be for Sage's room. Here, Valerie." I slide the key under the door, and she picks it up.

"Be right back!" she reassures me.

"Talk to me, girls. Maybe I can still help," I offer.

"The key worked for Sage's door!" Valerie hollers right before a metal door opens. "Holy shit, you weren't joking, Sage. There's a ton of shit in here." There's a few banging noises and what I assume is things being thrown around as Valerie looks through the room.

"What are you seeing in there?" I ask, just trying to get a feel for what they're working with.

"There are a shit ton of keys on the wall with letters on them, a big cabinet, and the weird cage thing that Sage is in. I'm going to open the cabinet and see what's inside, because it doesn't look like there's a lock on it."

Metal rattles for a few seconds, and then Sage asks Valerie what's in the cabinet.

"There's a pair of wire cutters and a piece of paper with a bunch of letters on it… Ugh. Not *another* math puzzle," she groans.

"Hey, at least getting Sage out should be easy. Just need to use the wire cutters, right?" I say, hoping to reassure her.

"That's true. Okay, hold on, I'm going to get her out."

A few minutes later, something—wires, I assume—clatters to the ground.

"I'm out, Baylor!" Sage updates me. "So, this piece of paper has letters on it, but the keys all have numbers on them. So we're just trying to figure out which one gets you out."

"What's on the paper?" I ask, trying to help as much as I can without being able to see what they see.

"Just all of the letters of the alphabet. Not even a code, it's just the alphabet," Sage replies, her tone a bit uncertain.

"What numbers do the keys all have?"

"There's a lot of them, Baylor. I'm not sure…" Sage's voice trails off. "Well, all of them have three digits except for seven of them. Those ones have seventy-three, fifty, thirty-two, seventy-two, ninety-one, eighty-nine, and twenty."

"Maybe the alphabet is a code?" Valerie suggests. When she's met with no response, she explains. "A could be one, B could be two, and so on. It's a common way to convert letters to numbers. But we'd just have to figure out what letter combinations add up to the ones on the keys."

"It could take all day for us to figure that out," I sigh.

Valerie's probably right, though. I can't think of anything else that would work. And from the sound of it, it would take just as long to try every single key that's on the wall.

"Wait, my name adds up to thirty-two!" Sage exclaims. "Try your name, Valerie."

After a few moments, Valerie confirms that her name adds up to seventy-two.

"It's gotta be all of our names. What if the key that unlocks Baylor's door is just her name?" Valerie suggests.

"That's gotta be right. It's seventy-three, guys! Come on!" My heart is pounding in my chest, and I can only hope that we have enough time left…and that the other team hasn't already figured out their clues.

Feet pound from the next room over until a door slams and the steps get closer to my door. The key fits into the lock, and the door creaks open, granting me freedom.

"Congratulations, Baylor, Sage, and Valerie," Jarrod's voice booms from a speaker in the corner of the hallway. "Your team has broken out of the rooms. However, your challenge is not over. You haven't officially won until you are out of the warehouse. The race is still on. And if I were you, I'd act fast."

"That either means that time is almost up, or the other team is close. We've gotta go." I hope the urgency in my voice is enough to motivate us.

Sage wrings her hands, but Valerie nods, and we all take off running down the hallway. The inside of the warehouse is a maze, full of twists and turns. That's why we were blindfolded in the beginning—so we wouldn't have an idea of how we got in.

"Should we split up?" Sage asks, huffing out breaths, as we run into our third dead end.

I shake my head. "No, no, we have to all be out to win. What happens if someone gets lost? We stick together."

"We need to retrace our steps and remember which ways we turned. We need a map or something," Valerie mutters.

"Wait, that's it! Sage, do you still have that piece of paper from the cabinet?"

She nods, her eyebrows furrowing in confusion. She digs out the piece of paper from her pocket and hands it to me.

"Come on, let's go." I take off running back the direction we came. And when we reach the fork in the maze, I tear off a piece of paper and let it fall to the ground. "Breadcrumbs. That way we'll know where we've already been."

The plan works perfectly. We hit a few more dead ends, but we aren't running around in circles anymore thanks to the pieces of paper we've left lying around.

We're close to sprinting now, because this stretch of hallway we're in keeps going. "We have to be close to the end, guys! Keep pushing!" I encourage them, even as my lungs burn. I am *not* a cardio girl.

There's a left turn at the end of the hall, and once we round the corner, street lights shine up ahead.

"We made it!" Sage cheers.

We race out of the old warehouse, panting once we come to a halt. I drop my head down as my hands rest on my knees.

A slow clap begins, and I look up right as Jarrod Stone starts walking toward us. "Well done, ladies. You made it out with only a couple minutes to spare. Now, let's see if your competitors are as lucky."

I look around, something I hadn't thought to do in my exhaustion. A digital clock counts down the time; two minutes and thirty seconds remain.

As the clock winds down, there's no sign of the opposing team. Only after two minutes since the timer stops do Aspen, Katherine, and Jade emerge from the warehouse. And they look *pissed*.

"Ladies, welcome back. I'm so sorry to inform you that not only did the other team beat you out, but you didn't make it out in the hour's time." Jarrod frowns as he delivers the bad news to the losing team. He turns to my team. "Baylor, Sage, and Valerie. Congrats, you have won the team escape room challenge and you are all immune from this week's elimination."

the confessionals

Aspen: That [bleep] challenge was a joke.
Producer: What happened in there? Walk me through it all.
Aspen: My team sucked. That's what happened. And now *I'm* at risk of being eliminated because my team couldn't get [bleep] done.

Katherine: You know, I try to give everyone the benefit of the doubt, but that was exhausting.

Jade: Aspen is my friend, but sometimes she can be a bit...intense.
Producer: She mentioned that your team couldn't get anything done.

Jade: Mhm. But what Aspen will never admit is that it was all of us. Not just me and Katherine.

Producer: What do you mean by that?

Jade: I mean, it's a team effort. Everyone has to pull their own weight, and that just wasn't being done. And now there's a chance I could be going home.

Producer: There have been some rumors swirling around about the intentions of some of the girls. What are your thoughts on that?

Baylor: I mean, in an ideal world we'd all be here with good intentions, right? Only here for Dusty Wilder and nothing else. But that's just not realistic, is it?

Producer: Any theories on who isn't here with good intentions?

Baylor: *(laughs)* Yeah, I have my theories. But I'm not going to say them out loud.

Producer: Walk us through your thought process on your conversations with Sage and Aspen this week.

Dusty: I heard some things you never want to hear in this position. And I wanted to get to the bottom of it.

Producer: Do you think you did?

Dusty: That's still up for debate.

17
baylor

The Battles

A WEIGHT HAS BEEN LIFTED off my shoulders with the knowledge that Valerie, Sage, and I are all immune for this week's elimination. Dare I say, an Aspen-shaped weight? That is, if she's eliminated. I'm not going to get my hopes up too high, though, because knowing her, she'll somehow make it through to the next week.

We were informed this morning that we'll be able to watch the elimination tonight after the episode airing concludes, so when the producers tell the three of us to follow them after Aspen, Valerie, and Jade are escorted to the stage, it comes as no surprise.

We're led down the hall into the auditorium. During the early weeks of the show, there's no audience, just the camera crew, but the last four weeks will include live concert performances. Colette had described it as a "mini tour," as *Heart Strings* will travel to three different cities and then come back to Nashville for the concert and the final decision at the Ryman Auditorium.

We're seated near the middle of the theater, so we don't block the cameras or get in the way of the crew.

"I wonder what's going to happen this week for the elimination," Sage murmurs.

It must be something different than the last two weeks. If it's the same, it seems odd for the producers to allow us to watch.

"I don't know, but I'm glad we're not the ones at risk tonight," Valerie answers. Her voice shakes a little as she reaches the end of her sentence. I know she and Katherine are close, and I'm crossing my fingers that she's not the one sent home tonight.

"We're live in ten!" someone calls out, and the crew frantically finds their places.

The stage lights kick on, and Jarrod Stone walks out.

"Welcome back to *Heart Strings*. Those of you at home just witnessed a heart-hammering fourth episode, but we're not finished yet. Unfortunately, tonight is an elimination, and each of the members of the losing team from the escape room challenge are at risk." He pauses for effect. "Tonight's voting is going to operate a bit differently from the past episodes, so don't get up from your seats quite yet. Your voting matters more than ever, and this will also be the first time you'll get to hear three of the six contestants perform live."

Sage, Valerie, and I all exchange glances.

"Yes, you heard me correctly, folks. Tonight, each of the ladies at risk of elimination will be performing, but they don't know what." Once he finishes his sentence, a screen on stage shows Katherine, Aspen, and Jade all in different rooms with noise-canceling headphones on. "All three of the women will perform the same song—the song that earlier this week you all voted for on social media—and America, you will get to decide who moves on based not only on what you've seen from tonight's episode, but also the voices and talent of our contestants."

"The same song?" Valerie's eyes widen like she's processing what Jarrod just announced.

"Let the battles begin." Jarrod shoots a smile at the camera, and then the lights go dim.

Jade comes out on stage first. She looks a bit nervous, and even though we're sitting far from the stage, I can tell she's gripping the microphone tightly as the curtain behind her rises, revealing a full band who starts to play the introduction to Pam Tillis's "Maybe It Was Memphis."

Right off the bat, it's clear she's either extremely nervous or doesn't know the words to the song. Valerie cringes from her seat next to me as she misses the cue to start singing the verse. It looks like she has ears in, too, so she shouldn't have missed it if she knew the song.

Jade's voice doesn't fit the song. I'm not sure what she sang during the auditions, but it must've been something in a different genre or something modern.

The song ends, and I let out a long breath. I feel for Jade, because that performance was rough. It's probably going to take Aspen or Katherine performing horribly for her to make it through the elimination.

Katherine performs next and completely steals the show.

"She was made to sing nineties country." Sage bites her bottom lip as Katherine exits the stage. "It was like being transported back a few decades."

"She's definitely a frontrunner when it comes to performing," Valerie agrees, nodding.

I think we can all agree that Katherine has secured her spot in the next week.

"Now, Aspen," I sigh as I train my eyes on the stage.

"Is it wrong of me to hope she messes up worse than Jade?" I say it under my breath, but not nearly quiet enough that the others don't hear. Sage lets out a soft chuckle as Valerie quickly shakes her head.

The same intro of the song starts playing, and while the song doesn't fit her voice as well as Katherine's, Aspen still gives an incredible performance. Not only does she have a great voice, she has great stage presence. I'm not sure what the producers were trying to do by letting us watch, but if it was to intimidate us, I'm afraid it's working —even if it is only a little bit.

It's a bit frustrating. Even though we're all guaranteed to stay another week, the audience is getting to hear the other three girls sing, which could give them an advantage. They've only heard us sing in the auditions, and potentially any dates I haven't been on. If voice and performances play a large role in whether someone wins *Heart Strings*, then Sage, Valerie, and I are being handed the short end of the stick right now.

Jarrod Stone walks back out on stage, switching places with Aspen. "Well, folks, there you have it. Those were our performances of the night. Now, you'll be able to cast your vote for your favorite singer. Voting will end after this break, when we'll come back and reveal the results. And remember, the contestant with the least amount of votes will be eliminated."

"I wish we got to vote," Sage mutters.

"I wish we got to sing," Valerie says, like she took my thoughts straight from my brain.

"It puts us at a bit of a disadvantage, doesn't it," I agree with her, my comment coming out as more of a statement than a question.

"Hopefully we get dates that showcase our musical

talent instead of axe-throwing or rollerblading," Sage remarks.

The group date during the week that Valerie and I had our solo dates must have been rollerblading, then. I chuckle quietly to myself, thankful I wasn't put on that date.

Our conversation is cut short by music playing and the stage lights kicking on once again.

"We're back, America!" Jarrod declares. "Before we went to break, you watched three performances. Each woman gave us their own rendition of 'Maybe It Was Memphis' by Pam Tillis, but none of them knew they all had to sing it. You've now heard three different voices on the same song, and the voting results are in for best performance tonight! Let's bring out the ladies! Welcome to the stage Jade, Aspen, and Katherine!"

I imagine millions of people sitting at home watching their TV screens intently, hearts pounding as they wait to see if their favorite singer is moving on. Makes me wonder if I'm anyone's favorite, or if my parents know I'm on the show. I can't imagine they'd be too eager to watch if they do.

"Ladies, it's the moment of truth. One of you will, unfortunately, be eliminated tonight. How are you all feeling?" Jarrod asks, leaning in like he's close friends with all of them.

None of them speak at first, but the look on Aspen's face radiates confidence.

"I'm feeling great, Jarrod, thanks for asking." She gives a beaming smile as Jade shrinks back a little.

"Jade, how are you feeling?" Jarrod calls her out.

She shifts nervously on her feet. "It wasn't my best performance… I know that. But I hope the people at home see enough in me and my relationship with Dusty that they want me to stay. I really want to be here, and I hope I'm given that chance."

Jarrod wastes no time, despite Jade's heartfelt answer. "Let's find out, then, shall we?"

A screen drops behind Jarrod and the three girls, displaying a live count of the votes. To no one's surprise, Aspen leads, with Katherine following closely behind in the polls.

When the votes are all tallied, Katherine ends up being in first place, Aspen in second, and Jade in third.

"Katherine and Aspen, congratulations! You've made it through this week's elimination." Jarrod turns to Jade. "Jade, I'm so sorry. Unfortunately, you've received the least amount of votes and that means you'll be going home. You can say your goodbyes."

For supposedly being close friends, Jade and Aspen's goodbye is short. I wonder if something happened between them during the escape room challenge and Jade saw Aspen's true colors. I'm starting to think everyone's beginning to see through her, and it comes as temporary relief—until I remember why *I'm* here.

It doesn't matter what they think of Aspen. As long as they don't also see through me.

That night, I'm writing down lyrics in my journal when a light tapping on my door gets my attention. Thinking it's Daniella, I set my journal down on the bed, not bothering to hide it.

To my surprise, when I open the door, there's a sticky note attached to it.

Meet me on the rooftop.
- DW

I shake my head in amusement before catching myself smiling because of the note.

What the hell am I doing?

There's no way I'm *actually* falling for Dusty Wilder.

I debate whether I should follow the note's instructions, listing out the pros and cons in my head.

Pros: I can spend more time with Dusty and get to know him. I'm already bored out of my mind, so getting to talk to someone would be nice.

Cons: If I get caught, I could lose my job.

The rational part of me knows I should rip up the note and never speak of it with anyone, but a small part of me wants to take the risk.

I've tried for so long to convince myself the only reason I came on the show was to save my job, but in the past few weeks going on dates, both secret and planned, I've come to love it. I never thought I'd have fun being on a reality TV show, but meeting Dusty and the other girls has exceeded my expectations.

I never pictured a career in music for myself, having set my sights on politics in Washington D.C. and making my parents proud. I always thought that was my dream—my life's purpose—but now I'm not sure.

Pushing away all logical thoughts, I make the decision for myself. Not the decision for Colette St. James or my job or my parents.

I'm choosing myself, I repeat in my head as I sneak out of my hotel room and head to the stairwell.

The night air bites against my cheeks when I open the

rooftop access door. I hold the door open as I look around. There's no one up here.

Dejected, I drop my shoulders. Maybe it was just some sick prank. But then fear settles in at the idea that it could have been a tactic by Aspen to get me caught.

Footsteps approach from around the corner, and my heart drops.

This is it. This is how you go down.

"Baylor?" The voice that calls my name isn't Aspen's or a producer's, and I let out a sigh of relief as Dusty moves into my line of sight.

"Hi. I wasn't sure if you were really up here." I stumble over my words, nervous energy pouring out of me.

He steps closer to me and takes my hands in his. "Don't worry, I wouldn't do that to you. I just wanted to see you again. How are you feeling after the elimination?"

"I wasn't on the chopping block, so I feel okay. I can't believe we're already down to the final five, though," I admit.

"It's flown by. I wasn't sure how all of this would work in the beginning, but I'm starting to really believe in this process—in all of you here…" His voice trails off, but he recovers quickly. "Come on, I have something to show you."

He leads me around the corner where a blanket is set up under a small pergola strung up with lights.

"Do you like it?" he asks, his voice a bit unsure.

"This is… You set this all up? For me?" I stare at him, a bit stunned at the gesture.

"I like you a lot, Baylor. You've taken up space in my mind, have occupied almost every waking thought, and I want to show you how glad I am that you're here."

My mind wanders to whether he's also planning secret

dates for the other girls, and my eyebrows pinch together as I fight my emotions. "Thank you. No one's ever done something like this for me, so…thank you."

"You mentioned lyrics last time we spent time together, so I wanted to show you what I've been working on. See if you have any thoughts?" He walks over to the blanket and grabs his guitar before sitting and patting the ground.

I follow and take a seat next to him, crossing my legs beneath me.

Dusty starts strumming a slow, soft chord progression. A love ballad. Then he begins singing.

*I've fallen down, felt my heart slip through my
hands. Not the type to write a song so easily.*

I close my eyes to let the words wash over me.

*I wish I could be where you are. That look in your
eyes, the way you smile.*

He starts the second verse, and I hum along with him. By the time the chorus begins, I've found a way to harmonize with his melody.

A few minutes later, he strums the last chord, letting it hang in the air between us.

"What did you think?" he whispers.

"It's beautiful. Why don't you take it to your label?" I ask, turning so I'm facing him and our knees graze.

He huffs out a laugh. "The label wouldn't go for a song like that. It doesn't fit my image." His words come out harsh, biting.

"That's too bad. It really is a great song. Maybe once

this is all over, you can have a conversation with them," I suggest, but he just shrugs.

"Maybe." He pauses then quickly changes the subject. "Want to do a song together?"

The corner of my lip rises as my stomach flutters. "Sure."

He starts strumming another song, a country duet from the nineties. We sing song after song together until we lose track of time. It's only when thunder rolls in the distance and rain threatens to drench us that we pack up and head back inside for the night.

And it's in those moments when I can really picture a future with Dusty Wilder.

18
dusty

Final Five

ONLY HALF of the women remain after Jade's elimination last night. The show is in full swing, and the final decision looms over me, even though it feels like we just started.

I was informed there wouldn't be an elimination this week, but I was also told the girls didn't know so I have to keep it a secret. Knowing I'll get to spend an extra week with the five of them gives me some comfort, but it also means the next elimination is going to be even tougher.

I'm taking one of the ladies on a date today. As much as I want to take Baylor, especially after last night, I still need to get to know the other girls. They're talented, and I want to help them as much as I can.

The only person I haven't gotten to talk to about the Aspen-Baylor drama is Valerie, so my plan is to take her. I don't want drama to cloud our entire date like it did with Sage's—and Aspen's, but that was different—so I'm going to try my best to get the conversation over with quickly so we can enjoy our day.

I also want to talk to Baylor, but I want to hear from everyone before that happens. I'm ready to move past whatever this is, even if it means that Aspen has to go home. I hope it doesn't come down to that, of course, but right now, if I had the choice between Aspen or Baylor, I'd choose Baylor.

Instead of meeting Valerie at the date spot, I'm staying at the house until the girls arrive so we can all eat breakfast together. It'll be a good opportunity to see the dynamic of the contestants together and maybe see where the root of the drama is coming from—that is, if any manifests.

The cars pull up to the house thirty minutes later, and the girls all pile out. We only have two more weeks before we go on the road for what Ace High is calling a "mini tour." Truthfully, it's just three different cities, and two of them are in Tennessee. But it'll give the girls a taste of what touring with me might look like, and give me an opportunity to perform with them live in front of an audience. Because at the end of the day, this is also about who I want to continue my career with.

"Hi, Dusty!" Katherine waves at me as she walks into the house before walking over to pull me into a hug.

"Morning, ladies," I greet the rest of them as they follow behind. Once they're all here, we take a seat at the dining table and the caterers who arrived early this morning start passing out plates of food.

I take a few quick bites, knowing I'll be leaving here soon before asking, "How was everyone's night?"

I don't enjoy small talk, but there's not much else to discuss right now. The deeper conversations happen during solo dates or one-on-one conversations.

"It was good. It's wild that there's only five of us left. It feels like we just arrived," Valerie answers first, and the other girls nod in agreement, even Aspen.

"Jade and I were pretty close, so I was sad to see her go." Aspen hangs her head a little, and I can't tell if it's genuine or an act now that the cameras are here. Jade was the one person, besides Valerie, who I hadn't gotten to speak to about Aspen, and part of me wishes I had spoken to her. Especially now, knowing that they were somewhat friends.

"I'm just glad to be here another week." Sage laughs, lightening the mood a bit.

"I'm looking forward to this week." I cut into the conversation after dabbing my face to get the syrup from my pancakes out of my mustache. "There are some important conversations to be had, but we've got some amazing dates lined up as well."

Any chatter amongst the girls has ceased as they wait for me to announce who will be going on the first date this week.

"I won't keep you waiting." I chuckle as I look around the table. "Valerie, would you like to go on this date with me?"

A sigh escapes the lips of one of the girls, but my eyes are locked on Valerie as she smiles and nods.

"Absolutely, I'll go on the date with you." She scoots her chair out from the dining table, leaving her breakfast untouched.

Before I follow suit and slide out from the dining table, I grab a piece of bacon for the road. "Have a great breakfast, ladies, and I'll see you later."

As we walk toward the front door of the house, I place my free hand on the small of Valerie's back and whisper, "I'm excited to have this time with you today."

She looks over at me, practically beaming, and replies, "Me too."

The producers bring us to a farmers market in the heart of the city. When we arrive, there are two big open-air buildings—one on each side of us—housing vendors. Straight ahead are the gardens and a stage where a band plays live music in front of a seating area with picnic tables.

"This is amazing," Valerie gasps as she takes it all in.

Before today, I'd never been to any of the farmers markets in Nashville. I'd never had time with my busy schedule and touring, although supporting small business owners is high on my list of priorities. Back in Oklahoma, my family often sets up at local markets, and being here causes a rush of childhood memories to flow through my mind. But I push them away as quickly as they come, not allowing guilt to rise in my chest.

I left home to make a better life for myself *and* for my family. I don't—*can't*—regret the decision I made, because what's done is done. But the pressure to succeed, knowing that one wrong decision could be the end of it all, continues to weigh on me.

"Where do you want to go first?" I ask in an attempt to completely clear my mind and focus solely on today's date.

"Should we just make our way down the line?" she suggests.

I nod, taking her hand and leading her toward the building to our left. Immediately, we're greeted by stands and stands of fresh fruits and vegetables.

"Good morning, folks!" one of the vendors greets us, even as camera crews follow us around.

"Oh, look at these!" Valerie points to some tomatoes as she moves down the line of vendors. "Do you like to cook?"

"I'm not very good at it." I laugh. "But I'll occasionally cook meals for myself. Do you?"

"I love cooking. Especially for my friends and family. My mom is Greek, so growing up, she frequently made a dish called strapatsada for family breakfasts," she explains. "She didn't want me and my siblings to forget about our roots, and food is such a wonderful way to bring people together, so she taught us how to make several traditional dishes."

"Your mom sounds wonderful." I turn to the seller behind the stand. "How much for a few of these tomatoes?"

"Oh, you don't have to do that!" Valerie protests.

"I insist. Come on, let me do this for you. That way you can teach me how to make your mom's dish. I can use all the cooking tips I can get." I wink at her before handing the vendor a twenty-dollar bill.

She hands us a bag filled with tomatoes and the change.

"Wait, okay, so if we're going to make a recipe from my family, we have to make one from yours, too. It's only fair," Valerie declares as we continue walking through the market.

"My mom makes this incredible strawberry shortcake," I reminisce.

"We can make my recipe as a late brunch and yours can be dessert later. I'm always up for a good shortcake. And I love strawberries." She looks like she's stuck in a daydream, and it would be impossible for me to say no to anything she asks at this moment.

We shop for all the ingredients we'll need for our cooking venture later this afternoon then head toward the gardens.

"There's something I've been meaning to discuss with you." I don't want to ruin the fun we're having, but the topic of Aspen still needs to be addressed.

"Yeah, what's up?" She looks up at me, taking her attention away from the flowers she was inspecting.

"I don't want to put a damper on our date, because I've really had an incredible time with you so far, but I've been trying to get to the bottom of this for a couple weeks now and I want to hear everyone's perspective," I lead into the conversation, but she beats me to it.

"Oh, this is about Aspen, isn't it?" Her voice has a tinge of disappointment to it, like she was hoping to talk about anything and anyone but Aspen.

I nod. "It is."

She sighs, looking down at the flowers, and starts rolling a petal between her fingers. "I'm guessing you've talked to mostly everyone, so you've probably heard a lot of what's going on?" She waits for me to nod before continuing. "There's been some...tension...between Aspen and Baylor. Aspen's gone on about how she's here to win and not here to make friends and that if Baylor was here for the right intentions that she wouldn't be trying to make friends either. It's messy, to say the least. I try to stay out of all of it, but there are only five of us here and we're always together, so it's difficult. Aspen's also got it in her head that the producers have something to do with Baylor being here.

"I mean, I know she's here because the viewers chose

her to be here. And the producers would have had to make an executive decision to bring someone on who didn't audition, but other than that, I'm not really seeing a connection between production and Baylor being a contestant. At least from my interactions with her, she seems genuine. She's always been kind to me and the other girls, aside from Aspen, but I can't exactly blame her. If my character was being called into question, I probably wouldn't be friendly either."

I don't interrupt, letting her get all of her thoughts out before asking any questions or making any remarks. "I appreciate you being so open about this."

She shrugs, like it doesn't affect her, but I know it has to in some ways. It doesn't feel great to be bringing up other drama during our time together, and I hope I can make it up to her later. But I'm one step closer to getting closure on the situation. A relief, considering we're already halfway through this process.

"Hey, let's not let this affect the rest of our day, yeah?" I lightly kiss her forehead to try to reassure her and show her that I'm still present, or at least as present as I can be with Baylor still in the back corners of my mind. "Pick out some flowers, I want to buy them for you." It's probably a shitty way of making it up to her, using more money to save this date, but it's the only thing I can think of doing.

"You don't have to do that for me." I can tell Valerie is trying to be polite, but a traitorous blush creeps into her cheeks.

"Pick out your favorites. Come on, now." I nudge her playfully with my elbow as she smiles and starts to walk around the greenhouse, scoping out all the florals. A few minutes later, she has a pretty bouquet of lilies, white roses, lavender, and daisies.

"Thank you for all of this, Dusty. I had a really fun time." Valerie leans her head into my shoulder as we walk toward the street where the car is waiting to take us back to the house.

"The day's not over yet. We still have to try out these recipes."

19
baylor

Take My Life Into My Own Hands

THE PRODUCERS BRING us back to the house later in the evening. Breakfast was uneventful, without any drama, a small stroke of luck I'm grateful for. Part of me hopes that because there are only five of us left, and Dusty has begun asking questions about Aspen's feud with me, she'll give up on whatever plan she has to get me eliminated and tone it down a bit.

While Valerie and Dusty were on their date, we all talked about our families and careers outside of the show. Well, *they* talked about their careers outside of the show. Katherine's a pediatric nurse, Sage works in a legal office, and Aspen…

Now that I think about it, Aspen didn't talk about her job, either.

"Hey," I whisper to Sage. "Do you know what Aspen actually does for work?"

She stares blankly at me. "I…I don't know? I think she does something related to music?"

I hum, thoughts whirling through my brain before

muttering. "If she works in music, why hasn't she been signed to a label?"

"That's a great question," Sage muses. "I'm curious now, too."

Maybe Daniella can do some digging for me, I think. It's risky, but any information I can use is information I want.

Boots clank across the hardwood floor, interrupting our conversation. Sage and I turn our heads at the same time as Dusty walks into the living room.

"Good evening, ladies. I'm looking forward to spending time with you all tonight."

He grabs Katherine first, leaving the rest of us sitting on the sectional.

"How was your date today, Val?" Sage asks to break the silence.

"It was good!" She nods. "We went to a farmers market and picked out ingredients from recipes our families made when we were kids. Then we came back here and made them. There are leftovers in the fridge." A flush creeps into her cheeks, and it's not difficult to pick up on their connection.

"That's great. Do you think your relationship is in a good place for next week?" Sage continues, her question coming out carefully.

"I do. I don't want to speak too soon, but I think we really see each other for who we are, you know?"

We all nod, without anyone interrupting, not even Aspen. It seems she also wants to hear what Valerie has to say.

"We talked about his family a lot and everything they've done to support Dusty. There's a lot more to him than being a famous country singer."

It's a similar, if not the same, conversation that Dusty

and I had when he snuck up to my room last week, and a sinking feeling settles in my stomach as she continues to describe their day. I'm happy Dusty's family is so supportive. That's all anyone could ask for. But I can't lie and say it doesn't make me a bit sad for myself. All I want is for my parents to be proud and support whatever dreams I have. To not have to prove myself every time there's a bump in the road, a wrench in my carefully thought-out plans.

"Who do you think will get the next date?" Aspen speaks up.

My eyes shift toward her, wary.

Valerie shrugs. "We don't really talk about his other connections. I just worry about my own."

"Has anyone here not gotten one yet?" Sage asks, and we all shake our heads. "I think you're the only one so far to have had two, Val."

"Lucky girl," Aspen sighs. "It'll be interesting to see who gets the dates next week and if that plays into who gets eliminated."

A few murmurs of agreement rise before Katherine and Dusty walk back into the room.

"Baylor, do you want to go talk?" he offers before anyone else can pull him aside.

I nod, standing from my spot on the couch. Before following, I give a small smile and wave to the other girls. Not to brag, just a genuine act of kindness.

We walk outside, heading toward a plush sofa on the patio, the night air cooling my face. Dusty gestures to the couch, and I sit before he joins me, taking off his jacket and wrapping it around my shoulders.

"Listen, I wanted to talk to you about Aspen." Dusty cuts straight to the chase. "I'm sure this isn't news to you, but she brought up her concerns that you might…you might be here because of the producers. And I just want to clear the air and move past this drama for good."

I fumble with my jacket lapel as I sigh. "I knew you'd probably bring it up. I just want to preface by saying I'm not trying to throw her under the bus or anything, but Aspen's had an issue with me since the very beginning. And I don't know what her problem with me is, but I'm here because I want to be here. I'm here because of you. Not the producers. I mean, I left my job to come on *Heart Strings*. I'm making sacrifices to be here, but I wouldn't have it any other way."

God, has it always been this easy to lie?

I hate it. Especially since I feel like Dusty and I have had great moments together, but they've mostly been off camera. And it's not like I can bring up those dates now. Not with the producers breathing down our necks.

"Thank you for that. I really appreciate you being so honest with me."

I smile at him, all while my lie gnaws at my stomach.

"Wait, what were you doing for work before you came on the show?" Dusty asks. "I don't think we've ever talked about that before."

I pause for a moment, trying to think of a believable answer, especially since he *definitely* saw me that first day of filming interviews.

"I worked in social media and public relations." It's the obvious answer, although it's also one that might raise suspicion, so I have to tread lightly here. "I worked in Washington D.C. in the government sector." *Even if my dreams have shifted, there's no harm in manifesting it still, right?*

"Wow, what made you want to leave that to pursue music?"

Dig deep here, Baylor. You're in this far, you may as well keep going.

"I've always done what others expect of me. Or at least tried to. I've spent my entire life trying to prove that what I want is worth something to others. But with this show, with music, I realized it's what *I* am passionate about. What *I* want to do. So I went for it. Even if it's not what everyone else wants from me." I didn't mean for all of that to come out, but it did. Deep down, I think I have wanted to try a career in music, but the pressure from my parents and wanting to prove myself to them has always overshadowed my own dreams. It's about time I take my life into my own hands and stop worrying about whether or not it pleases someone else, even if it's risky.

Daniella would be so proud if she were here right now.

Dusty doesn't say anything, and I worry for a moment that I've said something wrong.

"Did I—" The words falling out of my mouth are cut short as Dusty cups my face with his hands and leans in, our lips brushing gently. This kiss, unlike the ones we've shared off camera, is soft, unhurried.

My eyes flutter shut as I lean into him—his touch like waves crashing over me, both of us taking small breaths before diving back under the surface. His thumb strokes my cheek, and I wrap my arms around the back of his neck.

"I thought I might have said something wrong," I whisper into his mouth.

"No, Baylor, you didn't. That was exactly what I needed to hear." He plants a kiss on my forehead then pulls back, gazing at me for a moment, his lips quirking up in a quick smile.

We stay there, embracing each other for a while longer,

like we don't care if we lose track of time and let the night slip away from us. He's in no rush to get back to the other women, and I'm just following his lead.

He's the same Dusty from the rooftop, but I'm not the same Baylor.

I don't like being dishonest with him, but when the cameras are on, so am I.

I just hope he can't see the truth behind my lying eyes.

the confessionals

Producer: So, how has this week gone so far? I know there were some important conversations you wanted to have.

Dusty: I think I'm at the point where I'm able to put all of the drama in the past. I believe I've gotten the clarity I need on the Aspen-Baylor situation, and I'm ready to move forward.

Valerie: Baylor and Dusty were gone for a long time. I wonder what they talked about.

Aspen: It's really not fair that he spent so much time with her. We all deserve to have time with Dusty.

20
dusty

A Future with You

WE'VE REACHED the turning point of the show, where relationships start to become deeper and decisions are more difficult.

Today, we're in downtown Nashville on lower Broadway, with security and producers flanking us on both sides to prevent fans who recognize us from getting too close.

It's slightly annoying, having so many watchful eyes on us, but I understand the concern with it being the whole group. If it were only two of us on a solo date, the security wouldn't be as necessary because, hypothetically, it would be easier to blend in.

"Oh my God, is that *Dusty Wilder?*"

"It is! They must be filming today."

"Ugh, those girls are so lucky."

Whispers and faint squeals can be heard as we pass people on the sidewalk.

One of the girls next to me stifles a laugh, clearly hearing the comments being made as we pass. I focus more on their reactions, rather than the attention from fans.

"How do you deal with this all the time?" Baylor mutters, and I flick my eyes toward her, amusement probably painting my features. She catches me looking at her, and her eyes drop to the ground, like I wasn't supposed to hear her comment.

Aspen, on the other hand, seems to be soaking in the attention, holding her head up high and flashing smiles to the people who stare a bit too long.

We eventually enter a bar at the end of the strip. Security guides us to the V.I.P. section directly in front of the stage.

Valerie and Sage sit at a table to the right of me, and Katherine and Baylor find their place at my table. Aspen tries to squeeze her way in, too, but when she realizes there isn't room, she rolls her eyes and surrenders to the other table.

The stage is empty for now, top country hits playing from the speakers. Before I can process the song that's playing, Katherine nudges me with her elbow.

"Isn't this your song?" She laughs, and I strain my ears, recognizing the familiar kick drum beat before I even hear my own voice.

I let out a slightly nervous chuckle. "Yeah, I guess so. What a coincidence." The bar probably changed the station specifically to the one that's always playing my music, knowing we'd be here today.

Jarrod approaches us out of nowhere. You'd think by now I would expect him to turn up out of the blue since he's the host.

"Hello, Dusty. Ladies," he greets all of us with a wave. "Exciting plans for this afternoon."

Curiosity must get the better of Sage, because she raises a hand. "What are we going to be doing?"

"I thought you'd never ask, Sage. You'll all get the chance to sing today on this very stage..."

Aspen's eyes widen, a smile creeping onto her face.

"...as a group." Jarrod finishes his sentence, and Aspen's smirk vanishes. "Don't worry, Aspen." He chuckles. "I'm not finished. You'll all perform a song as a group, and then the audience will get to choose one lucky woman to perform with Dusty."

Sure enough, a crowd has gathered behind us, security and a velvet rope the only things separating us. I face forward again as a band steps onto the stage and the radio stops playing. Jarrod jumps on stage as well, heading to the microphone.

"Good afternoon, ladies and gentlemen! I'm Jarrod Stone, the host of the new hit reality TV show *Heart Strings*. We've got some incredible talent with us here today, and they cannot wait to perform for you!" He looks down at the women and gestures for them to come up. "Come on up, ladies. Folks, let me introduce you to our final five women: Aspen, Katherine, Valerie, Sage, and Baylor!"

One-by-one, they all file onto the stage. Aspen immediately heads for the microphone, but Jarrod waves her away and hands the first microphone to Baylor. I stifle a laugh, because *of course*, but then the bar staff brings over four more microphones.

Jarrod quietly talks to each of the women, Katherine and Valerie nodding along with what he has to say, while Baylor has a blank expression and Aspen just glares.

Once he finishes, he exits the stage and nods to the band, who starts playing the opening notes of a popular Pistol Annies song.

Valerie, Aspen, and Baylor start the song off with a harmony, and I can't lie, they sound *great* together. Their voices mesh effortlessly. Baylor sings the line about breaking a million hearts, which is fitting, because with the way she looks on stage, she could give a man a heart attack.

Katherine takes over the first verse, singing a solo, and when Miranda Lambert's verse approaches, I fully expect Sage to start singing. I assume she expected to start singing, too, but instead Aspen cuts in, her more powerful vocals drowning out Sage's softer voice.

Murmurs from the crowd rise behind me, but the girls recover quickly and Sage picks up the next verse. I make a mental note about their ability to adapt. It's an important trait to have, especially on tour.

I also take into account Aspen's selfishness, but I already knew she possesses that trait.

Valerie and Baylor split the next chorus, then all five women harmonize the final one, and the song ends with a roar of applause from the crowd.

Jarrod claps as he enters the stage again. "Well done, ladies. How about that, folks?" He pauses as the crowd cheers again. "What you in the audience don't know, is that Dusty Wilder is also going to perform a song for you all. And he's going to perform with one of these lucky women."

A hush falls over the bar as the audience listens intently.

"You all have the chance to vote and pick the special girl who gets to perform. I'll have each of the women say their name once, and then voting will be determined by the loudest cheers and applause. Are you ready, Nashville?"

Hoots and hollers rise from the bar patrons as Jarrod gestures for Valerie to start. They go down the line until Aspen and Baylor are the only two left.

"My name is Aspen," she says confidently, arrogance radiating off her as though she's the obvious choice for the crowd.

"Hi, I'm Baylor," Baylor introduces herself then gives the crowd a closed-lip smile. She does that often in public, like she wants to save her true smile, the radiant one. The one she's given me during our secret, off-camera dates.

"As I raise my hand above each contestant, cheer loudly for the one you think should get to sing with Dusty!" Jarrod instructs.

He starts with Valerie, and the crowd gives an uproar of applause. Sage gets a similar response. Katherine gets a few more cheers, but it's nothing compared to the response the audience gives Aspen. For a moment, I think the roof might blow with how loud it gets.

"Finally, Baylor." Jarrod hovers his hand over her head, and the crowd goes into an absolute frenzy. "Well, folks, I think we have a clear winner here. Congratulations, Baylor."

Aspen looks like she's going to explode as her jaw ticks and she stomps off the stage. Valerie, Katherine, and Sage look disappointed, but still happy for their friend.

I stand, wiping my hands on my jeans as I walk toward the steps to get on the stage.

"You all looked and sounded great up there." I give the other girls an encouraging nod. I don't want them to lose their confidence from this, because they all sounded incredible.

Valerie and Katherine smile, and Sage nods as they walk past me, but Aspen grabs my arm.

"I wish it was me up there with you, but I understand," she whispers before planting her lips on mine.

My eyes widen at the contact. I'm a little bit taken

aback, and this is clearly an attempt to throw Baylor off. The camera crew catches sight of us "kissing" and immediately points the cameras at us.

I gently push Aspen away, the movement discreet enough that no one will notice.

"What?" She furrows her brows.

"I need to go on stage," I reply then leave her standing there with a confused look.

In the five seconds it takes to walk up the steps, all my annoyance with Aspen melts away when I see Baylor. She turns toward me and flashes me a smile, a real one this time. She probably doesn't save them just for me, but I'm okay with pretending.

"Hi." I smile at Baylor.

A flush creeps into her cheeks as she whispers, "Hi."

"Second time performing together, might as well make it official, huh?" I tease, although it's not a joke, not really.

I can't pinpoint the emotion on her face, whether it's amusement or contemplation. But she laughs it off, responding, "Don't get too ahead of yourself, superstar. There are still five of us here."

Yeah, but only one of you matters.

The band starts playing a song by Flatland Cavalry, interrupting all my thoughts. I don't take my eyes off Baylor as I begin singing the lyrics—about what the future could look like if we worked out and ended up together.

Baylor picks up the second verse where the lyrics talk about the nicknames we'd call each other and the things we'd do together when I'm not on the road.

While it's not necessarily a happy song, it makes me hopeful for the future—preferably one with Baylor.

Before the chorus starts, I step closer to her, holding my microphone to the side and leaning close enough to share hers. Close enough for me to feel when she takes a breath in between lines.

I've all but abandoned my microphone at this point, singing the final verse with hers. The lines alternate, and at one point she draws her bottom lip between her teeth as though she's holding back a smile. When the song ends, instead of pulling apart, we freeze, gazing into each other's eyes like the audience and the cameras and the other women don't even exist.

It's only when the crowd starts chanting, "Kiss! Kiss! Kiss!" that I'm brought back to reality.

"Let's give the people what they want, darlin'," I whisper before leaning in and kissing her. Her lips meld to mine, like puzzle pieces fitting perfectly together. Like *we* fit perfectly together.

The crowd swoons and cheers as we break apart. In the absence of her, my lips tingle, a burning want creeping into my chest.

I look down at the V.I.P. section where the other women are. Katherine picks at her nails, Valerie won't make eye contact with me, and Aspen looks like she wants to murder Baylor. I can't imagine it's fun having to watch your competition kiss the person you're dating, but that's the name of the game.

We exit the stage and join Jarrod and the women.

"There won't be an elimination this week, ladies," Jarrod announces, signifying the end of the date and the day. "Head back to the hotel and relax. You've all earned it. Congratulations on making it this far."

Oh, I plan on doing something at the hotel, but it won't be relaxing.

21
dusty

Over the Edge

I **KNOW** I'm taking a huge risk showing up—yet again—to the hotel, but I can't stop thinking about Baylor. Kissing her isn't enough. I need to know what she tastes like, feels like, the sounds she makes. The need rising in my gut is desperate, like an animal trying to claw its way out of a cage.

I take a deep breath as I enter the lobby. The front desk receptionist is busy and there aren't any producers around, but I don't want to risk an elevator run-in, so I walk as fast as I can down the hall to the stairwell.

I take the stairs two at a time until I get to the fourth floor.

My knuckles rap against the wood grain of her door, and within seconds, the lock clicks and the door swings open.

A mix of shock and confusion paints Baylor's features, but I don't give her the opportunity to ask questions before I wrap my hands around her waist, smash my lips against hers, and walk her backward into her room, letting the door slam behind us.

"What are you doing here, Dusty?" she gasps between kisses. "Do you need something?"

"You. I need you," I rasp out as her hands wander up my body.

"We could get in so much trouble for this. I could get kicked off the show." Her actions don't match her response, as her hand fists my hair and she pulls me closer to her.

"I don't care. Fuck the rules." I pull away slightly, looking down into her deep-brown eyes. "Tell me you don't want this."

She tries to ignore me, standing on her tiptoes to kiss me again, but I pull away more.

"Tell me you don't want to do this, and I'll stop, Baylor."

"I can't. I don't want you to stop." She looks up at me through thick eyelashes, and *fuck*, I'm a goner. "I want this. I want *you*."

A guttural, nearly animalistic noise escapes me, and I place my hands on her jaw, lowering my mouth to hers. I lightly nip at her bottom lip, sucking on it as she lets out a soft moan. As she parts her lips, I take the opportunity to deepen the kiss, our tongues entangling with each other in a slow, sensual dance.

I run my hands down her neck and torso until they find their place on her hips, and I lift her up so her legs are wrapped around me. She grinds her hips into me, her center rubbing against my hard length.

"Fuck," I groan. I walk us over to her bed, lowering her down in the middle of the mattress as I climb on her.

"Shoes." She laughs.

"Great idea," I mumble into her neck. "Shoes, clothes, all of it can go."

I back myself up so I can stand again and kick off my boots, tossing them near the dresser and television. Baylor lies on the bed, resting on her elbows, looking at me with a mix of amusement and lust.

"What are you waiting for, darlin'? Take them off." My voice rumbles in my throat, and a breath catches as she hooks her fingers in the waistband of her leggings, peeling them off slowly, teasing me.

Every second is torture as she reveals each inch of her skin. Finally, she bends her knees, pulling the pants completely off and leaving her in her shirt and underwear. Before I can move, she grabs the hem of her shirt, pulling it over her head at another achingly slow rate. But it gives me the time to really look at her, to admire her body and her beauty.

"Fuck, Baylor. The things I want to do to you right now." I step closer to the bed, fully intending to climb on top of her, but she sits up and places a hand on my chest to push me away.

"Not so fast, superstar." She looks at me again with those siren eyes before her hands fumble with the button on my jeans, unhooking them. In one fell swoop, she pulls down my jeans and boxers, letting my cock spring free.

Her eyes widen at first glance, but any concern she may have had disappears in a split second as she climbs off the bed and lowers herself to her knees. She fists my cock, pumping it in her hand a couple times before wrapping her mouth around the head.

Baylor swirls her tongue around the tip then takes me deeper in her mouth. I swallow the lump in my throat as I close my eyes. She's so good at this. Too good. Any longer and I might burst.

"Baylor," I moan as she hums around me, my tip hitting

the back of her throat. "Baylor, please." I'm stuck between wanting more and wanting to stop. The urge to grab a fistful of her hair and fuck her mouth is strong, but the desire to feel her clench around me is stronger. I manage to muster enough strength to pull myself out of her mouth, the suction making a popping sound as my cock leaves her lips. "Get up."

She listens, standing so the backs of her knees are pressed against the bed.

I hook my hands around her back, unclasping her bra and letting her breasts spill out. Moving her so she's sitting on the edge of the bed, I lower my mouth to her nipple as I palm her other breast. As her back arches, pushing her tits closer to my face, I glance up at her. Her eyes are shut, her mouth gaped in pleasure.

I lightly nip, my teeth grazing her sensitive peak before unlatching my mouth and moving to the other one, giving it an equal amount of attention. "Your tits are perfect."

She hums in approval as I kiss down her stomach, reaching the hem of her panties.

"How wet am I going to find you, Baylor?" I purr, kissing the thin fabric covering her.

She doesn't answer as her breath hitches in her throat. I slide my hand under her waistband, reaching down the front of her. She's soaked, her arousal already coating my fingers.

"Dusty, please," she gasps.

I remove my hand from her underwear instead of giving her what she wants, but only to hook my fingers in the elastic to bring them down her legs, baring her to me.

I take a moment to admire her. I thought her body was perfect before, but that word doesn't seem good enough to describe her now. She's absolutely ethereal, fully naked and exposed to me. Her curves fit perfectly in my hands, and I'm desperate for a taste of her.

"My turn to kneel for you, darlin'," I murmur as I lower myself to the ground and rest her legs on my shoulders, pulling her to my face.

I run a finger through her slit, teasing her and spreading her wetness before circling her clit. Then I latch my mouth onto her, devouring her like she's my last meal. My tongue laps at her center, and she throws her head back in response.

My mouth never leaves her body as my fingers work in tandem with my tongue. And when she practically screams my name, panting that she's coming, I drink up every sweet drop.

"I need you inside me, Dusty," she begs, as though the orgasm I just gave her isn't enough.

Unfortunately, it's at this moment I realize I don't have a condom. "I-I don't have any protection." I swore I'd put one in my pocket, but I must have forgotten in my urgency to get to her.

She huffs out a breath, and disappointment settles in my stomach. But I'm not done with her.

"Sit up," I say, as I climb on the bed and lie on my back.

"What are you doing?" she asks.

"Come here." I pat my chest. "Ride my face. Take what you need."

"Oh, God," she moans. But she does what I asked, settling herself over my face.

My hands grab her hips, and I yank her down, pulling her weight onto me. Then I lick and suck, dragging orgasm after orgasm out of her.

After two more, Baylor pushes away from my face, her legs trembling around me. "I can't."

"Yes, you can. Give me one more." I dig my hands into her hips, and this time when she sits, I fuck her with my tongue as she soaks my face, calling out my name as the last wave crashes into her.

When she comes down from her high, she collapses next to me, her chest rising and falling at a rapid pace. Her cheeks are painted red with a flush, and I know I've done my job.

"Let me…help you," she pants.

"Darlin', that was enough for me. Making you come was my goal tonight." It's a half-truth. My goal was to feel how tight she would be around me, but tonight has given me enough to get myself off later when I'm alone. I can still taste her in my mustache, and it's enough to keep this night replaying in my mind until the next time I see her.

Baylor rolls over so her head rests on my chest and her leg drapes over my body. I wrap my arm around her shoulder and brush my hand up on and down her arm.

She looks up at me with an expression that I can't quite read. Uncertainty?

"What's up?"

Her eyebrows pinch together as she softly shakes her head. "Nothing."

I'm not sure it's nothing, but I let it go as she lowers her head again. We lie there for a while, tangled up in each other, until soft snores next to me tell me she's fallen asleep, so I carefully pull the sheets over her and turn out the light before redressing and sneaking out her door.

Hopefully no one noticed my absence, but I honestly don't care if they did. Even if they chain me up, nothing is going to keep me away from Baylor.

I'm in it too deep at this point. All I want is her.

22
baylor

Bed Chem

SOFT SHEETS, cool against my bare skin, greet me when I wake up.

Oh my God, it wasn't a dream. My eyes widen as I realize what happened last night. Dusty was here. Again.

And he gave you some of the best orgasms of your life.

The memory of his tongue and his hands makes me press my thighs together, like there's still a phantom touch between my legs.

I reach my hand down my body, desperate to relieve this feeling of lust and want. I shouldn't feel this way. Nothing about this relationship is real.

Or is it?

Everything about Dusty Wilder's bedroom skills was definitely real. And it's pretending that Dusty is here again, fucking me with his fingers and mouth, that sends me over the edge for the fifth time in less than twelve hours.

Someone bangs on my door, both startling and prompting me to jump out of bed.

"Hold on!" I yell when they pound it again. I get dressed in record time and then look through the peephole to find Daniella on the other side. "What's up?" I ask as I swing open the door.

"Good morning to you, too." She lets herself in, walking right past me. "What did you do last night?"

I shut the door and slowly walk over to the bed. "W-what?"

Daniella raises an eyebrow. "I was just curious what you were doing, but that look on your face tells me something happened." When I don't respond, she puts her hands on her hips. "Bay, what the fuck? I'm your best friend and you're not even going to tell me?"

I still don't say anything, engaging in a stand-off with Dani. I pinch my brows, and her eyes widen in expectation. We could do this all day; we're both stubborn enough.

"Wow, I see how it is," she scoffs.

"Fine! I hooked up with Dusty," I rattle out, my words spilling too fast to be coherent.

Daniella's jaw practically drops to the floor. "Excuse me? You did *what*?"

I shrug. "I don't know. The last couple weeks, he's been sneaking up here to spend time with me. He even planned a secret rooftop date. And we've kissed…a few times. Off camera."

"Baylor Sommerfeld, are you telling me you're catching feelings for Dusty Wilder?" Her smile widens. "Oh. My. God. You are! You're literally blushing right now!"

"I didn't plan to, okay? It just…happened."

"I can't believe this. My best friend is going to be a famous country singer." Dani pauses. "You need to be careful, Baylor. I mean, get it, but if Colette or any of the other producers catch you…"

"I know, I know. I've been telling him that, too, but I don't think Dusty is very good at listening and following directions."

"If it's worth anything, I support whatever is going on and I won't say a word."

I laugh. "Thanks. What would I do without you?"

"You certainly wouldn't have anyone to share your sex adventures with Dusty with. I mean, the guy already gives off big dick energy, I'm sure the actual thing is—"

I groan and cut her off. "Stop. Last night was the first time we did anything like that, and we didn't even go all the way."

"You're going to tell me when it happens, though, right? I bet you guys have amazing bed chem." She sighs like a lovesick schoolgirl.

"You are absolutely ridiculous!"

"I'm *honest*."

I grimace. "Can you be honest about literally anything else? Something that's *not* my sex life?"

"Sure, but talking about you and Dusty is so *fun*." She wiggles her eyebrows. When I shoot her another glare, she sighs. "Fine. How are the other girls, then?"

Now seems like as good a time as any to bring up Aspen. "Funny, you mention them. I need you to do me a favor."

Her brows pinch together. "What is it?"

"Can you look into one of the other contestants for me?"

She purses her lips and narrows her eyes. "Why?"

"One of the girls, Aspen, seems to be out for my blood. But I feel like she's hiding something, too, and I want to have all the information I can. You know, in case I need to defend myself."

"You know that's risky." She hesitates, but then she seems to give in. "But I'll do it for you. In the name of love. And so you and Dusty Wilder can have gorgeous country music babies."

The familiar chime of Daniella's ringtone interrupts our conversation, and she looks down at the screen.

"Oh, that's Alex. I've gotta go, but I'll look into Aspen for you, okay? And I want to hear *all* the details of you and Dusty later."

Shortly after Daniella leaves, there's another knock at my door—one of the producers letting me know we're heading back to the house for the day. Something about getting footage of all the contestants spending time together.

The only reason I'm somewhat excited to go is the possibility of seeing Dusty. However, I'm not sure if I can keep a straight face if he does show up. Memories of last night are still rolling through my mind like a broken record, and I have to squeeze my legs together on the car ride there to relieve some of the ache. I just hope the other girls don't notice.

While I was okay with telling Sage about the first time Dusty and I kissed, there is no way in hell she can find out about last night. Kissing off camera is breaking the rules, but engaging in sexually intimate activities off camera would be enough for me to not only get kicked off the show, but likely be fired on the spot and blacklisted from other publicity firms. Not being able to follow the rules— no matter how attracted you are to the other person—is not a desirable trait in any profession. And it would jeopardize Dusty's career as well.

So, for now, it has to stay a secret. Preferably until either I get eliminated or the show is over. Probably until Dusty finishes out his contract with Sparks Studio Productions, too, to be safe. Daniella can be the only person outside of me and Dusty who knows. And she's my best friend, so I know she would never tell anyone.

When we arrive at the house, Dusty is nowhere to be seen. Which is fine—I'd rather not watch him kiss other girls knowing where his mouth was less than twelve hours ago.

"We just need to get some shots of you all talking and some other B-roll footage," the producer explains when we sit down inside. "Talk about whatever you'd like. Conversations about your relationship with Dusty are great, but do whatever is most comfortable." He cues us to start talking, making a wild gesture when we don't immediately strike up conversation.

"Okay…" Katherine glances to the side. "How is everyone feeling about Dusty? Baylor, what was it like performing with him on stage at the bar?"

I wasn't expecting her to call me out like that. "It was fun. I'm really grateful to have had the chance to sing with him on stage."

"I'm honestly a little bit jealous," Valerie adds with a laugh. "I felt like I was interrupting something watching you two together. You have great stage chemistry, it must feel really good to have been able to show that off."

"Yeah, I mean, I was just doing what felt natural, I guess." I'm not really sure what to say. I like Valerie, but it feels wrong to brag about our relationship. It would feel wrong to brag about my relationship with Dusty even if we weren't on a television show.

"I got to record a song with him a couple weeks ago," Aspen cuts in, and for once, I'm glad she took the attention off me.

"You did?" Sage raises her brows.

"Yep," she pops the P. "At Ace High Entertainment's recording studio."

"Wow…" Katherine sighs. "Have any of you ever done anything like that before?"

We all shake our heads.

Sage turns her head toward Aspen. "Wait, you haven't? I thought you worked in music?"

I don't know if the other girls noticed at all, but Aspen flinches. It's a tiny movement, one I would've easily missed if I wasn't paying attention.

"You must be mistaken," she replies dryly. "I've been *trying* to get into the music industry, just like all of us, but I don't already work in music, no."

"Huh, I guess I'm thinking of someone else, then." Sage shrugs then changes the subject. "Do any of you have siblings? Or what's your family like at home?"

"I'm the oldest of five," Valerie answers first, her face gleaming with pride. "My family is super important to me. Knowing how hard my parents worked to set up our futures, getting a record deal with Dusty would be life-changing for me *and* for them."

The difference between me and Valerie is stark. I'm an only child, and judging by the way she speaks about her family, Valerie's parents probably love her and are proud of her regardless of what she accomplishes in life. I know it's wrong to make assumptions, but I'm guessing her family supported her coming on the show. Meanwhile, my father would probably have an aneurysm if he knew I was dating a man—who's also been dating nine other women—on live television.

"Baylor?" Valerie's voice jolts me out of my thoughts.

"Hm?"

"Do you have siblings?" she repeats what I assume was her question.

"No. I'm an only child." I leave it at that. Talking too much about my family will lead to more questions, and frankly, I don't want to get into it with my competitors right now.

"I'm an only child, too." Aspen purses her lips and flashes me a look. I suppress a laugh at the irony. Of course, Aspen and I would have that in common, too. But I feel like we're nothing alike, and that's a small comfort. Because even if I don't win, at least I don't have to be her.

The producers shoot a couple more hours of us just hanging around the house. They also pull us aside one-by-one to do some interviews about the previous weeks. By the time the day is over, I'm exhausted and ready to go back to the hotel to decompress.

23

dusty

Face Your Fear

"ARE YOU A DAREDEVIL?" I ask Baylor as we walk hand in hand to the location for our date. This is our second on-camera solo date, and although we've secretly spent more time together, I still feel like there's a lot I don't know about her. I want to know what gets her heart racing, if she's the type of person to jump blindly into love or dip her toes in first.

"I'm not sure," she admits. "I wouldn't say I'm an adrenaline junkie, but I'm not scared to do crazy things."

"Good. I hope you're not afraid of heights," I hint at what our date has in store for us.

"Oh no." Her face pales. "I'm guessing you're not going to tell me what we're doing, though, are you?"

I give her a mischievous grin. "That would ruin the surprise." I haven't really gotten to see Baylor in an uncomfortable situation yet. Sure, the drama with Aspen wasn't pleasant, but it wasn't something fear-inducing.

"*Please* tell me we aren't jumping out of an airplane or something."

"If I said we were, would you still do it with me?" I ask.

She squeezes my hand. "I'd probably shit my pants"—she lets out a laugh mid-sentence—"but yeah, I'd still do it with you. I'll face my fears, if that's what it takes."

"Atta girl." I squeeze back and wink. "Come on, we're almost there."

About a quarter-mile later, our destination comes into view, a towering skyscraper. My stomach swims with anticipation, and I just hope Baylor won't be too nervous when she finds out why we're here.

We both look up when we reach the base of the building.

"What are we doing?"

"We're going to the top," I reply, wrapping my arm around her shoulder and pulling her into me.

She lets out a nervous laugh. "Just for the view, right?"

In convenient timing, a cheer cuts through the air, prompting her to look up at the person hanging from the side of the building.

"You're joking, right? There's no way we're jumping off a building!"

"We're *rappelling* off a building," I correct as she pulls her bottom lip between her teeth. "Don't worry, I've got you. We'll do it together."

"I swear, if we die because—" Panic fills her voice, but I press a finger to her lips.

"I won't let anything happen to you. We've got professionals who are going to get us through it." I'm not sure if my attempt at reassuring her works, but she reluctantly nods and we enter the building to take an elevator to the top floor.

Neither of us says a word in the elevator. I can tell Baylor's nervous, and I don't want to make her more anxious by speaking. So I just hold her hand, rubbing gentle circles with my thumb.

When the elevator dings, signalling our arrival at the top floor, she sucks in a deep breath. Before we exit, though, I cup her face with my hands.

"If you don't want to do this, just say the word and we'll go back down. I would love for you to do this with me, but the last thing I want to do is pressure you into something you're uncomfortable with."

She nods, closing her eyes for a moment. "I want to do this with you. I want to face my fears and take the leap… literally." She chuckles, and my shoulders immediately relax before I plant a kiss on the top of her head.

Jarrod is already waiting for us with more of the camera crew, who help the professionals set us up with GoPros on our helmets.

Resting my hand on Baylor's hip, I whisper in her ear, "How are you doing?"

"A bit nervous," she admits. "I've never done anything like this before."

"Neither have I. To be honest, I'm a little nervous, too, but everything is going to be great."

The technician waves us over to get on our harnesses and the rest of the gear we need then goes over a brief overview of how to rappel down safely.

Before I know it, our harnesses are attached to the belay device and rope, and Baylor and I are standing next to each other on the edge of the tower.

I reach over to grab her hand and check in. "You doing all right?"

She nods, even though the grimace on her face says otherwise.

"I'll be right here with you the whole way," I reassure her as best as I can, trying to keep my own nerves at bay.

"Ready?" the technician asks.

"Ready," we confirm at the same time.

"All right, have fun. Don't forget you've got a radio if you need anything."

To make our way down, we have to make our bodies perpendicular to the building so we can take steps as we feed the rope through the belay. Finding my position is a lot easier than it is for Baylor, and I can tell she's struggling to get started. Her torso is lower than her legs, her feet still on the ledge of the roof.

She squeezes her eyes shut, her expression mimicking a person in pain.

"Hey, you're okay." I get her attention, and she slowly opens her eyes. "Talk to me."

"I don't know if I can do this," she mumbles.

"You've got this, Baylor. Just use your weight to help you take your first steps. Slow and steady, baby." I catch myself off-guard calling her the term of endearment, but I don't think she even notices as she takes a long, slow breath and steps off the ledge.

Her first few steps are slow and a bit wobbly, kind of like a fawn standing for the first time. But once she gets her footing, she whips her head toward me with the biggest grin. Then she makes the mistake of looking down the twenty-six or so stories, and her face blanches.

"Hey, hey, hey, look at me." I'm talking to her before she even has the chance to speak.

"I d-didn't realize how high up we are." Her eyes snap up to mine.

"Don't think about that, or it'll make it worse. Talk to me. What's your favorite color?" It's the first thing that comes to my mind, even though it's a pathetic attempt at a distraction.

It works, though, because she lets out a laugh. "Orange. My favorite color is orange."

"I don't know if I've ever met someone whose favorite color is orange," I reply, keeping the conversation flowing. "My favorite color is green. But forest green. My bedroom as a child was neon green, which gives me a headache just thinking about it."

We're slowly inching our way down, and I think my efforts to distract Baylor are working, because she doesn't look as tense anymore. Her shoulders have relaxed, and she's not white-knuckling the rope like she was when we first started our descent.

"My bedroom was just white. My parents didn't let me paint my room, because they didn't have time—family of doctors," she adds. "As a kid, I was obviously devastated, but looking back I'm oddly grateful. I probably would have chosen the worst color combinations known to man."

"As long as you didn't want to paint your room baby-puke green, I'm sure it wouldn't have been that bad."

We laugh together, throwing out the worst color combinations that we could have used for our childhood bedrooms. I look up to see how far we've come, finding that we're about halfway down the building. I don't mention it to Baylor, because I don't want to freak her out, but pride rises in my chest at how she's facing her fears.

"If you had to choose only one artist to listen to for the rest of your life, who would it be?"

"Do I only get their existing discography or do I get future albums?"

"All existing and any future music they release," I confirm.

"Even with that, this is probably the hardest question ever. I can only have *one*?"

I nod, taking a few more steps. "Yup. Only one. Everyone else is wiped off the face of the Earth."

Baylor actually *giggles*. "Are you going to be offended if I don't pick you?"

"I think I would be more offended if you did pick me over all of the options you have," I tease. "My artist would be Elvis."

"Even though you won't get any more new music?" She gives me a quizzical look.

"As much as I would love to hear new music, I would hate to never be able to hear Elvis again."

"I think that's reasonable. Man, I don't know. I don't think I've ever thought about that question before. I would hate not having the luxury of listening to all my favorite singers. I feel like I'd want someone with the largest catalog of songs, but there are so many," she rambles on, and I stare at her in awe.

"Think about it and tell me later." I wink.

We're getting closer and closer to the ground, but selfishly, I don't want this to end. I know we're being recorded from our GoPros, but it's been a nice reprieve from having a camera crew and producers in our faces.

"Look how far we've come!" Baylor looks up in awe.

The ground is much closer now, and the producers and crew on top of the building are smudges in my vision. Like tiny ants.

"*You* did that." I smile, and she reciprocates.

"Maybe, but I couldn't have done it without you, Dusty."

24
baylor

Taking a Risk

I'M WALKING down the hallway of the production studio to head to my "confessional" interview, as Colette likes to call it, when I'm suddenly yanked into one of the storage closets.

"What the—" My elbows are locked and loaded when a large hand covers my mouth.

"Shhh," Dusty whispers in my ear.

I rip his hand off my mouth and spin around to face him. "What are you doing here? We're going to get caught," I hiss.

"I'm making up for the other night. And we won't get caught if you're quiet." He winks, and then his lips are on mine, greedy and wanting. Frantic.

I kiss him back, our tongues tangling as he hooks his arms under my thighs and lifts. I wrap my legs around him as he carries me further into the closet, setting me on a random desk flush against the back wall.

"I've missed you," he murmurs, his lips only millimeters from mine.

"You just saw me yesterday." I pull back to look up at him.

"That's too long when it comes to you."

"What about the others? There are still four other women here, you can't be missing me *that* much," I tease, running my fingers through his hair, despite the growing pit in my stomach at the idea he could be sneaking around with them, too.

"Don't talk about them. They don't hold a candle to you. Not now, not before, not ever." He presses his forehead against mine.

My legs are still wrapped around his waist, and his fingers draw lazy circles up and down my arm.

"What are you waiting for, then?" I challenge, and that's all he needs for a fire to light behind his eyes.

"Arms up," he orders, and I lift them to give him access to pull my shirt off before he unclasps the hooks of my bra. He takes in the sight of me. "God, you're gorgeous."

I don't say anything as I grasp the cotton of his T-shirt and pull it over his head, revealing his chest and toned stomach.

"We need to be quick," I say. "They're expecting me for an interview."

"The last thing I want is for our first time to be quick, but we can do that. Later I get to have you for as long as I want, though. Deal?"

He looks me in the eye as if waiting for an answer, so I nod.

"Take these off." He grabs the hem of my jeans before running his hands down my legs. He kneels, placing the tip of my right shoe on his knee before undoing the straps on my sandal to take it off. Then he repeats with the left side.

When he's done, I pull my jeans off, letting them fall to the floor, leaving me only in my underwear.

Dusty stands and hooks his index fingers in the waistband, slowly removing my panties, leaving me naked on the desk.

"You have no idea how badly I want to taste you right now, but I know you have to go, so that will have to wait. But trust me, I will be taking my sweet time savoring you later," he groans as he rakes his eyes up and down my body.

"Please," I whisper.

That's all it takes for him to undo his belt buckle and jeans. He pulls them down to his ankles, along with his boxers, letting his erection spring free.

He pulls me to the edge of the desk with one arm, using the other to pump his cock.

I gasp as he runs a finger up my entrance, stopping to rub my clit.

"Fuck, you're so wet for me, Baylor." Stopping for a moment to reach down, he grabs a condom.

He rips it open with his teeth then hands the silver package to me. "Do the honors, baby."

I carefully take the condom out of the packaging and move to put it on him when he reaches forward again, plunging a finger inside me.

"Oh, God," I moan, fumbling as my hand tightens around his cock. "Dusty…"

He smiles as he removes his finger, allowing me to catch my breath and slide the condom on. Dusty wastes no time, lining himself up with me and slowly pushing in, filling me.

"Good?" He's not moving, just waiting for me to respond.

Meanwhile, I'm craving his touch, his movement. "Yes. Move, Dusty, please." My tone is desperate, pleading.

He does what I ask, thrusting deep inside, causing my walls to tighten around him. But it's not fast enough, not hard enough. I want *more* of him. No, *need* more of him.

I grasp his shoulder hard enough that I know my nails will leave a mark and try to pull him even closer, my legs wrapped around him.

"Tell me what you want." His voice is low and husky.

"I want you to fuck me hard. Don't hold back," I whisper in his ear before nibbling on it, sending a shiver up his body.

"As you wish."

And he doesn't hold back. He places his hands under my ass, squeezing as he lifts me off the desk and drives into me repeatedly. The sounds of skin on skin and our tandem breaths fill the room as I climb closer and closer to my high.

"I-I'm going to come, please don't stop," I moan before I bury my face in his shoulder.

"I'm almost there," he rasps, never slowing his pace, even when he lowers his head to latch onto my nipple and sucks. The sensation combined with the tip of his cock hitting my G-spot is overpowering, and a wave of pleasure rolls over me. My head rolls back with my orgasm, and I feel Dusty's cock twitch as he finishes with me.

He kisses me gently, pushing a wild strand of hair behind my ear. "There. Now you're extra glowy for the camera."

"Oh, thanks." I playfully roll my eyes. "I'm sure the viewers will love that."

"Don't worry, baby. No one will even suspect that you just got fucked in a supply closet." He kisses me on the cheek before taking care of the used condom and helping me get dressed.

"Okay, I have to go for real." I laugh as he steals another kiss. "They're going to be suspicious."

"Find me later tonight, okay?"

"I will. Now, let me go," I tease as I steal one last glance and open the supply closet door. The hallway is clear, so I smooth out any wrinkles and take a deep breath.

Damn, that man sure knows what he's doing.

"Baylor! There you are, where have you been?" Daniella's tight grip on my arm breaks me out of my trance when I walk into the room where my interview is taking place.

"Sorry, I got…er…caught up doing something." I'm a horrible liar. Always have been. Especially when it comes to Dani.

She lowers her voice. "You smell like sex and your shirt is on inside out. Come on." She pulls me away from the film crew into a dressing room. "Here. You need this." She hands me a bottle of perfume, and I spray a small amount on my wrists and neck. She hands me a new shirt next, because apparently I hadn't smoothed out my clothes enough.

"Thanks," I mutter.

"You're welcome. Speaking as a publicist, you're taking a risk. But as your best friend, you know I want *all* of the details later." She grins and sends me back out to the confessional room.

25
dusty

Dust

I HAVE to rush to my date with Aspen after my run-in with Baylor at the production studio. I just happened to be coming directly from filming some interviews when I caught a glimpse of her walking toward the confessional room. Getting to spend that time with her, even if it was in a supply closet, was well worth the time crunch.

"Where the hell have you been?" Brett snaps when I finally show up. He sniffs the air. "Also, you smell like… dust. What have you been doing?"

Oops. That desk did look like it hadn't been used in ages. Better to smell like dust than sex, though, right?

I ignore Brett's question. "None of your business, Ben, but I…" *Think of something, Dusty.* "…I got hit by a biker on the way here. Knocked me right into the dirt." It's not believable at all, especially considering my clothes are anything but dirty, but it stops him from asking any more questions. I like my other producer, Alex, better. Half of the time, he's not even around, so I'm able to do whatever I want. He monitors me in the evenings, and I'm stuck with Brett during the day.

He throws his hands up in surrender as he walks toward the car. "Sure, okay. Come on, let's get going."

We're meeting Aspen by the Cumberland River, because today's date is a kayak tour. When we get there, I change into swim trunks. By the time I'm done, Aspen is already dressed in a bikini—a tiny one. I'd be lying if I said she didn't look good, but my mind keeps flashing to Baylor.

We've shown each other all of ourselves physically, but I intend to show her all of myself emotionally, too. I want to know her on a deeper level. And I think music has a way of doing that. Performing is a gateway to the soul.

"We'll get started over here," a producer instructs, and the daydream of Baylor disappears. He walks us over to some kayaks and a pile of life jackets.

I shrug mine on, zipping it up and snapping the buckles. Aspen can't quite get hers on, so I help her, but I'm careful not to touch her for longer than necessary.

"Everything okay?" she asks, her voice low, hardly a whisper.

"Mhm, yeah. Everything's fine. You ready?" I gesture to the kayaks.

She nods, but the suspicion on her face lingers even as we push our kayaks off the shore and step in.

Similarly to my date with Baylor, the camera crew set us up with GoPros so they wouldn't have to come out on the water. Our tour guide paddles a little bit ahead of us, so it still feels like an intimate setting.

Being out on the water is peaceful, the opposite of the woman in the kayak next to me. Aspen knows what she wants and she's not afraid to go out and get it, I know that for sure.

Our tour guide drones on about the landmarks next to us, but we've both lived here for years, so although we do our best to listen and stay engaged, we also engage in our own conversation.

"Do you like Nashville?" I ask as I paddle along slowly.

"I love it here. I couldn't see myself being anywhere else," she replies.

"You mentioned on our last date that you've been trying to get signed by a record label, and it just got me thinking a lot. I can't see why a label wouldn't want someone like you. You've got an incredible, powerful voice."

She lets out a breath. "I mean, yeah, I've submitted demos without luck. But I was really close to getting signed onto a label a couple years ago."

"Really? What happened?" I'm intrigued.

"I was on this TV show." She huffs out a small laugh. "It wasn't too different from *Heart Strings*, actually, but it was purely a singing competition. I ended up making it to the final three, and even though I got an offer from a label afterward, I was dropped. I still don't know why."

"That's..." I start.

"Crazy, right? It was put on by SSP, too. I don't think anyone remembers me, though. I looked quite different back then, and even though I was a finalist, they probably deal with so many people it's impossible to memorize all the names. I remember some people who worked with the company, however..." she trails off, like she's deep in thought.

The guide turns over his shoulder. "We're going to pull off here, you two! We've got a nice little lunch set up so be ready!"

Aspen doesn't finish her sentence, but what she said sticks in my mind. I didn't realize she had already been on one of these shows before. One would think it'd give her an advantage, but maybe it's the opposite.

We paddle toward the shore, leaving our kayaks on the grass before heading over to the "lunch" that the producers set up for us. There's a blanket laid out on the grass with a picnic basket, very reminiscent of my date in Centennial Park with Valerie.

I shuck off my life jacket and sit cross-legged on the blanket. Aspen follows suit, but she's much less clothed than I am, so I do the gentlemanly thing and take off my shirt, handing it to her so she can cover up. It's not even because I want to prevent myself from looking at her, either. I'm attracted to her, of course, but not in the way I am to Baylor.

"Thank you." She pulls the shirt over her head. It's a bit large, coming halfway down her thighs.

"So, before we got cut off by the tour guide, you were talking about the show you were on? You were saying how you remembered some people that worked for the company." Out of the corner of my eye, I see a couple producers exchange wary looks. One of them starts talking furiously into their radio, although I can't hear what they're saying. My intention was only to talk more about what Aspen told me earlier, so I can learn more about her career trajectory, but in a turn of events, she…shuts down.

Her body shakes as her eyes water and a tear rolls down her cheek. "I'm sorry, I just…it's hard to talk about. I don't really want to talk about it. That was my chance, you know? And I don't know what I'll do if this…if this doesn't work out."

"Aspen."

She wipes away her tears, even as more seem to pour out. "God, I'm sorry, this is so embarrassing."

"No, it's not. Listen, I know this is hard. But you have talent. If this doesn't work out, I know there will be something else out there that will."

"Thank you, Dusty." She flashes her eyes up at me, tears still gathering at the brims, and for a moment, I almost feel sorry for her. But then I remember who she is and that if she really wants to break into the music industry, she'll do whatever it takes to get there.

We open the picnic basket and dig into the lunch the producers provided, making small conversation about our favorite places in Nashville and other random topics that come up.

Once we finish our date, Aspen's taken back to the hotel, but a producer pulls me aside.

"What did you and Aspen talk about while you were on the water?" There's a bit of bite to her question.

"Um, we talked about living in Nashville…" I begin listing off the conversations we had, but the producer cuts me off.

"No. About the TV show."

My eyes narrow. "She just mentioned that she was on a TV show a few years ago. A singing competition that Sparks Studio Productions put on."

"Did she mention anyone's name?"

"No? She just said that she remembered some people who worked for the production company, but didn't think that anyone would remember her because of how many shows y'all work on."

She ticks her jaw, her nostrils flaring, but then she lets out a harsh breath and claps me on the shoulder. "Thank you, Dusty."

"Did she do something wrong?" I ask as she starts to walk away.

Looking over her shoulder, she mutters, "Not yet."

26
baylor

I Know Who You Are

SOMEONE IS GOING HOME this week, which means that at least until I know I've made it to the next week, my little fantasy world where Dusty and I can be together without any consequences is just that—a fantasy.

Daniella hasn't found out any information about Aspen yet. Nothing she's told me, anyway. But she also hasn't come around a lot, either. Now that I'm thinking about it, every time Dusty has snuck into my hotel room has been when Alex is supposed to be monitoring him. He takes his job seriously, so I can only think of one reason—or rather, one person—that would be enough to distract him. We've never kept secrets from each other before, but it feels like she is now.

In the days leading up to the elimination, I've spent most of my time with the other girls at the house and writing in my journal.

I've had a burst of inspiration since joining the show, so I find myself writing down fragments of lyrics almost every night. They're not anything I'm brave enough to share, but then again, Dusty shared a song he'd been working on with me. If there's anyone I'd share the lyrics with, it would be him.

Footsteps approach from behind me, and I snap the book closed and tuck it under my legs.

"What are you up to?" Sage asks over my shoulder.

"Oh, nothing. Do you want to sit?" I pat the cushion next to me.

She plops down, the drink in her hand sloshing around, before letting out a big sigh. "Do you ever wonder what you'd be doing if you didn't come on the show?"

I huff out a laugh. I know *exactly* what I'd be doing if I didn't come on the show, but it's not like I can tell her. "Not really. Do you?" I redirect the question back to her.

"It's not that my life back home isn't interesting, but I'd probably just be going through the motions. Going to work, swiping on dating apps, going on bad dates with said matches." She laughs. "God, I've been on some bad dates."

My dating life before now was basically nonexistent, but I nod and say, "Same."

Sage doesn't seem to notice my short answers, because she jumps right back in. "I went on a first date once with a guy who showed me his tax returns on his phone. He kept droning on about how he made a million dollars in a year and just had to prove his income to me."

"He did not!" I gasp, trying my best to hold in my laughter.

"I wish I was lying. Then when he took me back home, he asked if he could kiss me, and I said I was more comfortable with just a hug. But when we went to hug, he tried to kiss me anyway!" She takes a long gulp of her wine.

I scrunch my face, internally cringing with secondhand embarrassment for the guy. "Damn, that's…rough."

"Yep. His name was Jeremy. Which, in hindsight, was probably my first mistake. Claimed to be this tech guy who works on AI billboards."

I snort. "Sounds fitting."

She palms her forehead with the hand not holding the wineglass. "I'm just glad Dusty's not like that."

Normally, Dusty tells the producers who he wants to save and the bottom two or three contestants face the elimination. This time, we'll be on stage where Dusty will announce face-to-face who he wants to continue next week.

The producers escort us down the hallway to the auditorium—the same hallway Dusty kissed me in a few weeks ago. Butterflies flutter in my stomach as I think about it, but they dissolve just as quickly when we walk on stage.

Spotlights flood the area, catching me off guard. I squint to avoid being blinded by them until my eyes adjust. Not sure I'll ever get used to that.

Jarrod Stone walks out as the cameras start rolling. "Good evening, ladies, and congratulations on making it to the final five. Unfortunately, tonight, there is an elimination and one of you will be going home. Dusty?" He looks off to the side of the stage, and Dusty appears. His hair is a bit messy, like he's run his fingers through the strands, and his eyes seem to sparkle in the light.

I tug my lip between my teeth as we make eye contact. I wonder if the camera is catching the look in his eyes. A look I want to believe is reserved for me and me alone.

"Hello, ladies. The past two weeks have been very eye-opening, and we're getting down to the final weeks of the competition. While this was an extremely difficult decision to make, I believe it was the best one for my heart and for my career." He surveys each of us. "The three women who I would like to continue next week are…"

One of the girls sucks in a breath next to me.

"Katherine."

Katherine dips her chin and slowly smiles.

"Valerie."

That leaves me, Aspen, and Sage.

Oh, God.

"Finally…" He pauses, and it's like my heart is trying to break out of my chest, pounding so hard I can feel it all the way in my ears. "Baylor."

A gargled sound leaves Aspen's throat as she looks at Dusty in disbelief.

"Valerie, Katherine, and Baylor, you may all follow me." Jarrod beckons us offstage. "Sage and Aspen, you are now at risk of elimination. This week, you'll each have the opportunity to perform a song. There will be no audience voting this week. Instead, the women who have already made it through to the next week will determine the winner of the battle."

Valerie gasps.

Aspen's mouth twists into a frown. "You're kidding, right?"

"I'm afraid not," Jarrod deadpans.

"How is that fair? We're their competition!" she screeches but then calms down like she remembers she's live on national television.

"Best of luck, ladies. We'll be back after this break." Jarrod winks at the camera.

Producers start rattling out instructions of who is supposed to be where and what's going to happen next. I can't hear much, but Sage is set to perform first and is given three different song options. Aspen will get to choose either of the two that Sage doesn't pick. She's at a disadvantage in every way, it seems. But there's no denying she's a powerhouse on the stage.

"This is kind of a lot of pressure on us, don't you think?" Katherine mutters as we sit in the front row.

I scoff and roll my eyes. "Anything for good television. I wouldn't put it past Col—" I stop myself before I say anything further. The other contestants don't have a relationship with Colette. They wouldn't know what she's like to work with, and neither should I.

Luckily, neither Katherine nor Valerie seem to notice. But out of the corner of my eye, I notice Aspen shooting me daggers.

What the hell does she know?

"And we're back, ladies and gentlemen. Welcome to *Heart Strings*. We have two incredible singers who are at risk of elimination, and tonight they will battle it out for a spot to continue on to fight for a record deal and Dusty's heart."

The classic, cheesy reality dating show lines from Jarrod will never get old. And by never, I mean last week. He really needs some new material.

"First up, we've got Sage!"

The lights dim, and the drummer taps his drumsticks together to count off the beat. The band starts to play a short intro to "Burning House," and after a few measures, Sage joins in with haunting vocals filled with emotion.

She's really bringing her all for tonight's elimination, and I can only hope Valerie and Katherine agree. The song may be slower, but it really showcases how well Sage conveys the lyrics. She sells the story.

When she finishes, I can't help but let out a whistle of encouragement, despite the disapproving glance I get from one of the producers.

"Now, give it up for Aspen!" Jarrod calls out. His wording is ironic, considering there's no live audience, just the cameramen, producers, and us.

No one knows what to expect from Aspen normally, but I can confidently say *no one* was expecting her to start belting out the lyrics of "Crazy" by Patsy Cline with a growl and pain to her voice none of us have ever heard before. I can also assume Dusty wasn't expecting her to look directly at him when she sang about him leaving for someone new, judging by the way his mouth gapes.

Her facial expression on the surface gives off the impression of a heartbroken woman, but her eyes say something else. They bite. I've always known Aspen was dangerous, but after tonight, I'm afraid I've underestimated the lengths she'll go to get what she wants.

No one says a word when she finishes her song. The auditorium is utterly silent, and I wonder for a moment if I've stepped into an alternate universe, into some twisted haunted house.

Jarrod walks on stage, his eyes wary as he looks Aspen over. "Thank you, ladies. Tonight we have something special for you all watching at home. There won't be any viewer voting—instead, the three women who are safe will be the ones to decide who will join them next week.

"Let's begin shall we? Katherine, you're first. Who do you think should move on?"

A producer hands Katherine a microphone as a camera swings around to face her.

"I love both of you, truly. But tonight, my vote goes to Aspen." She swallows, and I wonder for a moment if she actually wanted Aspen to move on, or if she's doing it out of fear of retaliation.

"Thank you, Katherine. Valerie?"

Valerie is more brave. "My vote tonight is for Sage."

"Thank you, Valerie." Jarrod nods. "Ladies, we have one vote for Aspen and one vote for Sage."

Oh, fuck. That means *I'm* the tiebreaker.

"Baylor? Who is moving on to next week?"

A shiver travels down my spine, and my pulse roars in my head. Do I pick my friend, or do I pick the girl who seems like she's out to destroy me just to protect my ass? It would be so easy to get rid of Aspen. But if I'm the reason she goes home, there's no way she won't take it out on me later.

"Baylor? Are you good?" Valerie taps me on the arm. Everyone is waiting for my response.

I close my eyes and take a long, slow breath. "Sage. Sage is moving on."

"Thank you, Baylor. Congratulations, Sage, you have made it into the final four. Go ahead and join the other girls." Jarrod waves her off. "Aspen, I'm sorry, but this is the end of the road for you."

"I can't say I'm not disappointed, Jarrod, but it was a good run." She gives the diplomatic answer to the cameras, but once the attention is taken off her, she looks at me dead in the face and mouths something that looks a lot like *I know who you are.*

the confessionals

Producer: That was a tough decision you all had to make out there. How are you doing after that?
Katherine: I'm fine. It was a lot of pressure, but at least I didn't have to be the deciding factor.

Valerie: I'm just glad I didn't have to completely decide someone's fate.

Producer: Baylor? Are you okay?

A producer off camera is heard yelling at someone to get Baylor water. Baylor's face is ashen, and she's unresponsive.

Producer: Cut the cameras, damn it!

27
baylor

Dating Show or Dateline

I'VE BEEN SLOWLY SPIRALING since the elimination. There's no way Aspen knows who I am. That's probably not even what she was saying.

But what if it was? The voice in my head nags at me, sending me deeper into a rabbit hole of anxiety over my secret identity being exposed.

I pace around my room, clutching my head as I wrap my mind around this whole thing. I don't know how she would've figured anything out, but knowing Aspen, there's a strong likelihood this will come back to bite me. I wouldn't put it past her to tell the world what she thinks she knows just to get back at me for sending her home. And once she does, I have no hope of making it to the end. I'll lose my job and all of this—joining the show, believing a career in music could be a possibility, wanting to prove my parents wrong—will have been for nothing.

Even worse, I'll probably lose Dusty, too.

No. *No.*

Dwelling on hypotheticals isn't going to help me. Until

something happens—*if* anything even does—I can't let myself worry about it.

I take a few deep breaths, mentally running through this week's schedule. All four of us remaining women have solo dates before we pack up and head to Chattanooga for our first live concert. My date is first, followed by Valerie, Sage, and Katherine. Going first is both a blessing and a curse. A blessing, because I'll get to see Dusty sooner. A curse, because after our date ends, I'll have to wait longer to see him again. That is, unless he sneaks away from Alex *again* to come see me. I have a feeling that will happen less often now that we're getting down to the wire, though.

I've been waiting for Dusty in this clearing for at least an hour. I shift my weight back and forth as I twist the rings on my fingers.

Maybe he's not going to show up. Maybe this was some kind of test.

There's no one else out here, either. Just me and the microphone pack attached to my back. My heart races at the idea that this could be a ploy to get me alone in the middle of nowhere. I look down, surveying my wardrobe choice for today. I'm wearing jeans and boots, so horrible choices for running away from a serial killer. I'm not Catholic, but I still sign the cross as I send up a desperate plea to not get murdered out here. This *dating* show would turn into *Dateline* real quick if that happened.

Before my thoughts spiral even more out of control, the sound of hooves clomping against the ground gets my attention. I look over my shoulder, and sure enough, Dusty is on a horse. He's leading a second one behind him, and he may be a country singer, but his farm roots sure are showing.

"Hello, darlin'." He waves from his seat, high in the saddle. "Sorry to make you wait so long. Petunia here was a bit fussy."

I nearly snort at the horse's name. I stifle the laugh in my throat as I reply, "That's okay. I only thought I was going to be murdered for about twenty minutes."

"I'm quite relieved that didn't happen." He chuckles as he dismounts from his horse then struts over to me. "Other than fearing for your life, how's my girl?"

I dip my head in amusement before tilting it back up to look at him. "I'm not too bad. Better now, for sure." I wink.

He takes the sides of my face in his hands and leans down to plant a kiss on my lips. "Good. I'm better now, too." Neither of us make any effort to break apart, not until the camera crew slowly trudges through the trees where Dusty entered the clearing. It was naive of me to think there wouldn't be *any* cameras today. For all I know, the production company has invested in drones and they're getting footage from above us.

"So, is this my horse?" I point toward the bay horse standing next to *Petunia*.

He nods. "That's Biscuit."

"Uh-huh. Who named these horses?" My shoulders shake slightly as I eye the horses in amusement.

Dusty just shrugs as he tosses the reins over my horse's head. "I'm not sure. Some young kids, probably. Want help?" He offers a hand as I slip a foot into the stirrups. I wave him off as I grab hold of the saddle horn and swing my leg on the ground over Biscuit's back. "You're a pro. You ride a lot?"

"As a kid," I tell him as he mounts his horse. "I didn't live on a ranch or farm by any means, but my parents put me in horseback lessons when I was young. I don't ride much now, but it comes back like muscle memory when I do. And you?"

"I try to go as much as I can, but my schedule is pretty demanding. I also don't have my own horses here, so that makes it difficult, too," he explains as we head toward the woods, the camera crew following.

"What do you do to destress besides music?"

His head tilts to the side at the question. Then further. "I… You know, that's a good question. Music has always been the thing to calm me down. And even though I'm in the *music* industry, it's hardly ever the music itself that's causing me stress. If that makes sense."

I nod. "There's a lot of external pressure that comes from being a public figure. You see it a lot with social media. There's pressure from fans to be genuine, there's pressure from your label or agency to look and act a certain way, and sometimes you just want to *be*."

He looks at me like I've grown a second head. "You get it. I don't know that I've ever met another person who gets it. Most people would tell me to be grateful for my success."

A laugh slips from my lips. "As if you aren't grateful." Then, under my breath, I say, "I'd like to see some of those people in your shoes and see how they handle it."

"I guess it just comes with the territory." He shrugs. "If it was easy, everyone would do it."

As we continue riding side by side, sunlight streams through the treetops, speckling the ground with pale, buttery light and the shadows of leaves. A gentle breeze blows through my hair, cooling the nape of my neck.

"That's true. Guess that just makes us a special breed, huh?" I joke.

"Exactly. We should probably stick together in that case. Makes it less lonely."

"Do you?"

His brow quirks up.

"Get lonely, I mean." Maybe it was a stupid question. Everyone gets lonely now and then. But Dusty always seems to have people around him. I mean, he's got the other artists at his label and Brooklyn James, and—

"Sometimes, yeah. It's odd." He pauses. "A profession where you're constantly surrounded by people who 'love' you is sometimes the loneliest one." When I don't respond, he continues. "Everyone thinks they know who I am. That they're entitled to every aspect of my life because they know my entire discography or have been a fan since the beginning. Sometimes, I just..." he trails off.

"Sometimes, you just..." I parrot his words back at him.

"Sometimes I just want to show them the true side of me. Who I really am, where I grew up. But I'm afraid they won't love this Dusty as much as they love the Dusty they think they know."

We've talked about this before, briefly. But it was a conversation behind closed doors, not in front of the cameras.

"If they don't love the real Dusty as much as the country singer Dusty, then maybe they're not real fans," I suggest but then wince, because I don't think that's any more reassuring than not having fans at all.

"What's the point, then?" He looks at me with curious eyes. "If the only version of me they love is the idea they have of me, why continue?"

"Do you love it? Singing. Performing," I elaborate.

He nods. "I do. I love performing, and I know I'm here for a reason."

"Then that's the only thing that matters in the end. It shouldn't matter what other people think, because there's nothing more important than doing what you love."

He hums in agreement. "That's true, Baylor. It *shouldn't* matter what other people think." He repeats my statement, and he's gotten his point across. It's about time I start taking my own advice.

We finish the remainder of the ride in comfortable silence, hooves against dirt and soft huffs from the horses as our soundtrack. When we step out of the woods, we're not in the same clearing where we started. Instead, next to a couple small posts to tie up the horses, is a small hot tub and a few small panels to change in privacy.

"Thought we could rest our muscles here for a bit before heading back," Dusty explains as he brings Petunia up next to Biscuit. "Give the horses a break, too. There should be a swimsuit for you behind the panels." He dismounts and ties up Petunia before approaching Biscuit, on the side where I would dismount, and offering his hand for me to grab.

This time, I take him up on his offer as I slide off the saddle. He's already tying up Biscuit, so I take the opportunity to step behind the privacy panels. Just as Dusty suggested, there's a swimsuit hanging inside for me. I change quickly, noting how modest the suit is, unlike other dating shows where the bikinis leave little to the imagination.

Still, I have to resist the urge to cover myself up when I step back out. It's not like Dusty hasn't seen every inch of my body. But people on the Internet haven't, and people on the Internet are *mean*. I don't want to leave this social-media-free bubble just to find trolls critiquing my body.

My insecurities don't last long, though, because moments later, Dusty steps out and rakes his eyes over my body like he wants to store the image of me in his brain forever.

"You are a vision." He doesn't take his eyes off me for a second, and I'm filled with gratitude over the small boost to my confidence.

"Oh, this old thing? Practically rags," I tease, doing a spin.

"You could wear a potato sack or a garbage bag and I'd still think you look beautiful." He gestures to the hot tub. "Ladies first."

I climb the small steps and gingerly dip a toe into the water before lowering my body inside. I don't think I realized how tense I was. I practically groan from the warmth enveloping and soothing my muscles.

Dusty slides in next to me, his reaction to the jets similar to mine. The tub is just big enough for the two of us, and our legs brush if we move too much.

He gently squeezes my thigh, giving me a soft smile. "How are you feeling?"

Content. But also like I want you all to myself.

"I didn't think I'd feel so…relaxed this late in the process. I mean, we're down to the final four. I assumed I'd be more stressed," I admit then let out a shallow laugh. "Then again, I wasn't sure I'd make it this far."

"Really? What makes you think that?" His gaze is filled with curiosity.

Besides the obvious? The fact that I wasn't supposed to be here in the first place?

I shrug. "I don't know, there were just so many other

talented women. I never expected Aspen would be gone already."

He tenses at the mention of Aspen, which, same. But his reaction only piques my interest, and I raise a brow.

Dusty just takes my hand, rubbing circles across my knuckle. "I don't want you to worry. I don't want you to think about the possibility of leaving. I like you a lot."

"I like you, too," I whisper. *Maybe a bit too much.*

As much as I try to push it away, anxiety bubbles up in my stomach and uncertainty gnaws at me. Would he still like me as much if he found out who I am? What I *actually* do for work? If he found out the real reason why I'm on the show is not because I'm an aspiring musician who was also looking for love, but because I was forced to join to save my career?

"What's going through that pretty mind of yours?" Dusty's soft voice brings me back to the moment.

"Nothing," I lie. It's easier than explaining what's really going on. To prevent him from asking questions, I maneuver myself so I'm straddling his legs. His eyes widen in surprise but then darken as lust creeps into his features. His tongue darts out, wetting his lips before he places his hands on my waist, tugging me closer.

Warm breath tickles my face as my eyes trail from his down to his lips and back up again. Then, in a split second, his lips are on mine, stubble tickling my chin. The kiss is slow, sensual, unhurried. These kisses are my favorite, because they remind me that, although time is ticking on our relationship with only three weeks remaining until the final decision, we don't need to rush. We're allowed to savor each other, savor the moments we have together, because that's what makes the time we do have together special. These types of kisses are like my own reminder to slow down and appreciate the man before me.

My hips grind against his, creating delicious friction between us. His fingers dig into my skin, hard enough that I'm confident I'll wake up with tiny bruises in the morning.

With a strained groan, he breaks the kiss, despite the small protesting noise that escapes my lips. His mouth moves along my jawline, and I hope the microphone isn't sensitive enough to pick up what he whispers in my ear, because it's enough to make heat rise to my cheeks and desire pool between my legs. Combine his filthy mouth with how dangerously close his fingers are to the strings on my swimsuit bottoms, we're about five seconds away from making an X-rated film instead of a reality TV show. The awareness of the cameras is enough for me to slide off his lap back onto the wooden seat.

"Give me a few minutes then we can head back." He chuckles as he discreetly adjusts himself under the water. Then he leans in close again to whisper, "I just can't get enough of you. If the cameras weren't here, there's no telling the things I would be doing to you. Later."

I mumble back jokingly, "Is that a threat?"

"It's a promise."

28

baylor

Road Head

THE PAST FEW days flew by faster than I expected. Dusty went on his solo dates with Valerie, Sage, and Katherine, but, unfortunately, hasn't had any opportunities to sneak out to see me.

"You're coming on my tour bus with me," Dusty whispers in my ear from behind me as he walks by. I stand there shocked for a minute. Bold of him to suggest that in front of the other girls. "I already let the producers know I wanted…extra time…with you."

"You coming, Baylor?" Sage waves me over from the contestant bus.

"I…uh…" *Dammit, Baylor get it together.*

"There's something on my bus that I need to give her, right, Baylor?" Dusty calls from the stairs of his bus.

"Right. Yes. I have to grab that. Don't wait for me!" I tell Sage, who gives me a suspicious look but lets me go.

"Smooth, darlin'." Dusty laughs as I get on the bus.

"I could say the same thing to you." I flip him off. "What did you need to give me?"

He grabs me by the waist, pulling me close to kiss me. I

find it hard to pull away, as our mouths explore each other and only separating to come up for air, so he finally does. "I'll give you a hint," he hums as he guides my hand to the front of his jeans.

"The other girls are going to wonder where I am." I try to reason with him.

"We'll be fine. They won't even notice you're gone."

Doubtful, but…

He hoists me up, bridal style, and I can't hold back the sound that leaves my lips as he walks us into the bedroom part of the bus and slams the door shut.

He throws me onto the bed, which is surprisingly soft for being on a tour bus. *Is this memory foam?*

My thoughts are forced elsewhere when Dusty climbs onto me, not wasting any time as he pulls my panties down. I bend my legs to make it easier for him.

"Black lace. My favorite," he purrs as puts them in the inside of his jacket pocket. "These are mine now."

Before I can protest, he reaches under my skirt again, sliding his hand up the inside of my thigh until he reaches the apex of my leg. His touch alone is enough to turn me on, and when he finally inserts a finger, he groans with pleasure.

"Fuck, you're already soaked. Can you feel how wet you are?" he asks as he withdraws his finger, spreading my arousal over my clit and the outside of my pussy.

"Mmm," I moan as he rubs circles over the most sensitive part of me then plunges his finger back in, picking up his pace as he fucks me with his hand.

I not only feel how wet he's making me, I hear it as he adds another finger, thrusting them inside me and then switching to a "come here" motion.

Just as I'm about to come undone, he stops and hikes

up the flowy fabric of my skirt so I'm entirely bared to him.

"I'm going to taste you when you come," he explains as he plants kisses up my inner thigh, his mustache tickling my skin. When he finally latches his mouth onto me, he moans. The vibration sends a shock wave up my body, causing me to arch my back and buck my hips closer to his face. His tongue works me in tandem with his fingers, and a blaze ignites in my toes.

"Oh, God," I cry out as my orgasm washes over me. A warm, wet sensation trickles down the inside of my thighs, and I can't tell if it's from me or his tongue.

"You are fucking gorgeous when you come. I could taste this pretty pussy and make you squirt on my face all day if you'd let me," he praises.

So it was me. But holy shit. I'm about to come again from his words alone.

"Will you let me fuck you all day, Baylor?" he asks as he lowers his mouth just above my clit.

"Y-yes."

When he sucks on my clit, I cry out again. This man is going to absolutely destroy me. Before I can push him off because the sensation is too much, he stands and takes off his shirt. Then his pants. And his boxers.

"Take off your clothes. I want to see those beautiful tits."

I do as he says, stripping until there's nothing left between us. He straddles me, palming one breast and pulling the nipple of the other between his teeth.

"Fuck." His voice is low and dripping with lust and attraction to me. "I want to fuck you bare, baby. Do you want that too? Look at me." He tilts my chin up to look him directly in the eyes. "I'm clear. Had to get checked out to be on the show. But if you'd rather me use a condom, I will."

"You mean you haven't been with any of the other girls?" I snort, disguising my anxiety as humor.

His eyes narrow, and he pulls back slightly. "What? No."

I let out a breath, the tension in my shoulders melting away. "I just…" I look away for a second. "I wasn't sure if you've been planning secret dates with the others, too."

"It's only *ever* been you, Baylor. We can stop if you want, but—"

"No, I want you," I interrupt. I believe what he says. I can see it in his eyes, in the way he looks at me. "I want all of you. I have an IUD, and I'm also clear. You're the only person I've been with in months. Please, I want to feel you come inside me." I plead with my eyes, and he practically growls as he stands. He pumps his cock in his fist before pulling me so my hips are at the edge of the bed and lines himself up.

He slowly glides his tip in, and I watch as he enters me inch by inch. It's painfully slow, and I grab his ass, digging my nails in to pull him closer, giving him a sign that I need him to move. He takes the hint and drives into me. Hard.

I gasp as he fucks me. He's rough, rougher than he's been before, and he reaches his hand down to my neck, adding the slightest bit of pressure. My head lolls back, and my eyes roll as I wrap my legs around him, wanting him even deeper.

"You like my hand around your throat? Fucking filthy girl." He tightens his grip and somehow quickens his pace, pounding into me. "You take my cock so well. Flip over."

I whine at the absence of him, but the moment I flip

over, he's filling me again, and the angle at which he's fucking me is heaven.

"Do you touch yourself as much as I do when we're apart?" He leans in and bites my earlobe, and I nod. "Show me."

I reach down to my clit and slowly rub circles. His cock brushes against my hand when he pulls out and thrusts back in, and each time the touch coats my hand with arousal. It's erotic and brings me closer and closer to the edge. I speed up my pace as my release builds.

"I'm so close," I whimper, working my hand faster as the sound of Dusty's skin slapping against mine fills the space.

"I'm right there with you, baby." A few more hard thrusts, and I reach my high, crying out Dusty's name as the warmth from his release fills me. It drips out of me onto my fingers, and I rub it against my clit as we both start to come down from our highs.

"You've made a damn mess of me," he murmurs as he peppers kisses along my back, pulls out, and smacks my ass.

I moan at the sting of it. I'd guess there's already a handprint forming.

"Stay," he orders when I try to roll over and get up to get dressed. Then he grabs a towel and cleans me up, but not until after he pushes his cum back in, fingering me again to mix it even more with mine.

It's a good thing I'm on birth control, because if I wasn't... damn. I wouldn't be able to say no to him coming inside me again if this would be the outcome every time.

"I probably should go back to—" My sentence is cut off by the sound of the bus engine starting.

"Guess you aren't going anywhere, which means my

request to fuck you all day gets to be granted." He smirks, and I melt.

He doesn't waste any time, either. He has his mouth on me and me moaning his name again within minutes.

This is going to be the best bus ride I've ever been on.

"Does everyone have their places? Know where to go?" the frontman of Dusty's band asks once we've walked through our stage positions a few times. Although Dusty is the true frontman—being the lead singer and all—his lead guitarist, Charlie, is the one giving out instructions of where to be.

We all nod, having gone through the motions for the past thirty minutes. We haven't performed anything yet, just walked through where everyone needs to stand for the live concert and transitions between songs. With this being the first live concert of the season, it was expected that we'd spend a bit longer figuring out where everyone would go.

While it is truly a Dusty Wilder concert with the contestants acting as openers, the four of us will get to perform one song individually and one song as a duet with Dusty throughout his set. We'll all perform as a group to kick off the concert, and then again as a group—with Dusty—to finish out the setlist.

The order of performers was predetermined by production as well. Katherine will be the first solo performer, then Sage, myself, and Valerie will go last. The order will be the same for duets with Dusty, although they won't be back-to-back.

"Let's do a sound check, then." Charlie claps. We

already have our in-ear monitors fitted, so we take our places on stage for the group performance. Without Aspen here, the performance seems to be going smoothly, with no surprises or hiccups.

As a group, we decided that the song we'd perform to open the concert would be "9 to 5" by Dolly Parton, to really set the mood and get people excited. Besides, who doesn't love Dolly? And there isn't going to be an elimination this week, so we'll perform the same songs next week in Atlanta.

The venue we're performing at has a larger stage than anywhere I've performed before, not that I have a *ton* of experience performing, just the small stages at bars in Nashville for the show. Before I joined *Heart Strings*, I didn't really show off my singing abilities. I was strictly a shower performer and occasionally drunken karaoke.

But, for whatever reason, I'm not nervous. Not like I thought I'd be, knowing I'd be performing live in front of thousands of Dusty's fans. Fans who've been judging me for the past six weeks. I'm sure the nerves will hit me in the actual moment, but for now I'm soaking it all up. My childhood dream of performing is coming true.

29
dusty

The First Live Concert

I GLANCE over my reflection in the dressing room. "You're Dusty Wilder, international country music superstar," I mumble to myself as if I need a reminder. "This is what you do."

It's been so long since I've toured, I'm a bit worried I'm out of practice. Performing in the studio and in bars around Nashville is different than performing in a stadium.

Tonight's concert is in a smaller venue, with a max capacity of 1,500 people. But as the weeks go on, the sizes of the venues will increase. The concert venue in Atlanta houses just over two thousand, and Thompson-Boling Arena in Knoxville accommodates about fifteen thousand. I've performed at Neyland before, but over a hundred thousand fans would probably be overwhelming for the girls and counterproductive to the reality show.

The finale concert, however, is being held at the legendary Ryman Auditorium. It's an honor and a privilege to perform on the hallowed stage of the Grand Ole Opry, so the catch is that only the winner will get to sing in the circle with me after the final decision. I truly believe any of the four finalists would thrive on the Opry stage, but there's only one woman I want standing next to me at the end.

Baylor.

A hollow knock at my dressing room door startles me, and I clear my throat before adjusting my cowboy hat.

"Come in." I make my voice as gruff as possible. The door swings open to none other than Brooklyn James. "Brooke, what the fuck are you doing here?"

"Wow, Dusty, what happened to 'Hello, how are you?' I came to support my favorite country singer, of course."

"You're your favorite country singer." I playfully roll my eyes.

"Fine. My favorite *male* country singer," she corrects.

"We both know that's Riley Green, not me," I scoff, shaking my head in amusement.

"I do love that man," she sighs before plopping down onto one of the couches. "But, no, seriously. I came here to give you some moral support. Maybe offer some advice on who should make it to the end of this little competition here."

"Trust me, I already know who I want to make it to the end."

"YOU DO? And you haven't spilled the tea yet?" She slams her palms down on the plush couch, not that it made any kind of noise at all or had any dramatic effect. "I want to know everything, Dusty, I swear to God."

"Technically, I signed an NDA, so I don't owe you shit." I laugh, teasing her. "But remember the girl you saw on the solo date with me?"

"Yes! Baylor, right?" She leans forward, her elbows resting on her knees and her chin in her palms.

"She's special. She makes me *feel*, Brooke. I've been at

an impasse with songwriting, but her being here sparked something in me. It's not anything the label would want, but the only thing that matters is the inspiration. That has to mean something. And we have pretty good chemistry, too, I'd say." The last part I mumble under my breath, hoping Brooke won't catch it.

She gasps. "You had sex, didn't you!" It's more of a statement than a question. A *loud* statement.

"Shh! Be quiet!" I hiss. "Physical intimacy in that manner isn't allowed on the show. I could lose my contract."

"It's a risk you're willing to take, though, isn't it?"

Both the angel and the devil on my shoulders nod along with me.

"I think I'm falling for her. We've had some secret dates off camera, and I've learned a lot about who she is. Her dreams and fears and her family. I've also told her things I haven't told many others. About why I came to Nashville in the first place." Brooke already knows my story. We've supported each other from the very beginning, navigating the music industry together. "It's like there's a string tugging me toward her. I can't get her out of my head."

"Look at you!" Brooke juts out her lip as she gets up to walk over to me. "Dusty Wilder, all grown up and falling in love. I'm proud of you."

"Don't get all sappy on me now, Brooklyn. You're gonna make me think you've gone soft."

Her arm reaches out in a flash as she slaps me on the arm. "I can be a strong, independent woman and a romantic all at once, thank you very much."

"Maybe we ought to get you on the show next. I'd pay good money to see you fall in love."

She sputters out a laugh, dismissing the suggestion.

"That's all right. I like seeing you on my television a lot more than I like seeing myself. Well, I'd better let you go. Good luck out there. I'm proud of you, D."

We share a quick hug, and then she slips out the door.

"You're Dusty Wilder, international country music superstar," I whisper the mantra to myself again as the door clicks shut.

"Chattanooga, how're you doing tonight?" Jarrod greets the crowd, who roars in response. "Welcome to the first stop on the *Heart Strings* live concert series! We're down to the final four women who have been vying for Dusty's heart and a record deal with Ace High Entertainment. Give it up for our women—Katherine, Sage, Baylor, and Valerie!"

That's the cue for the women to enter the stage. The band starts to play the intro to "9 to 5," the song the ladies chose to open the concert with. The audience is already into it, clapping along to the beat as Katherine starts singing the first verse. She's a natural out there; her stage presence is lively and engaging. Even with the small amount of space she was given in blocking, she's able to work the crowd, a sign of a great performer.

The final four women are a force to be reckoned with, all equipped with powerful vocals and their own unique style. I'm pleased with the choices that led me here.

Once the first number is complete, all the girls except Katherine exit the stage. I wasn't informed what solos they would be performing, but when one of the stagehands brings out a stool, I know her song's going to be slower.

Katherine's style has stayed true to classic country

roots. It's what she's good at, no doubt, but part of me wishes she would branch out a little. Experiment. Be brave.

"Hey," a feminine voice distracts me from the performance on stage. When I turn over my shoulder, Valerie places a hand on my arm. "How are you feeling?"

I've always appreciated the way she checks in on me. We've developed a sort of friendship outside of what was expected to be a romantic relationship in the past few weeks.

"I'm excited. It's been a while since I've done a full concert, but I'm ready to go back out on tour. This at least scratches that itch until the finale is over," I explain without meeting her eyes. By this time, Katherine's finished her song and Sage has already replaced her.

Both of us are watching the stage, and I can't decide if she's not looking at me because she's genuinely interested in Sage's performance, or because she wants to avoid what's become inevitable. Although Valerie and I have a good relationship—I could see a musical partnership working between us—there aren't sparks. And *Heart Strings* is about more than finding a business partner. From the beginning, it's been about finding someone to navigate music *and* life with.

"How are you?"

Her eyes shift to the floor then back up. "I'm just grateful to be here. I want so badly for this to work out in the end, but I'm soaking up every moment just in case."

Guilt twists her knife a little deeper into my chest. I've tried my best the past few weeks to stay engaged in my other relationships for the sake of the show, but trying doesn't make the situation any less unfair. On my last solo date with Valerie, she brought up her concerns about leaving the show alone, and I wasn't able to give her the validation she was seeking. Not without it being a bold-faced lie. I told her I want her to find love and success, whether it's with me or not. If she understood the deeper meaning, she didn't show it.

"You deserve to be on this stage, Valerie." I reach down to give her hand a quick reassuring squeeze, not too quick, but nothing lingering either.

She tilts her head up, and as her eyes meet mine, she gives me a soft smile. "I'd better get ready. Baylor's about to go on." She gestures toward the stage.

Sure enough, Sage finishes her song and the lights dim as Baylor walks out. My breath hitches in my throat at the sight of her, even from backstage. Her hair falls down her back in loose curls, her jeans hug her curves in all the right places, and her black top is cropped above her belly button, showing off her toned midriff. She's my dream woman in more ways than one.

When the lights come back up, cheers rise from the audience, evidence that she's cemented herself as a fan-favorite over the last few weeks.

I'm not the only one whose eyes are glued on her throughout her performance. Producers and other crew members pause in their tracks when they hear her voice. The song is over too soon, but as she exits the stage with a beaming grin, I intercept her, pulling her in for a kiss.

"You were incredible out there," I murmur against her lips.

"You think so?" she hums.

"May as well be a Baylor concert, not a Dusty concert," I tease, pulling away slightly. "You'd think you were the headliner with how the crowd was reacting."

A flush creeps into her cheeks, and she shakes her head. "We all know they're here for you. Half of them probably wish they were up on stage singing instead of me."

"You don't give yourself enough credit, darlin'." I kiss her forehead. "Seriously, you were amazing out there." *And I look forward to the day it's both of us performing an entire show together.* I, of course, leave that part out, even though it's probably written all over my face. Baylor deserves to be reminded of how much I care for her, though. How much I want it to be us at the end of all this.

"Thank you so much, Chattanooga! You've been incredible so far tonight!" I take the microphone out of the stand so I can walk around the stage. "I've got a few more songs for you, but first, I wanted to invite back to the stage another one of the incredible women here on the show with me. Y'all went crazy for her earlier, and I expect the same energy again."

A few laughs rise from the audience.

"Give it up for Baylor!" I extend my arm toward the side of the stage as she walks toward me.

We're nearing the end of the concert, and I've already had the opportunity to sing my duets with Katherine and Sage. Both of them performed really well tonight, but the song I chose for me and Baylor—with a little help from Brooke—is going to be a hit. I can just feel it.

The stagehands bring out stools for both of us, and after Baylor takes a seat, I look at her and mouth, "Ready?" She nods, and I start picking the beginning notes of "Don't Mind If I Do."

While the song isn't exactly a sappy love song, the lyrics still prove to be true. Not being able to hold her in my arms every night like a normal couple is killing me from the inside out, and I do my damndest to make sure she knows, locking eye contact and singing the words to her like we're the only people in this entire venue.

She joins in with the harmonies, and our voices blend seamlessly. When she takes over, singing the last verse on her own, the entire venue falls silent, every single person in attendance listening intently to Baylor.

Listening to my girl.

the confessionals

Producer: First live concert is over. Tell me what's going through your mind right now.
Katherine: I just can't believe I actually performed in front of a thousand people tonight and didn't mess up the words.

Sage: It was surreal. I've always dreamed of performing in front of a big audience like that.

Valerie: Like I told Dusty, I'm soaking up every minute I have on stage. On this tour. I never want it to end.

Producer: You and Dusty look like you have a lot of chemistry out there on stage.
Baylor: We understand each other.
Producer: Do you think you're falling in love with him?
Baylor: Yeah… I think I am.

30
baylor

Storm Warning

AFTER THE LIVE concert in Chattanooga, we come back to Nashville for a couple days before we hop on a plane to Atlanta later this week. We'll each have a solo date again, but an elimination will take place at the end of the live concert, so it's important this week to not only further my relationship with Dusty, but also maintain a positive impression with the viewers so I can stay another week.

Because that's what I want. To stay.

I'm walking through the production building hallway again when I'm yanked into an office.

"Ow!" I yelp. "Dusty, we can't keep—" I start to protest, but I cut myself off when I see it's not Dusty who pulled me out of the hallway. It's Daniella.

"I'm going to ignore what you just said in the name of love, but we need to talk." She shuts the door and locks it, pulling the shade over the window so no one can see us.

I've never seen Daniella act so serious. "What's going on?"

"I found some information on Aspen, Baylor, and it's

not great." She huffs out a breath as she sets up her laptop on the desk in the corner.

"Not great, how?" I proceed slowly as my eyes narrow.

"This is how." She flips the computer to show me what's on the screen. I have to really train my eyes to understand what's in front of me. It's a picture of Aspen singing on a stage, but she looks about four years younger and has blonde hair instead of her current dark color.

"What exactly am I looking at?"

"The background of the image. Look familiar?" She puts her hands on her hips after she zooms in closer on the image. It looks like the set of a television show… *oh no.*

"There's no way." I shake my head.

"She was a fucking contestant on that other singing competition show SSP put on, Baylor. She literally placed third."

My head starts pounding, and I press my fingers against my temple. "How the hell did no one realize it was her? How did *Colette* not realize? This is bad, Dani. I worked directly with those contestants. What if she remembers who I am?"

"Well, first of all, none of us thought you would end up being on the show and she was chosen for auditions before I made the drunken mistake of posting that video of you online. Still kinda feel guilty for that, by the way, but then again you're literally fucking Dusty Wilder, so you're welcome. Secondly, she's gone, so even if she did remember you, it's unlikely anything will come of it."

"What if she goes to the media?"

"I highly doubt she would do that. She signed an NDA, and Colette would squash any gossip articles immediately. I don't think Aspen is that stupid. I wouldn't worry about it too much." As if she senses I would ask her why she even brought it up, she says, "You wanted to know if I found any information on her, and this felt important for you to know."

"I appreciate it. Do the producers know?" I ask, wanting to cover our bases.

She nods. "Alex knows." I don't miss how she breaks eye contact with me for a split second and her face has a slight pink tint to it.

"Hold on. Are you and Alex—"

At the most convenient timing, Daniella's phone starts ringing. "I'm so sorry, I really need to take this. Don't worry about Aspen, okay? Just keep doing what you're doing. Maybe besides sneaking around with Dusty Wilder, but in terms of your on-camera chemistry, you're doing great!" she babbles as she quickly slips out the door.

I take a few breaths before following, careful not to let the office door slam and alert anyone who might be in the hallway.

It doesn't matter, though, because once I pick up my head to continue walking down the hall, I run directly into Colette, nearly stepping on her feet.

"H-hi, Colette. So sorry, I didn't see you there," I fumble over my words as I try to step around her. Instead of stepping out of the way like I expect her to, she grabs my arm to stop me. "Did you need something?"

"Final four, Baylor. Who would have thought? You must feel pretty good about yourself."

I squint, giving her a sidelong glance, as I try to figure out if it's just Colette being passive aggressive or if there's something else she's trying to say.

"Yeah, I don't know what happened." I shrug, trying to be as nonchalant as possible while keeping my voice low. "I trust Dusty's judgment, though." I'm not going to let

Colette St. James scare me. I mean, she *does* scare me, but now that I know what I want, I'm not going to let her take it away.

"Hopefully he makes the right choice in the end." She purses her lips as her eyebrows raise just a little bit. "Don't you agree?"

"Mhm," I hum, finally deciding to just step around her so I can get away from this uncomfortable situation.

"Oh, and Baylor? No one can know who you really are, remember." Her condescending tone makes me pause. "It would be bad for ratings. Imagine what would happen if the viewers knew you worked for us. Not to mention what Dusty would think."

My back is still turned to her, so I nod, acknowledging her…warning? Threat? There's no telling when it comes to Colette.

"It would be career-ending," she continues, and my shoulders tense. "I know you have big goals. Just keep that in mind."

I do have big goals, or at least I did before I came on the show and realized music was something I actually wanted to pursue. I never thought about what would happen if I didn't make it to the end. I assumed my job would still be there, but now Colette has me questioning things. She must suspect my intention to eventually leave Sparks Studio Productions and pursue public relations in a different sector.

I slowly turn around, ready to ask her what she meant or make some kind of retort, but she's already walking away.

31
dusty

Bluebird

IT'S BECOME obvious the producers are trying to push me toward Valerie or Katherine as my final pick, based on the nature of our dates. My solo with Valerie last night was a private dinner and firework show, and Katherine's was a couple's spa day.

I'm not sure why Baylor isn't higher on their list. I feel like I have the most romantic chemistry with her, but I've begun to catch onto the producers' reactions when I give them updates on how I'm feeling and who I'm liking the most. There's always a subtle exchange of concerned—or maybe confused—glances from the crew. The thing is, no one ever asks questions, they just make faces then go on about their day. It throws me off my game a little bit each time, but I don't have the guts to ask them why they react the way they do.

Today's date is going to be special, though. The producers wanted to film it yesterday, but I convinced them to move it to today. I might regret it tomorrow when we're all on a plane headed to Atlanta for the next live concert, but that's a bridge I'll cross when I get there.

The car pulls up to the hotel where the girls are staying, and I hop out of the backseat just as Baylor walks out the front doors.

"Careful, you'll catch flies with your mouth open like that," she teases.

"Can't help it when you look like that."

She's got on a navy-blue dress that falls mid-thigh with loose, puffy sleeves, a plunging neckline, and straps that tie into a bow on the back. Her hair's straight today, and I get a whiff of her perfume: cashmere and vanilla. I take another moment to appreciate her, but when she reaches for the car door handle, I snap out of it.

"No, ma'am." I wave a finger at her before opening the door. I grab the top of the door, holding it for her as she slides onto the leather seats. "Good to go?" I ask, waiting for her nod before shutting the door and walking around the back of the car to get on my side.

"You look nice today," Baylor says once I've buckled myself in. I do look nice, wearing what I typically wear—a pearl snap shirt with the sleeves rolled to my elbows, jeans, and a cowboy hat—but not as nice as she does.

"Nothing compared to you, sweetheart." When I reach over to place my hand on her knee, brushing my thumb over her soft skin, Baylor looks away. But not before I catch a glimpse of her pink-stained cheeks. I love that I affect her as much as she affects me.

"Where are we going?"

"Somewhere special. Don't worry, I know you're going to love it." I slide my hand off her leg and grab her hand, entwining our fingers.

About thirty minutes later, the car pulls up to the Bluebird Cafe.

"I've always wanted to go here," Baylor murmurs softly.

"You've never been?"

She shakes her head. "That probably sounds crazy, considering I've lived here for years, but I've never gotten around to it. I'm glad my first time will be with you, though." Her face immediately reddens, like what she said made her feel awkward.

"Honored to take your Bluebird Cafe virginity." My teasing probably doesn't help any, but I can't resist.

Baylor just shakes her head, playfully rolling her eyes with a subtle smile on her face.

"Come on, let's go inside." I race around the car to open the door before she can and offer her my hand. I help her out of the car, then instead of dropping her hand, I interlock our fingers. When she looks at me this time, there's no confusion in her expression, just what looks like pure contentment.

There isn't a huge crowd yet when we walk through the doors. Enough people that only one table is available, but not so many that the building is packed and there's no place to stand. We snag the last high-top table just as the host steps onto the small stage.

"Good evening, everyone! If you've never been here, welcome, and if this isn't your first time, welcome back. We've got a full lineup of singers for open-mic night."

Leaning in toward Baylor, I whisper in her ear. "I signed you up, darlin'. Better think of which song you're going to perform, because it's all original content." Maybe it was wrong to put her on the spot, but I know she writes and I have no doubts that she's talented.

She whips her head toward me. "You did *what*?"

I shrug. "I signed you up."

Her eyes blink rapidly as she aggressively shakes her head, like she's trying to wake herself up from a dream. "I-I don't have anything prepared. I—" I can tell she's panicking, but I've seen the journal she carries around. She's ready for this, ready to be a singer and songwriter. She just needs a little push. That's where I come in.

"Hey, relax. It's okay. You're going to be great. Play the song you know best."

"I don't know if I have it in me."

"You do, Baylor. I wouldn't have asked you on this date if I didn't believe in you and your abilities. Now you have to trust yourself."

During the first few singers' performances, I catch Baylor shaking her leg and continuously stirring her drink.

"You don't have to go up there if you don't want to, but I think—no, I *know* you're going to be incredible, and everyone else is going to think so, too."

"I just don't know if I can measure up to some of these songwriters. I mean, that last girl was amazing. Her lyrics were so poetic." Her gaze softens as her eyes shift to the right then down to her feet.

"Next up, we have Baylor!" the host interrupts.

I give Baylor an encouraging nod, and she hops down from her stool, gingerly walking to the stage. She grabs the guitar already there for performers to borrow if needed, pulls the stool away from the mic stand, and sits.

"H-hi, everyone. My name's Baylor." Her voice shakes slightly, but she clears her throat and slowly starts to strum chords as she looks around the crowd.

I can't read her expression, but it looks like nerves. Whatever it is, though, melts away when she begins the first verse.

Like a rose that's never seen the light, they blinded
your heart to make you feel like you're less than
you are.
The words they say behind closed doors make you
feel so small.

The entire café is silent, no one daring to make a sound as her voice fills the room. There's a slight crackle to it, like the words bring up deep emotion.

Always thinking that you must compete with the
people next to you.
Boys be careful, did no one tell you the nice guys
always lose?
Succeed and you're too conceited but fail and they
think you're weak.
Every time you make a mistake, they're always there
to critique.
But you're worth so much more than the things that
they say… You don't need to prove that you are.

She strums the last chord, and the audience erupts, going as far as to give her a standing ovation. I stand with the crowd, whistling as I clap. She doesn't need my approval, because she's got it from every single person here. Pink streaks stain her cheeks as she looks around at everyone applauding for her, flashing a radiant smile. But when her eyes lock on mine, it's like the entire world around us disappears and we're the only ones here.

After my solo date with Baylor, I asked the remaining three women to join us on Broadway. There haven't been many group outings, not since the early weeks of the show. But now we're down to the final four and tensions are rising. It feels like a good opportunity to have fun, let loose, but also see how my friendship with everyone can grow.

Baylor and I are sitting in a booth along the wall at Tin Roof. There's still time before the rest of the women arrive, so I place my hand on Baylor's thigh.

"What's up?" She looks down at my hand, which is resting just underneath the hem of her dress, and then back up at me.

"You look sexy as hell, you know that?" I pull at my lips with my teeth to wet them before leaning in to kiss her.

She leans into the kiss then deepens it, hungrily fighting for more. I nip at her bottom lip, which elicits a moan.

I slide my hand further up her dress, playing with the string of her thong. "How wet are you right now, baby?" I whisper into her ear.

"We're in the middle of a *packed* bar." She gasps as I dip a finger under her underwear, feeling the warmth radiating off her.

"That just means you'll have to be quiet." I drag my finger up her center. "Such a bad girl, you're absolutely soaked. Does the thought of me making you come in front of all these people turn you on, Baylor?"

"Yes. Fuck, yes," she sighs, closing her eyes. The bartender shoots me a look, and I raise my unoccupied hand in acknowledgment and flash him a cocky smile.

"You're going to give us away, Baylor." I nip at her ear as I plunge a finger inside her. "Open your eyes and keep a straight face while I fuck you with my fingers."

She snaps her eyes open and looks at me, her facial expression already clouded.

"Talk to me," I order as I add another finger.

"I-I really enjoyed our date earlier today."

"I had a great time, too." I smile at her, giving no indication that I'm currently moving my fingers in and out of her tight pussy. Her walls clench around me with each movement, and I ask her, "What did you like the most about it?"

She sucks in a breath as I start to circle her clit with my thumb. "Probably listening to all of the live music. T-that was my favorite part."

I lean into her ear. "Not performing?"

She shakes her head.

"Interesting. Regardless, your moans are music to my ears. Better than any performer. I can't wait to hear you scream my name again."

Apparently, my girl likes dirty talk, because as I rub her clit and fuck her with my fingers, her walls begin to clench around me. I continue the motions, smirking when warmth trickles along my palm and a sigh escapes Baylor's mouth.

"God, you are beautiful when you come. Wait five minutes and meet me in the restroom. Knock four times," I whisper as I remove my hand and try to stand as discreetly as possible, popping the buttons on my shirt open to reveal my T-shirt underneath. I think the bartender is onto me, but he says nothing as I disappear down the hall to the restrooms. It's a single stall, so we won't have to worry about anyone barging in. Once inside, I shrug off the long sleeve and fold it nicely, placing it on the toilet's tank cover, and wait, taking a few moments to fix my mustache.

Five minutes later, footsteps sound outside the door and

knuckles rap on the metal door four times. I open the door slightly, pulling Baylor in and clicking the lock.

"I think the bartender was onto us." She laughs as she fists my shirt, pulling me close. Neither of us seem to care, though, as we devour each other's mouths, still fighting for dominance.

Baylor pulls away, a devilish grin on her face.

"What's going on in that dirty little mind of yours?"

She says nothing, just undoes my belt and drops to her knees, taking my jeans and underwear down with her.

My cock springs to life, like it knows what's about to happen. If I was hard before when I was fingering her, it doesn't compare to how I am now.

Baylor takes me into her mouth, using her tongue expertly around my shaft as she pumps my cock with one hand and gently squeezes my balls with the other.

"Fuck," I moan as I grab the back of her head and pull her closer to me, forcing my dick to go even deeper down her throat.

She's at the base of me now, taking all of me, until she starts moving, letting me fuck her mouth without me having to do anything. I'm at her mercy right now, and God it feels so good.

I hold her head still so I can thrust into her mouth. She looks up at me, and her eyes water as she takes each thrust like a champ. Fuck, that's so hot.

"You're taking me so well. Such a good girl, letting me fuck your mouth. I'm going to fuck your tight, wet cunt next, and I want you to watch." I pull out of her mouth, on the verge of coming on her face, and grab her hair, yanking her to her feet before turning her around. "Hold on to the sink and spread your legs."

She does exactly as I say, and I hike her dress up and

pull her thong to the side before lining my cock up with her entrance.

I slide myself in with ease, and a collective moan leaves our mouths as I start to move. She's so tight and full from my cock and the angle. God, fucking her from behind is absolute bliss. I don't know how long I can last, but I do know I'm going to make her come before I do.

Our eyes meet in the mirror, and I start thrusting faster, feeling myself hit the deepest part of her. "Look at how perfect you are, getting fucked in a bar bathroom with people right outside the door."

Her face is frozen in pleasure, her mouth gaped in a silent cry.

I pull on the tails of the bow on the back of her dress then slip the sleeves off her shoulders down her arms, dropping the bodice and causing her breasts to spill out. They bounce with each thrust, and I'm confident I could get off on the sight of them alone. I wrap one arm around her front, palming her breast and then rolling a nipple between my fingers before pinching it.

Her pussy clenches around me, and I pound into her harder, faster, giving her everything I've got. At least the music is too loud for anyone to hear the sound of my skin slapping against her perfect ass.

"Oh, Dusty! I'm going to come," she cries out, causing me to clamp a hand over her mouth.

The music may be loud, but it isn't loud enough to drown out a scream like that. My girl is vocal. A little too vocal for public sex, but it's fucking hot.

"Come for me, baby. Come all over my cock." I nip her earlobe as she falls apart. She tightens around me, and it's like I've died and gone to heaven. If there was any way to go, I'd be content with it being this, buried inside her, her release dripping down my shaft.

My release follows not too far behind her, and I grip her hips, digging in my fingers so hard it'll probably leave bruises, not wanting to collapse.

She turns to look at me, and I kiss her, feeling her tongue fighting for dominance with mine. Nothing compares to her. I'm convinced that no sex could be better than this. She lets me take full control, trusts me to try things with her.

I give her one last kiss before I reach down to pull my boxers and jeans up, giving her ass a good smack on my way back up.

"Let's get you cleaned up. The others will be here soon." I pull some paper towels from the dispenser by the sink and wet them so I can wipe the inside of her thighs.

"Thanks." She blushes.

I've never known Baylor to be shy. I guess it's different when anyone could walk in on us. It's not like the other times where we've been in a semi-private place.

I reach for the door handle, and she goes to follow me until I stop her.

"Wait. We probably shouldn't leave at the same time."

"Yeah, you're right." She hesitates. "Umm…how are we going to do this?"

I think about it for a moment. It's going to look suspicious as hell however we do it, but both of us are going to have to leave this bathroom at some point. It's a miracle the cameramen haven't already figured out where we are. I told them all to take a break when we arrived at the bar, and they actually listened. But if they come back and we're gone, it's going to cause a multitude of problems for us.

"I'll leave first since I came here first. The bathroom is at least hidden enough that people can assume you were just waiting for the restroom. Wait another five minutes or so and then you can come out." It's not a super solid plan, especially if there are people outside waiting for the restroom. I'm just crossing my fingers hoping there isn't anyone outside the door.

I take a deep breath and open the door, looking around to make sure no one is nearby and adjusting my cowboy hat. *Coast is clear. Phew.*

I head back to the booth where Baylor and I were sitting. The bartender has a stupid smirk on his face, and I want to wipe it off. I give him a nod, but also a look of warning.

A few moments later, by the grace of God, the cameramen walk in.

"Hey, Dusty," one of them greets me.

"Where's Baylor?" the other one asks.

"She's in the restroom," I reply. *Can they see me sweating? Does it look like I just fucked her in a dirty bar bathroom?*

"Right on. The other girls should be here any time now."

As if on cue, Baylor walks up to the booth.

"Sorry, I was in the restroom." She laughs. I will say, she's a great actress. Besides the slight flush in her face, you would have no idea she's sneaking around with me. She has this natural air about her, though. She sparkles so much already that a tiny post-sex glow has nothing on her.

32

baylor

Dancing Around the Truth

REHEARSAL HAS GONE a lot faster than it did in Chattanooga. While it did take some time to figure out our spots on the new stage, since we're performing all the same songs again, it's much easier to find our groove.

Having already played through the setlist once gives me more confidence during soundcheck as well. I'm able to experiment more and truly feel like I'm putting on a show, rather than standing and singing in front of an audience.

"You're doing good out there today, Baylor." Charlie, the lead guitarist, pulls me aside after a quick runthrough of the opening setlist.

I brush a stray lock of hair behind my ear. "Thanks, that means a lot. I'm trying to be more engaging on stage and move around this time," I poke fun at myself.

"Your last performance wasn't bad though, either. You had the crowd enamored." He pats me on the back. "I, for one, think you'd be a great addition to the group."

I'm sure I'm blushing from the compliment, but it's nice to be validated by Dusty's bandmates. I don't want to

272

seem too confident, though, so I add, "I'm sure any of the other girls would fit in just as well."

"Come on, now, don't be so humble. Give yourself some credit. You've got real talent." He winks as he walks away.

"Damn, if I didn't know any better, I'd think you were flirting with my guitar player." I whirl around, nearly tripping at the sound of Dusty's voice.

"I definitely wasn't." I laugh. "He was just complimenting me on my performance during soundcheck."

His lips quirk up in a playful smile. "I know, I'm just giving you shit. Charlie's engaged with a kid anyway. Don't think his fiancée would be too happy with him if he was flirting with anyone other than her. Especially since you've also been dating me. He's a good guy, though. Been with the band for years now."

"How did you meet?"

"My manager, Craig, actually introduced us. Charlie was looking for an opportunity, so we met up, immediately hit it off, and the rest was history."

"Better not be talking shit about me, Wilder!" Charlie calls over his shoulder from across the stage.

"Of course, I am. Only the bad things!" Dusty sends him a mock salute with a crooked grin, and Charlie flips him off in return.

My lips quirk up at their interaction. I remember Dusty saying he didn't have any siblings, but if I didn't already know, I would have thought he and Charlie were brothers just from how they acted. "You're close, then?"

"Oh, yeah. All of us in the band are. It would be fucking miserable on the road if we all hated each other." He chuckles. "We're a family. We take care of each other."

His words tug on my heart, especially the sentiment about family taking care of each other. I know my parents mean well and only want what they think is best for me, but it's been a long time since I've felt taken care of—supported—by them.

"Where's your head at?" Dusty asks, his voice low and rumbling.

"Just thinking about my family."

"Do you miss them?"

"Sure. But I'm not sure which version of them I miss more. Who they are now, or who they used to be," I admit. "My parents are supportive…as long as I'm doing what they want. If they knew I was here, they probably wouldn't be very impressed."

"I'm sorry."

My brows pinch together. "Why?"

"Support and parental love shouldn't be conditional. They should be proud of who you are as a person, not the career path you choose."

"Aren't they one and the same, though?" I whisper.

"No. God, no. You're so much more than what you do for a living. You're brave and empathetic and funny."

"What about you, then?" I tease, flicking my eyes up to meet his. "Don't you want people to remember you as a famous country singer?"

He shakes his head. "I'd rather be known as someone who loved the people around him wholeheartedly. As someone thoughtful, who uses their platform for good. Someone genuine…" He pauses then winks. "We're still working on the last one."

The media has painted a specific image of him, but the more I get to know Dusty, the more I believe he's all of the things he mentioned and then some. He's proven it every time he's risked his career to sneak out and see me, the way he's tried to get to know the real me. The music he writes, even if he's afraid to bring it to the label. How he interacts with the members of his band and his friends.

The real Dusty is so much more than a country singer.

"Shit," I mutter, halting my steps in the middle of the sidewalk. Katherine and Valerie are up ahead with the producers and crew, and they don't notice I've stopped.

"What's wrong?" Sage asks as she stops walking for a moment.

"I forgot my bag back at the venue. I have to go back."

"I'll go with you," she offers, but I wave her off.

"No, that's okay. Go ahead without me. I'll catch up." I spin on my heels to head back before a producer decides to tag along. It won't take long—I know exactly where I forgot it.

When I enter the building, the stage lights are off, leaving most of the venue shrouded in darkness, only a small trickle of moonlight shining through the stained glass windows.

"What are you still doing here?" Dusty calls to me from the stage.

I pick at the loose strands of fabric on my jeans as I walk toward the front row. "I, uh, forgot my bag. I told the others to just go ahead without me and I'd catch up. What are you still doing here?" I parrot back to him.

"It's peaceful in here, isn't it?" He ignores my question as he paces around. "Serene."

I nod as an eerie silence fills the room. "It feels like the calm before the storm."

He lifts his head, and when his eyes meet mine, his stare burns holes through me. "Come here." He walks over to the edge and extends a hand.

I take it, letting him help me up.

"I always like to get a feel for the venue before a show outside of soundchecks and rehearsals. It's easy to get caught up in the motions during a tour, so this helps me slow down. Something about standing in an empty auditorium or arena or stadium helps put everything into perspective. Tomorrow night this place will be packed, but for now it's just me and the space…and you."

I take a step back, suddenly self-conscious. "I'm sorry, I didn't mean to intrude on your time."

He steps forward to grab my hand. "That's not what I meant. I like having you here. It's nice to let someone in on this routine. No one else knows I do this."

"I wouldn't think someone like you would have secrets, what with all the media attention you get."

He steels his expression. "Everyone has secrets. I've just been waiting for the right person to share them with."

"Tell me a secret, Dusty." I close the distance, my voice only a whisper hanging between us.

His hand slides up to my jaw, a gentle caress. "I'm terrified of getting to the end of all this and it being the wrong person. I know the label has expectations, and I'm worried the person I want to choose won't fit their image."

I place my hand over his and look up at him through my lashes. "I think you just need to follow your heart. As cheesy as that sounds, no one knows you and your career better than you."

"What's your heart telling you, Baylor?" His eyes plead, like he's been waiting for this moment.

He leans down until our foreheads press against each

other. It would be so easy, too easy, to kiss him and avoid his question altogether.

My heart's been telling me about the risks, about the consequences if my true identity gets out. It's also been aching for the man in front of me. Every day we spend apart, it longs for him, and when we're together, it threatens to beat right out of my chest and land in his palms.

I've been waiting for the shoe to drop, for something to light what we have on fire and slowly send our relationship up in smoke. The fear of Aspen telling the world who I am has sat in the back of my mind since my conversation with Daniella.

But right now, I don't want to let my anxiety about the future hold me back.

I'm falling in love with Dusty Wilder. I know I am.

"It's telling me I'm falling in love with you." The admission is so quiet, I'm not sure if I even said it aloud or if it was all in my mind.

But then he murmurs back, "I'm falling for you too. I've *been* falling in love with you."

I'm not sure what to say, so I loop my arms around his neck. When he places his hands on my waist, I lean my head on his chest. A vehicle horn blares in the distance, but we don't break apart.

In the stillness of the empty venue, we sway to an imaginary tune. No cameras, no producers, just us. And for the first time in weeks, I let myself fully relax in his arms.

Maybe we're just dancing around the truth, holding on to each other as the metaphorical house smolders until only ash remains. Still, for this love—this desperate desire to learn and have every part of him, body, mind, and soul—burning is a risk I'm willing to take.

33
dusty

On My Knees for You

SHE'S FALLING *in love with me.*

I'm in love with her.

She's *falling in love with* me.

Baylor's head rests on my chest, and I draw circles on her back with my fingertips.

"Come on." I lift her chin with my index finger then lean in to brush my lips against hers.

"Where are we going? I should probably go. The others are going to get suspicious." She looks over her shoulder at the entrance.

"If anyone asks, you can tell them I needed help with something." I interlock my fingers with hers and lead her off the side of the stage toward the dressing rooms.

"Need help with what, exactly?" Her eyes sparkle with intrigue and a bit of mischief.

I close the dressing room door behind us, turning the lock before backing Baylor up against the wall. Dragging my hand along her side, down her thigh, I press my lips to her neck, peppering kisses up to her ear. "Memorizing every inch of you. I can't get enough, baby. And I can't wait any longer to watch you come undone." To drive the point home, I back up, resting my palm on the wall above her head, not quite giving her enough space to leave, but still enough space for me to rake my eyes up and down her perfect body.

She crosses her arms over her chest, and I let out a quick tut. "Uh-uh. You don't get to act all shy now, darlin'. Just last week you were begging me to make you come, and I need to hear that again."

But because my girl keeps surprising me, she ducks under my arm and crosses the room to lean against the vanity, putting too much space between us.

"What if this time I want to make *you* beg?" Her lips curl into a devilish grin, and God, I turn into putty on the spot.

"Just say the word, sweetheart, and you know I'll drop to my knees for you."

She raises an eyebrow, as if she doesn't believe me. But when the word, "Beg," leaves her lips, not only do I fall to my knees, but I crawl to her like I've been stranded in a desert, dying of thirst, and she's the last drop of water.

"Believe me now?" I tilt my head up from my position on the ground as my hand skims her leg from her ankle to her knee. Instead of answering me, she slides her hand up the side of my neck to my jaw. My mouth gapes as I look at her through my eyelashes and she drags her thumb down my bottom lip until the tip of her fingernail pulls at the skin.

Fuck, it's hot.

It's even hotter when she drawls, "Are you just going to stay there or are you going to say something?" and pushes my hand off her knee.

"Please, Baylor, let me make you come. Let me make you feel good."

Her hand still rests on my jaw, but in a smooth, subtle movement she grabs my chin and lightly tugs so my head falls back. I grab the crown of my cowboy hat, taking it off then placing it on the counter.

"Can I please touch you?"

"Yes," she breathes out. "Please."

I waste no time as I rise to my knees and my hands glide up to her waist. "Is this okay?"

She nods, and my fingers unclasp the button on her jeans and slowly pull the zipper. Hooking my fingers into the waistband, I slide the fabric down her thighs, revealing gooseflesh-covered skin and lace. I pull her jeans down the rest of the way, and she steps out so I can toss them aside.

One hand cups her ass and the other holds the outside of her leg as I pepper kisses along the inside of her thigh. Baylor sucks in a breath as I lightly nip the sensitive skin.

"Stop teasing," she whimpers.

"As you wish. Lean back on the vanity," I instruct as I remove her underwear and nudge her left leg to the side, widening her stance so I can settle myself between her legs.

She does as I ask, and I hook one of her legs over my shoulder as I run my finger along her entrance then slowly insert one finger while circling her clit with my thumb.

"You're so perfect, drenched like this for me and I've hardly even touched you."

She lets out a soft hum as I add another finger, curling them inside her. Before I can move, her hand is in my hair, tugging on the strands while simultaneously pushing my face toward her.

Say less, I think as I swipe my tongue along her pussy.

Her grip tightens as a needy moan escapes her lips,

urging me to continue, alternating between flicking and sucking her clit.

"Fuck, Dusty," she moans. "You're so good."

My dick twitches at the praise she's giving me, and it only makes me want to give her more. I remove my fingers and unlatch my mouth for a second, despite her protests and plea for me to come back.

But when I lift her other leg so she's straddling my shoulders, she clamps her mouth shut. I sit a little straighter so her ass sits on the edge of the counter instead of her back leaning against it.

"You're heaven. Come for me, baby," I purr, burying my face between her legs.

Her pants quickly turn into shattered breaths, which turn into whimpers then desperate cries not to stop. All the blood in my body rushes to my groin when she knots her fingers in my hair and her thighs close around my head. Death by pussy would be the way to go, yet I push them apart as I suck her clit into my mouth while pumping my fingers.

"Keep going. I'm going to come," escapes her lips before her body tenses and her thighs start to tremble around me. She bucks her hips against my face, and I grab her hips tighter so she can't pull away. When she comes down from her high, I'm still there, cleaning up every drop of her.

I pull away, taking a moment to admire her—flushed cheeks, a glowy sheen of sweat on her skin, and parted lips taking ragged breaths—before standing. My cock is rock hard, straining against my jeans. I need to be inside her, need to feel her clenching around me.

I remove her shirt then carefully unclasp her bra,

letting it fall to the floor. Dragging a knuckle over her nipple, I rasp in her ear, "I'm going to fuck you now."

"Don't hold back. I want all of you," she murmurs as she traces her fingers over my stomach. Baylor grabs the hem of my shirt and yanks it over my head.

I answer by unzipping my jeans and pulling my boxers down with the denim, letting my cock spring free. After swiping my fingers through Baylor's slit, wetting my fingers with her release, I stroke myself a few times.

"Hop down and face the mirror," I tell her. She gives me a curious glance, but doesn't argue with my request. Once she's turned round, I nudge her legs apart with my feet. "Lean forward, baby." I plant a kiss on the nape of her neck before brushing the head of my cock against her clit, guiding it down to line myself up with her entrance and slowly pushing myself inside.

She lets out a shaky breath, and I inch myself further until I'm buried to the hilt, her pussy stretching to fit my length. My hands grip the counter as I slowly start to thrust, pulling out for a moment then sliding myself back in.

"We fit together perfectly," I sigh into her ear. "Look at how well you take me."

Her eyes snap up to the mirror, and she bites her lip as she palms her breast, tracing her nipple. The sight alone is enough to get me off, so I slow my pace for a moment before wrapping her hair around my fist and pulling as I pound into her.

Baylor's eyes roll back when I bring my free hand to her front, adding pressure to her clit. Skin slapping against skin echoes in the empty dressing room. I let go of her hair to weave my fingers with hers as her eyes meet mine in the mirror.

She pushes her ass against me, matching me thrust-for-thrust in rhythm and intensity.

"I'm close," I choke out.

Our bodies work in unison, claiming each other as her sweet cries pierce the room and we both come undone, the warmth of my release filling her.

My head finds the crook of her neck, and we stay there, neither of us wanting to separate. My chest heaves against her back and sweat rolls down my cheeks, but I need this moment with her to last.

"Baylor," I press my lips against her neck, humming her name.

"Yeah?"

"Nothing." I let out a content sigh. It's not nothing, though. There's always been *something* between us, and I think I realize what it is then.

Baylor's always felt familiar. Whether it was our back and forth banter, or singing together, or just lying in the dark, holding each other. She reminds me what I want my future to look like. What my future *could* look like.

She feels like home.

the confessionals

Producer: You look happy.

Baylor: I am. I really am.

Producer: Do you think you'll make it to the end?

Baylor: I'm not sure. But I'm starting to think maybe I could.

34
baylor

Scandal

I HAVEN'T SEEN Dusty all morning. After our night in the dressing room, he walked me back to the hotel. We shockingly didn't run into any producers. But this trip, the contestants all have roommates, so Dusty wasn't able to sneak into my room and I wasn't going to try to sneak into his. It was too risky.

When I got back to my room, Sage was sprawled out on her bed, drool rolling down the side of her mouth. She left the lights on, so I got ready for bed, turned them out, and went to sleep. It's probably best she wasn't awake. Allowed me to avoid a potentially awkward interrogation.

We don't have to be at the concert venue until four this afternoon. Doors will open around five thirty and the show starts at seven, so it gives us plenty of time to relax. The producers offered to accompany us if we wanted to walk around and explore, but we're all exhausted from the day before, some of us (me) more than others and in different ways. The spot between my legs is still sore, and I wouldn't be surprised if I found small purple marks peppered around my body.

Katherine, Valerie, Sage, and I all sit at a table in the hotel restaurant.

"I can't believe it's already been eight weeks," Valerie mumbles between bites of her eggs benedict. "It feels like we just started."

"It's kind of bittersweet that there are only two weeks left of the show. But then again, that's only for two of us," Katherine replies a bit sadly.

"I wish all of us could get record deals and go on tour with Dusty," Sage adds, but there's some humor to her voice. "We could all just be country music sister-wives."

That gets a laugh out of everyone, at least for a brief moment. But it ends when Katherine whispers, "Who do you think will go home this week?"

It's the question everyone's been thinking, but we've all been too scared to ask.

The group falls silent. If Aspen were here, she'd have an opinion and would unabashedly share it. But she's not here, and there's an air of mutual love and respect within our group.

"It could be any one of us," I dare to answer. "It's going to be a tough decision."

The girls all nod in agreement.

"We'll all have to do our absolute best," Valerie agrees. "Luckily, we've already performed the set once, though."

The rest of the girls have already left the dressing room to wait backstage, but as I'm adding the finishing touches on my hair, someone knocks at the door.

"Come in!" I call out, not bothering to get up to let them in.

"How's my girl?" The mirror's reflection shows Dusty leaning against the door frame.

"I'm not your *only* girl." I playfully roll my eyes.

He walks over, letting the door shut, and wraps his arms around my shoulders. "No, but you're my *favorite* girl."

"I don't think you're supposed to be saying that kind of stuff. Takes away all the mystery."

"It's not a mystery that I've been falling in love with you for weeks now, Baylor. It's not a mystery that you occupy every corner of my mind." He brushes my hair to one side, and his lips move down my neck, placing gentle kisses that send shivers down my spine.

"It needs to be a mystery. You know, for the viewers…" I trail off, because what I'm saying isn't something a contestant would say.

"I'm afraid I can't pretend when it comes to you. You look absolutely stunning, by the way." With a gentle brush of his knuckles on my cheek, he heads toward the door. "I'll see you out there, darlin'."

My heart races in my chest. I'm not sure I've been able to pretend with him either. Not for a while, at least. I know this was all supposed to be fake and I wasn't supposed to fall in love with him, but it's not a game to me anymore. I'm not sure if it ever was. I close my eyes and take a deep breath to compose myself, fluff my hair one more time, then head toward the stage with my head held high.

"How are y'all doing tonight, Atlanta?" Jarrod waves as he struts out on stage, microphone in hand. "This is our second leg on the *Heart Strings* tour, and I know I can speak for the ladies and Dusty when I say we are so honored to be here. You'll be spending the next couple hours with us, so I hope you all thoroughly enjoy the show."

When Jarrod exits the stage, the lights go out—the cue for the four of us to go out and take our places.

The opening number goes perfectly, even smoother than the show in Chattanooga. My confidence has definitely improved since the first rehearsal for the tour, and I can only hope the viewers see that.

All of us except Katherine exit the stage, and Sage grabs my hand when we're out of the audience's view.

"You were amazing out there, Bay." She gently squeezes. "If it's not me tonight that makes it, I really hope it's you."

"What do you mean? You don't think we'll both make it?"

"Katherine and Valerie are going to make it. That's a no-brainer. I've seen the way Dusty interacts with them. He's smitten."

My stomach drops a little at the thought of Dusty having a strong relationship with them. But she's right. From what they've told us about their dates, the producers are setting them up to be the final two. The worst part is that even though we're friends, we're all competing for him.

It's kind of fucked up if I think about it too much. If I don't win, I don't think I can ever watch the show back. Even if I win, I'm not sure if I can watch it. It'll hurt to see Dusty kissing other women knowing what we've been doing behind the scenes.

"Mhm, yeah." I try not to sound wounded, but I don't think I succeed.

"I'm so sorry, Baylor, I didn't want to make you feel bad," Sage apologizes quickly, guilt laced in her words.

I place my hand on her shoulder. "Don't worry, you're

not. We all knew what we signed up for, right? I think you're on soon, you should probably get ready."

She purses her lips but then nods, even as her eyes glass over like reflective pools of sadness. And when Katherine kills her performance, earning a standing ovation from the crowd, I worry Sage might be right. If Katherine and Valerie both move on—something that's looking more and more likely to happen—it's going to be a battle between me and Sage tonight for the final spot.

Sage and Katherine trade spots on stage, and Sage begins her solo. Her vocals start off wobbly, but she finds her rhythm soon enough that I don't think many people notice. I wonder if she's as nervous as I am with the elimination hanging over our heads.

"How are you feeling about tonight?" Valerie sidles up to me. Her normally bouncy curls are straightened today, and the corners of her eyes are brightened with white eyeliner and highlighter.

Jealousy pricks at my skin when I look at her. She's *beautiful*. There's never been a doubt about that. I wouldn't be surprised if Dusty's label would want him to pick her. She's incredibly talented and would no doubt make her mark in the genre. They'd be remiss to let someone like her go. And she deserves it, arguably more than anyone else here.

"Baylor?" She raises a perfectly shaped brow.

What the hell am I thinking? Valerie's been nothing but kind and supportive of me, even in this competitive environment.

"I'm sorry, I'm just feeling overwhelmed," I admit. "The elimination is stressing me out. And I don't know, I was kind of jealous of you for a second." I choke out a laugh, but not because I think it's funny.

Valerie doesn't give me any pity laughs. "You're so talented, Baylor. Of course, all of us want to make it to next week, but I don't think you have anything to worry about. What you have with Dusty is special. I can see it in his eyes."

"Sage thinks you and Katherine will make it. She says Dusty is smitten with you both." I don't know why I said that. I'm not trying to discredit or invalidate their talents at all or throw Sage under the bus, but I think Valerie needs to hear that she's just as loved.

But she shakes her head. "Dusty may admire me and Katherine, but our relationships with him are nothing compared to what you two have."

I wonder if she knows something I don't, but I don't have time to ask, because Sage finishes up her song and one of the stagehands pulls me away.

I blink to adjust my eyes to the spotlights when I step out on stage. My song starts out with a simple guitar-picking pattern, and before I get to the microphone stand, Charlie is already playing it on a loop. He knows to give me as much time as I need before the song starts.

"Atlanta, you look amazing tonight!" I give the audience my biggest smile, even as nerves eat away at my stomach. I turn to the band and nod before moving right into the first verse.

The song I chose to perform tells the story of a breakup and the aftermath of a relationship. How everyone—media, friends, family—talks about the happy moments involved with falling in love and how beautiful it all is. But the song argues that love is weird and messy. The lyrics capture the reality of moving on from heartbreak and the acceptance that comes later. Slow drums enter on the chorus, creating cinematic imagery and emotional depth.

My voice cracks during the bridge, but I keep going, even as tears well in my eyes and threaten to fall. The song is my own recognition that I'm not the same person I was when I started the show and I won't be the same person after it ends. As bittersweet as it is to sing about, it's also healing.

When I look to the left wing, Colette is standing with her arms crossed, watching me. I don't let it throw me off, though, even when she raises her cell phone to her ear and shifts her body so no one can read her lips. I close my eyes and grab the microphone with both hands, singing the final verse of the song like it's the last time I'll ever perform. When I open my eyes again, she's gone.

The last line of the song leaves my lips and the guitar fades out, all while the crowd leaps to their feet. I blow a kiss to the audience, their cheers still echoing throughout the venue long after I exit the stage.

The rest of the concert flies by. I don't see Colette backstage for the remainder of the show, but a nagging feeling in my stomach tells me there is a reason she made an appearance for my song and no one else's.

"Ladies, after your closing number, you'll stay on stage and the elimination will take place immediately," a producer chirps in my earpiece. "Remember, the concert is being aired, so live voting will be taking place for the bottom two."

I do my best to clear my mind and not think about the

elimination during our final group performance, but my breathing quickens when Jarrod joins us.

"Ladies and gentlemen, tonight there will be an elimination. Dusty will choose two women who he would like to continue in the competition, and you will have an opportunity to vote to save your favorite contestant."

Right on cue, Dusty emerges from the right wing. He gives me an encouraging smile, and while I'm sure the intent was to help me relax, it only stirs the butterflies in my stomach.

"Dusty, who are the first two women you would like to—"

"Miss! Excuse me, you can't be on stage!" My head snaps to the right as I look off-stage where Aspen is strolling up without any regard for the producer who is yelling at her.

"Oh, trust me. The viewers are going to want to hear this." Her eyes shoot daggers as the producer stands down. Anything for dramatic television, right?

"What are you doing here?" Dusty meets her in the middle of the stage, his posture rigid and challenging. "You were sent home for a reason, Aspen."

"Yeah, and the person who you're apparently obsessed with shouldn't even be here." She gestures at me.

Oh no. God, no, please.

"What are you talking about?" Threads of accusation lace through Dusty's voice. He still has no idea.

"She's a fucking plant, Dusty. She was never here for you."

At this point, the producers are panicking, wanting to get Aspen out of here as quickly as possible. Silence falls over the live audience as they watch everything unfurl in front of them. As they process the nuclear bomb that was just dropped on everyone.

"Someone get her off the stage!" If anyone doubted what Aspen said, the reaction from the producers likely made them change their minds. It's obvious to anyone that they're trying to cover it up.

A producer runs up and grabs Aspen's arm to remove her from the premises, and she doesn't resist. She's already done her job. The damage was done, and I know I'm going to have to deal with the fallout.

"Dusty, we need you to choose who you would like to move on," the director cues him in our ears.

He looks at me with a pained expression, but it's only there for a split second before he sighs and looks at the four of us. "Valerie and…Katherine."

Sage and I look at each other.

"I'm so sorry," I mouth at her, because words won't come out. She doesn't say anything but squeezes my hand once before letting go.

"Live voting, starting in three, two, one."

The clock is running down, and the stage screen behind us shows the running tally of results.

Sage, then me.

Then Sage. Then me.

Fifteen agonizing minutes pass, and despite Aspen's outburst and exposing me on live television, the results read *Baylor - 55%, Sage - 45%*.

"Congratulations, Bay. I knew you'd make it. Prove them all wrong, okay?" She looks at me with glassy eyes, and I hug her before she gives one final wave to the crowd and walks off stage.

I'm left to join Katherine and Valerie. They both give me looks of acknowledgment. I'm unsure what their thoughts are. What Aspen said isn't false, but she also painted herself as the villain of the group from the very beginning.

All that matters is a conversation between me and Dusty. But the minute the cameras stop rolling, he gives me a defeated look and rushes off stage.

35
dusty

Playing With My Heart

MY MIND SWARMS with disbelief over Aspen's revelation that Baylor was a setup, a plant. That she was the mystery girl because the production company chose to have her come on the show. Even if I thought Aspen was lying at first, trying to get her fifteen minutes of fame, I couldn't ignore the response from the crew. If she was just trying to get attention, I have to believe they wouldn't have panicked like they did.

The minute the director yells cut and the live broadcast shuts down, I push past everyone on stage and walk off, pressing my hands against my temples, willing it all to be some kind of sick joke. Maybe this was all a prank and I'm on *Punk'd* right now. I know it's been a long-ass time since the show ended, but maybe they're bringing it back. The camera crew out there was all fake and the real crew will jump out at any moment.

Fuck.

"Dusty! Wait, Dusty, please, just hear me out." Baylor runs off stage after me, grabbing my forearm.

I spin around to face her, tearing my arm out of her grip. "What, Baylor? What is there to hear out?" My eyebrows draw together as I back away from her. "You've been lying to me this whole time!"

"I know. And I'm sorry. This truly isn't what I had intended to happen." Her lip trembles, and I have to force myself to look away from her deep-brown eyes. Eyes I've looked into so many times, seen them brimming with lust and what I thought was love. I've been a damn fool.

I clench my jaw and through gritted teeth force out the question I'm scared to ask. "Was any of this real to you, or was it all a game?" I don't give her time to answer before I fire another one. "How long have you been playing with my heart, Baylor? Tell me the truth."

She's silent, her head hung and shoulders slumped, and that should be all I need. The lack of a response should be enough for me to leave and never look back, tell Colette St. James that I want her gone. But I can't. I want—no, *need*—an answer from her. Something. Anything but what I heard out on that stage.

"Tell me, dammit!" I feel awful for yelling at her, but *fuck*, I thought I was falling in love with her.

No, I *was* falling in love. Just not with the person I thought she was.

"It was never a game to me, Dusty. Yeah, in the beginning I didn't want to be on the show, I was doing it to save my job, but that's not the case now. Please believe me."

Fuck. That's how it was for me in the beginning, too, wasn't it? I didn't want to be here either. But how am I supposed to continue this, not knowing if every connection I've made so far has also been a lie? What does it mean when the one woman I can actually see a future with has been lying to me for weeks? Sure, there's still Katherine and Valerie, but with Baylor it is—was—different.

Everything in me is screaming to grab her, pull her close, and crash my lips to hers. Forget everything that happened out on stage and believe her over Aspen.

But. I. Can't.

Pain over her betrayal and yearning for her war against each other in my brain, but the betrayal wins out, cutting like a knife.

"I'm sorry," I grit out. And then I do the cowardly thing and walk away. I don't look back as I leave her standing alone in the middle of the hustle and chaos of the film crew.

I don't look back as I call a car to take me to the hotel, and I sure as hell don't answer the door to my room when several people knock on it throughout the night.

I need time. Space.

I guarantee that's not what the producers want, but it's not about them. It's never been about the fucking TV show. I know it, and they know it.

Tomorrow, we'll fly back to Nashville.

I need to make a decision, a decision that will determine how the show proceeds, but I need a clear head to do that.

I know exactly who I need to talk to when we get back home.

He's already waiting in the conference room when I arrive, but the moment he sees me, he gets up from his chair.

"I saw what happened. Are you okay?" The question is almost enough to bring tears to my eyes, because the first thing Craig wanted to know was if I was okay. Not what I'm going to do about the situation, not what the production company has done to handle it, not what the label is going to think. He's always had my best interests at heart. That's why he's my manager.

When I don't answer right away, he pulls me into a hug, patting me on the back like I'm that eighteen-year-old kid again.

"I don't know what to do," I choke out. "She's the one, Craig. I *thought* she was the one. But everything has been a lie."

"Take a deep breath, kid." Craig is shorter than me, but when he holds my arms like he wants to shake me, I've never felt smaller.

I close my eyes, inhale a long breath, hold it for a few seconds, then push it out through my nose, repeating the action until my heart rate slows and my head clears.

"What are your feelings toward the other two women you have? Do you see a future with them?"

I shake my head. "Not like I do with her. Sure, I could see myself in a business partnership with either of them if it comes to that, but I'm not *in love* with them. And I don't think I could pretend to be in love with them."

Craig simply listens, nodding and occasionally tapping his lips as though in deep thought.

"I opened up to her, told her about my family, about the media portraying me as someone who I'm not. If I'm a lifeboat, then the feelings I have for her are the entire ocean, Craig. There's no limit to how she makes me feel. But I can't shake the thought of everything being a lie.

That she was just telling me what she thought I wanted to hear so she could stay on the show longer."

"You don't have to make a decision right now. But if it came down to it, would you be willing to let her go?"

"I don't know, Craig. I don't know."

baylor

The Girls

DUSTY'S BEEN radio silent since we got back to Nashville. I was informed by the producers that I won't be going on a solo date this week. They didn't give me a reason why, but I'm not an idiot. I can read between the lines. And I can't say I blame Dusty. Even though I hadn't told him any bold-faced lies since our first meeting, a lie by omission is still a lie.

Instead of taking us to the house during solo dates, we're stuck at the hotel, which means I'll likely be spending the week alone in my room. I'm not sure how Katherine and Valerie feel about me, and they're probably too concerned about their relationships with Dusty to want to spend time with me. I don't blame them. They came here with good intentions. They both deserve to be in the final three. Sage deserved to be here, too.

I sit cross-legged on my bed and pull out my journal, because if I'm going to wallow in my feelings, I might as well get a song out of it. I also flip through the pages I've filled since the week I came on the show. At some point between week two and now, I found my voice. Inspiration sparked in me, and I'll be damned if I let anyone snuff it out. I have to continue the show with my head held high, because if I don't, then everything my parents have tried to tell me—about a career in music not being worthwhile—will be true.

When I finally leave my room a few hours later, I catch Alex in the hallway.

I call out to him, walking at a faster pace to catch up.

He doesn't slow down for me. "What's up, Baylor?"

"Oh, you know, just staying out of the way," I retort.

That gets him to pause. "Listen, Baylor, I'm really busy right now. Dusty's been a mess, and I need to go deal with it."

This could be my opportunity to talk to him. No other producer would willingly take me to see Dusty, but Alex just might.

"I know this is a lot to ask, but—"

"Baylor," Alex warns.

"I just want to talk to him, Alex."

He lets out an exasperated sigh. "It's a bad idea."

"But—"

"He doesn't want to see you." Alex has never been so short with me. When he sees the hurt on my face, his voice softens. "I know this is hard. It's not easy for me either, but I can't lose my job by disobeying his wishes. Colette's already on everyone's ass for what happened in Atlanta."

I open my mouth to protest, but he holds up a hand.

"I know it's not your fault. But everyone is on edge right now, and it's best if you just lay low until the live concert. I'm sorry."

The day before the next concert arrives, and when we head to the tour buses, Dusty doesn't so much as look in my direction.

Valerie gives me a sympathetic smile as she boards, and my heart drops. It feels like someone's stabbing thousands of tiny needles into my chest as I trudge onto the bus and plop down in a seat.

"How were your dates this week?" I ask, not because I'm threatened by Katherine and Valerie, but because I want them to succeed just as much as *I* want to.

"Mine was good. It felt"—Katherine furrows her brows and looks down for a moment before bobbing her head back up—"right."

"I had a fun time. I'm sorry you didn't get a solo date this week, Baylor," Valerie replies.

I shrug. "I get it. Last week was rough."

"If it's any consolation, there were some moments when Dusty looked a bit out of sorts," she offers. It doesn't really do much to ease the sting, though. Especially if it impacted her time with him. She must see the guilt on my face, because she immediately adds, "It didn't affect our date, though. I just happened to notice it a few times when we weren't talking."

"If I go home, it is what it is. Of course, I want to continue, but I'll be so happy for you both if it's not me," I confess. "And I'm so glad I got to meet both of you."

Valerie gets up to switch seats, landing in the one next to me to give me a hug. "It's not over, Baylor. All we can do is our best tomorrow." The way she's supporting me, even after Aspen's shocking revelation, almost brings tears to my eyes.

Katherine also chimes in. "Any one of us could be

going home. Nothing's ever guaranteed. Keep your head up."

I give them a soft smile. "Thank you. I know what happened in Atlanta was pretty incriminating, and both of you could have rightfully turned your back on me, so it means a lot that you're still my friends."

"Let's be real. Aspen was drama from the beginning." Katherine laughs. "Sure, it was a bit unfair that you got to skip the auditions and everything, but you're here now, in the final three, and that's a testament to your relationship with Dusty and what the viewers think of you."

I nod, relief cascading down my spine. *Heart Strings* is designed for competition, to pit us against each other, yet I've never felt so supported and lifted up by the girls who are supposed to be my rivals.

What I assumed would be a long, uncomfortable bus ride to Knoxville turns into a road trip filled with laughs and hearty conversations.

Later that night, Charlie informs us that the setlist and order of the concert has changed. We'll still get to open the concert with a trio performance, but instead of both a solo and a duet with Dusty, we'll only have the opportunity to perform a solo. And those will take place after Dusty's main set, right before the elimination. We only get one chance to impress Dusty this week, and the viewers won't have any say in who goes home.

There's no live voting.

It's all up to Dusty.

"Baylor, let's run through your solo," Charlie suggests when the rehearsal hits a lull.

Dusty literally walks in the opposite direction when I walk on stage and try to approach him.

Charlie places a hand on my shoulder. "Give him time. He'll come around. Kid wears his heart on his sleeve."

I sigh, steeling my expression to not let anyone see that I'm just as hurt. "Let's just go through the song."

While the song I've been performing has—ironically—been a breakup song, this week I'm shifting gears in the hopes that a happier, more upbeat song will demonstrate my range and save me in the elimination. However, when we run through the song the first time, my heart just isn't in it. How can I sing about love when everything has already come crashing down around me?

"You good?" Valerie asks after we run through it another time. This time at least was better than the first go, but it's clear everyone can tell my head's not in the right place.

"I don't know. I'm just not feeling it."

"Take a break. Katherine or I can run through our song and maybe that will help?" she suggests, already signaling for Charlie and the rest of the band members to switch it up.

I flash her a look of gratitude before disappearing in the wing of the stage to decompress for a moment.

Hushed voices catch my attention on my way to the dressing room, and I strain my ears to listen.

"He hasn't seen her all week," a male voice mumbles.

"Good. Make it happen. Do whatever you have to do." I recognize Colette's voice immediately.

What the fuck is going on?

I'm not able to eavesdrop any longer as heels start to click across the floor. I dart away, closing the door to the dressing room before anyone can catch me.

37
baylor

Snake in the Grass

THE FUTURE of my job still hangs in the balance. Now that my identity has been exposed, I'm not sure what Colette wants to do. It doesn't look great on the production company that an employee was cast on the show, even if I wasn't necessarily a plant like Aspen accused me of being. Colette expected me to keep my identity a secret and—*wait a second.*

Last week when I ran into Colette in the hallway, she brought up how important it was that no one found out my identity. She said it herself, it would be *career-ending*. And she came out of nowhere. There was no reason for her to be in that hallway at that moment. The timing was too convenient.

Like she *knew* Daniella was going to talk to me about Aspen.

And earlier tonight when she was talking to the producer. I thought I was imagining things, but maybe she really was talking about me.

There's no way.

There's a chance Daniella will be asleep or not even in

her room, but it's a risk I need to take. I sneak down the hallway until I get to her door, softly tapping my knuckles against the wood grain. A few seconds later the door opens and I slip inside her room, immediately heading to her bed to sit on the edge.

"What's going on?" she asks with a yawn.

I draw as much air into my lungs as I can before blurting, "I think Colette set me up."

Her eyes narrow as she frowns, but she doesn't say anything so I continue.

"The day you told me about Aspen being on one of SSP's prior shows, I ran into Colette in the hallway. She said some cryptic things that I took as her just being her usual self, but I think she knew Aspen recognized me. I mean, she sees all of the footage. She would have known Aspen was gunning for me and once she realized my relationship with Dusty wasn't going to end anytime soon, she used that knowledge to her advantage."

"Wait." She holds up a hand to stop me. "You think Colette brought Aspen to Atlanta to expose your identity?"

"I'm almost certain that's what happened. When she ran into me, she said I must feel good about myself and she hopes Dusty makes the right choice in the end. Then when I started to walk away, she told me I need to keep my identity a secret or it would be career-ending. And she brought up that I have big goals for myself. She knows I'm not going to be here forever, and I think she used Aspen revealing my identity as an excuse to fire me. She was hoping Dusty and the viewers would send me home.

"I didn't get a solo date this week, and Alex mentioned that she's been on everyone's ass when I saw him in the hallway back in Nashville. Probably because I wasn't sent home and she's doing everything she can to get me eliminated tomorrow."

"Holy shit, Bay. I hate to say it, but you might be right. I thought it was weird that Aspen was in Atlanta, and it's even more strange that she had such easy access to the stage. That shouldn't happen."

"During my solo, Colette was on the phone with someone. I saw her."

"What are you going to do?"

"I don't know. But I'm not going to let her get away with it. I need to talk to her."

I storm down the hallway until I'm at Colette's door. She doesn't answer when I knock, so I start banging on it. "I know you're in there, Colette! Open the door!" I was going to approach this in a well-mannered way, but clearly she's not operating like that. I should have known better. She's always been a bit venomous, especially when it comes to me.

Heels click on the other side, and the door opens to a frowning Colette.

"Go back to your room, Baylor, it's late." She gives me a dismissive wave and starts to close the door in my face, but I grab it, holding it tight enough that my knuckles turn white. She tucks her chin and purses her lips before opening the door again. "What is *so* important that you can't wait until tomorrow morning?" Her tone drips with condescension, but I can't bring myself to care about what she thinks.

"I need to talk to you. It's urgent."

"Well, come in, then." She rolls her eyes.

I cut right to the chase. "I know you brought Aspen to Atlanta. I know you had her reveal my identity to the world. What I don't know is *why* you did it."

"You were *never* supposed to make it this far, Baylor. That was *not* the plan, and you know it." Her words bite, their poison dripping into my veins. "I had to do what was best for the company."

"But you never planned on letting me keep my job. You said it would be career-ending if anyone found out."

"Your career ended when you started sneaking around with Dusty Wilder," she snaps. "You're lucky I didn't tell Aspen to reveal to the whole world that you've been sleeping with him. But that wouldn't only make us look bad. It would ruin Ace High Entertainment's reputation, too, and they're paying us good money to put on this show."

"So that's what this is about? Money?"

Colette scoffs. "Foolish girl. Rob Acerra doesn't want someone like you at their label. You were never the first choice. And it's only a matter of time before Dusty sees that you're not fit for this. You'll never be good enough. The ideal scenario was for the viewers to vote you off in Atlanta, but after this week, I'm almost certain you'll be done. Then you can crawl back to your hometown, because no public relations firm is going to want you after this nightmare."

I shake my head in disbelief. "Why did you let me get this far, then? Why not just kick me off the show?"

Her eyes roll toward the ceiling in a dramatic display. "The viewers would have questioned it. You were too much of a fan-favorite. But, Baylor, honey, the viewers can't help you now. It's up to Dusty, and judging by the dates this week, it's clear he doesn't want anything to do with you." She turns her back to me, heading deeper into the room. "Don't let the door slam on the way out. Enjoy the rest of your time here, because the minute he lets you go, you're done."

I bite my lip, trying not to let frustration get the better of me. Crying in front of Colette would only make things worse. "You're wrong, by the way. Coming on the show may have just been a safeguard for my job in the beginning, but you have no idea how Dusty feels. How I feel. I'm going to prove it to you. You'll see." Even if it's not true, and I end up going home—because as much as I hate to admit it, Katherine or Valerie are the more ideal choices—I'm not just going to lie down and let Colette walk all over me.

I don't let her get another word in before I walk out of her room and head down the hall, but not in the direction of my room.

I have one last person I need to talk to.

"I have an idea, but I need your help," I say when the door opens before explaining all the details.

Charlie smiles. "I always knew I liked you. Come on in, we've got work to do."

the confessionals

Dusty: I have a huge decision to make tomorrow.

He places his head in his hands, visibly distressed.

Producer: Yes, you do.
Dusty: I have no idea what I'm going to do.

Producer: What are your thoughts on Baylor still being here?
Katherine: I'm not answering that, respectfully. Baylor may not have come on the show for the right intentions, but she's still my friend. And we don't know her side of the story, so I'm not going to speculate just for drama.

The camera picks up another producer off camera talking in a hushed voice saying, "We can cut it so it sounds like she's accusing Baylor of not coming on the show for the right reasons."

Another producer responds, "That's too risky. We can't have the viewers hating her. Not with the current objective."

38
dusty

Unpopular Choice

WE HAVE A SOLD-OUT ARENA TONIGHT. A little under fifteen thousand people will be in attendance to watch me make one of the most important decisions of my career, not to mention the millions of people at home. I didn't watch the opening song. Seeing Baylor around the hotel and at rehearsal was hard enough, but watching her sing is like having my heart ripped out and stomped on.

I know I'll have to watch her solo tonight, but I want to prolong this sense of security as long as possible. I just know once I hear her sing alone on stage, all the defenses I built up during this week apart from her will break down. I need to have a clear head to make my choice.

The TV in my makeshift dressing room displays Jarrod talking on stage, which means I'll be going on soon. Adjusting my pearl snap shirt one last time, I open the door to a wide-eyed Baylor.

"Dusty…" she whispers.

If I don't walk away, I'll kiss her. I'll pull her in and miss my cue. So, I do what Dusty Wilder, the famous country singer, would do and brush past her.

I wish I could tell her I'm sorry. That I didn't have a choice in whether I got to see her this week. That the producers took my hesitance as definiteness and made the final decision on dates for me.

But she's not running after me either.

Fear that she's accepted everything courses through my veins, but I push it down as I walk down the tunnel leading to the stage.

The show must go on.

My drummer starts playing a beat and Charlie and the other guitarists start playing the riff of the first song on the setlist as the stage lights begin flashing like a strobe.

Microphone in hand, I run out on stage, and the crowd goes absolutely *insane*. Our set opener is one of my most popular songs, because it gets everyone in the audience involved. Girls in the front row scream my name, trying to get me to look at them, and men raise their beer bottles. Everyone is singing along to the lyrics, and even if they aren't ones that I wrote myself, it still feels really damn good.

By the time the first song ends, my forehead is slick with sweat. I put the microphone into the stand and walk back to the riser where the drums are to grab my bottle of water. I take a long, slow drink, water running down the side of my mouth, before leaning up to the microphone and shouting, "Howdy, Knoxville, how are you feeling tonight?"

When the roar of the crowd dies down again, I grab my guitar from the rack and throw the strap over my shoulder.

"We've got a full show for you tonight, so kick back and relax…or don't," I add with a wink. "This one's called 'Backroad Baby.'"

Knoxville kept up the energy tonight, that's for sure. After I introduce my band, finish the last song, and we all exit the stage, the fans chant for three minutes for an encore. And I give them what they want, mostly to avoid the part of the night I'm dreading the most.

After the encore, each of the remaining women will perform one song, then the elimination will take place. The producers all expect me to send Baylor home tonight. They didn't have to explicitly say it for me to know. I'm also confident I'll get an earful from Rob Acerra if I choose her. He'll say she's not fit for the label. Choosing her would give Ace High Entertainment a bad reputation, and I'd be risking my career.

But for love? For love, I'll risk a whole lot more.

From the wings, I watch as Baylor glides onstage. She was wearing jeans for the opening performance, but now she's got on a black long-sleeved dress that falls to her ankles, except for the slits that cut up to her hips. The tulle gives the illusion that she's floating, the smoke machine only adding to the imagery.

She looks like a *star*.

I didn't watch much of her rehearsal, but I do know she wasn't planning to play the guitar tonight. So when she grabs one and Charlie places two stools in front of the microphone stand, I narrow my eyes.

Baylor adjusts the stand to her liking and takes a seat, crossing her legs. "Knoxville, I hope you're having a great time tonight," she addresses the crowd. "I'm going a little bit off script. My original plan was to sing an upbeat, happy love song, but during our rehearsals and soundchecks, I couldn't help but feel like my heart wasn't in it."

A hush falls over the crowd.

"Last week, a secret I've been keeping for the last eight weeks was revealed, and it blindsided us all. I won't lie to you. When I first joined the show, it wasn't for the reasons you all thought. You might remember the video that went live on the *Heart Strings* social media a week before the auditions aired. That was me."

A few gasps can be heard from the front row, but it doesn't seem to phase her.

"My responsibility with Sparks Studio Productions was to run the social media accounts. Mistakes were made, and I accepted the consequences: starring on the show. But somewhere between that blurry video and now, it became less about saving my job and more about the music. About a dream I've had since I was young that I've been too afraid to chase out of the fear of what people will think of me."

Charlie begins strumming soft chords, adding a soft ambience to her monologue.

"But I realized..." She pauses. "Even though the things I wanted out of the show became clearer to me, I was still living in a lie. And last week, I hurt someone I really care about." She looks to the wings where I'm standing then back to the fans.

"So, tonight, we're doing something different. This week, I'll admit I was quiet. I was scared of what the future holds for me." She looks back at me. "But now I'm ready to fight. This is an original I wrote just last night. Knoxville, I hope you like it."

I don't know if the rest of my band was looped into this change, because everyone but Charlie looks mildly confused. Yet, none of them bat an eye when Baylor starts strumming a familiar chord progression.

It's the same chord progression of the song I showed her.

The only difference is the words.

> *With every moment, every passing glance.*
> *I felt the spark between us and I took a chance.*
> *I learned who you are and ignited this dream inside*
> *of me.*
> *Don't want to lose this love because it makes me feel*
> *so free.*

The chords shift during the second verse, and as though they've caught on to the tone of the song, the band starts to back her up.

> *The moon to the tides, you keep pulling me in*
> *You're the glue that puts me back together again.*
> *And like my favorite song, I can't get you out of my*
> *head.*
> *Something draws me to you, there's an invisible*
> *thread.*

When she starts the bridge, phone flashlights start popping up in the arena one by one until the crowd is a sea of lights swaying back and forth. Something most artists can only dream of happening.

> *I've been told saying goodbye is the hardest thing*
> *to do.*
> *But I never really believed it until I met you.*

*Even if we end up miles apart, you'll always be
there like a tattoo on my heart.*

Her song ends on a haunting note, and the audience wastes no time to erupt into whistles, claps, and cheers. Like they're trying to send me a message.

"Thank you, Knoxville." She waves as she exits the stage.

"How about those performances?" Jarrod gets the crowd going again. "I hope you've enjoyed your evening, but we're not quite done yet. We've got one last thing to do tonight and that's an elimination. Dusty, my man, come stand next to me."

I walk to the spot next to Jarrod. I'm standing face-to-face with three women who I deeply respect. But only one of them stands out as someone who I could truly love.

"You've got a big decision to make, my friend. Who is moving on to the finale?"

You could cut the tension in the arena with a knife. The arena that once teemed with energy and a roaring crowd falls silent, eagerly waiting for my decision.

"The first woman who I want to move on is…Valerie," I say with as much confidence that I can muster.

Valerie smiles. Since the beginning, she's been someone I know the label would want me to choose. And I can see a partnership with her working out. She's confident, but also kind. And her voice is powerful. She was an obvious choice, and the nods and smiles from the audience tells me they agree.

Katherine and Baylor look at each other. Baylor has

now been in this situation for two weeks in a row. And it's been a trend this season that anyone who's been in the bottom two in consecutive weeks has been sent home during live voting. But this time, it's my decision and mine alone. Not the viewers'.

Both Katherine and Baylor would be amazing music partners. Katherine has proven time and time again that she's here for me. Not for a job, not to simply advance her career. But Katherine doesn't stir my heart the way Baylor does.

Baylor makes me want to be better. Not only for myself but for my family, my fans. She may have come into this experience with motivations that had nothing to do with me, but I can't deny the connection and the chemistry we have.

And she's still here, isn't she? If she truly was here just to save her job, wouldn't she have left after Aspen revealed the truth? Why would she have continued to fight for me? For us?

I hope I'm making the right decision.

"Baylor."

Both the crowd and crew backstage let out a collective gasp. I think the producers are just as shocked as the viewers seem to be. No one saw this choice coming, not even Baylor nor Katherine. It's evident by the looks on their faces.

I walk over to Katherine and pull her in for a hug. "I'm so sorry," I murmur into her hair.

"I get it, Dusty. It's okay. I wish nothing but the best for you," she tells me. Looking into her eyes, I know it's genuine.

39

dusty

Full of Hot Air

I GOT an earful from Rob for choosing Baylor in Knoxville. The producer he called looked like he was about to shit his pants before he handed me the phone.

"You're lucky if we don't terminate your contract for this!"

I could just imagine his expression—eyebrows slanted down, veins popping out of his neck.

"You heard the song she wrote. There's promise there," I muttered.

"You're treading dangerous water, Dusty. One more slip up and it's over."

He hung up before I could respond and left me with a raging headache the rest of the day.

I have one final date with Valerie and Baylor. I thought a lot about what the last two dates would look like, and the plans for each one are very intentional. It's my last effort to get the viewers to see what I see, to get inside my mind and understand my thought process, because although I can picture futures with both of these women, the images that run through my mind are different.

Despite it not quite being sunrise, it's warm. It's the perfect twilight hour, and there isn't a single cloud in the sky. I silently thank God the weather didn't ruin my plans for Valerie's date.

She's waiting for me up ahead with a radiant smile on her face. When I reach her, I pull her in for a hug, wrapping my arms around her as she buries her head in my chest.

She breaks away from me, and I get a whiff of her perfume. "It's so good to see you."

"I've got something special planned for us today." I rest my hand on the small of her back as we continue walking down the path.

"Is that where we're going?" Her mouth gapes as she points to the field filled with hot air balloons. I nod, and she lets out a small squeak, eliciting a laugh from my chest when she starts pulling me along faster. "I've always wanted to go up in one of these."

"Happy to be helping you experience it." A genuine smile tugs at my lips at her happiness. My hope is that the first half of our date will make the second half easier.

Hand in hand, we make our way over to one of the hot air balloons. The pilot greets us while the crew inflates the balloon. It's a smaller basket than some of the others to make it a more personalized and intimate setting instead of being with a large group.

"Welcome to SkyWonders! My name is Austin, and I'll be your pilot today. Is this your first time riding in a hot air balloon?" Valerie and I both nod, so he continues. "It's an honor to be taking you up into the skies. If you both will climb into the basket here, I'll go over a short safety brief then we'll be off."

Valerie's short and the basket's about four feet tall, so I help her before I climb into it. Once we're settled, Austin goes over everything we need to know, including where to hold on, what to do in an emergency, and what *not* to do. Before I know it, he's firing it up and we're floating off the ground.

I put my arm around Valerie, resting my hand on her shoulder as we watch the ground get farther and farther away.

"You two doing all right over there?" Austin asks.

"Yessir." I offer him a thumbs-up.

"This is incredible," Valerie exhales. "I've obviously flown in a plane before, but this is unlike anything I've ever done."

The people on the ground are mere specks as we approach three thousand feet, and the sun is beginning to rise, painting the horizon in streaks of orange and pink.

"Do you ever miss your family while you're out here?" Valerie's whispered question catches me off guard.

"Yeah, I do," I confess. "I try to visit as often as I can, but I get so busy that sometimes months will go by without seeing them in person. But I text my mother every morning and night. At least I did before I came on the show. This has been the longest I've gone without talking to her."

She looks out toward the horizon as she rests her forearms on the lip of the basket. "That's what I worry about. My family is the most important thing to me. And I want this, I really do, but I'm afraid I won't be strong enough without them. I didn't leave home for the longest time, and even when I did, I didn't go that far. Nashville is a long way from them, though."

"It took me a long time to get used to being away," I

explain. "I mean, I was just a kid when I came to Nashville. But knowing I'm supporting them financially pushes me."

She turns her head toward me as she nods, her deep-brown eyes wide. "That helps. I don't want to give off the impression that I want to leave or don't want this. Because I do." She smiles. "I don't know, I guess I was just saying what was on my mind."

I brush my thumb over her jaw. "You don't have to apologize. I understand. Sometimes talking it out is all you need. And no matter what happens this week, you can always talk to me. I'll be here."

"Thank you." She doesn't lean in to kiss me, just looks at me with understanding in her gaze.

"This is the highest point for today," Austin interrupts. "I won't be firing the balloon anymore, so we'll be descending soon."

The ride back down to the ground is silent, both of us appreciating the views and the sounds around us. The breeze rustling the balloon, airplanes flying overhead, and the chirping of birds and whir of traffic once we reach a lower elevation.

"I'm going to try to land us as smoothly as possible, but there are no guarantees, so make sure you stay seated," he warns when we approach the ground.

The landing is *not* smooth, and the basket tips over, causing Valerie to land directly on top of me. We thank Austin, though, laughing it off as we head back to the car —makes for a good story.

About thirty minutes later, we walk through the front doors of my favorite café for breakfast. We have a good amount of time before we have to be at our next location, and I heard Valerie's stomach rumble a few times after we got out of the hot air balloon.

"Good morning! Just the two of you?" the host greets us.

"Just the two of us." I nod. *And the camera crew following us, but you know.*

"Perfect. You can follow me back."

She leads us to a booth in the back corner, away from the other patrons, most likely so they won't feel uncomfortable with the cameras. But it's likely they aren't paying attention anyway. This is one of my favorite places because of that fact. I can come get breakfast without fans interrupting me. Here, I can just be Dusty.

"Wow, I can't believe no one's come up to talk to you or stared at the cameras or anything," Valerie mumbles. "How did you find this place?"

"Charlie and I just kind of stumbled upon it. The food here is incredible, so we kept coming back. It's kind of a hidden gem that tourists haven't found. The place has its regulars and they're not hurting for business, so they haven't said anything about this being my breakfast spot."

"That must be nice to have a place where you don't have to worry about being famous."

"It is. Don't get me wrong, I enjoy being a country singer, but sometimes I just want to be me."

A server walks up, forcing us to pause our conversation. "Hi, Dusty! Who's this with you?"

"Morning, Taylor. This is Valerie," I introduce them.

"Very nice to meet you. What can I get for y'all today?"

"Ladies first." I gesture to Valerie.

She looks down at her menu. "I'll do the waffle combo, please. And a coffee with cream and sugar."

When Taylor looks at me, I order my usual, chicken fried steak and a black coffee.

"I'll get these going for you two. Nice to see you again, Dusty."

"Okay, I can see why you like this place." Valerie giggles once Taylor's out of earshot.

"It's definitely special when all the employees are on a first-name basis with their customers. I selfishly hope the tourists don't find it, but at the same time, I'd be thrilled for the owners. Anyway, I did want to let you know that after breakfast we're going to head over to the label. I don't want you to feel overwhelmed or nervous."

Her eyes widen, and she opens her mouth, but then closes it like the words won't come out.

"It's a casual meeting, no pressure. They just want to meet you." And I want to use this meeting to ensure that I can set Valerie up for success—maybe even a spot at the label—even if she's not the woman I'm ending this experience with.

"W-wow, I don't know what to say." She manages to get the words out. "Thank you, Dusty. Seriously, you've done so much for me the last couple months, and I don't know what I did to deserve it."

I take her hands across the table. "You're amazing. And you deserve good things in life. You deserve to be happy."

The air in Ace High Entertainment is a bit stifling as I lead Valerie down the hallway to the elevator that will take us up to the conference room. The same conference room I sat in three months ago when Rob told me I was going to star as the lead of *Heart Strings*.

It's also been three months since I've had to see the guy, and I can't say I'm looking forward to facing him today, even if the meeting isn't only about me.

As if she senses my shift in mood, she takes my hand, giving it a reassuring squeeze.

Rob and a few other executives are already sitting at the table when we approach the conference room. Craig is there as well, and he gives me a nod of acknowledgment through the floor-to-ceiling windows.

I hold the door open for Valerie, and we both step inside. I can tell she's nervous by the way she shifts on her feet and wrings her hands.

Rob isn't making any effort to say something, so I take the lead. "Hello, gentlemen. Good to see you again. This is Valerie."

Rob finally stands, approaching us to shake Valerie's hand. "Very nice to meet you and congratulations on making it this far. We've been really impressed with you on the show here at Ace High Entertainment."

A flush creeps into her cheeks. "Thank you, that means a lot. I am truly so grateful to have this opportunity. And to have met Dusty in the process, of course."

"We're happy to have you here. Let's take a seat, shall we?" Rob gestures to the table.

I pull out a chair for Valerie and take a seat between her and Craig.

"So, Valerie, tell us a little about yourself. Your background, aspirations, where you see yourself, and how we, here at Ace High, can help you achieve your goals." Rob leans back in his chair. I don't trust him, but I know

Valerie can hold her own. I'll step in if I need to, but she's strong and I know she can handle him.

"I've been performing for about five years now. I don't live in Nashville, because I wanted to stay close to my family, but I'm willing to relocate if an opportunity arises. My hope is to break into the country music industry to help support and give back to my parents. They did so much for me to be able to be sitting in front of you today, and they're so resilient, so I want to make them proud. I would love to work with Ace High Entertainment. I've seen what you have done for Dusty, and I think we could be a strong fit." Even though she's explained a lot of her background already on the show, she doesn't leave out any details, speaking to them as if they haven't watched her on national television. She's so eloquent when she speaks. She'd be a great spokesperson and addition to the label.

"There's no doubt that you're incredibly talented. We're really looking forward to a potential partnership, and I want to wish you the best of luck this final week. If Dusty's smart, he'll be bringing you back." Rob winks and Valerie chuckles, but I also know it's a threat directed at me.

A warning to make the right choice.

"I personally think Valerie would be an excellent fit for Ace High Entertainment," I add when there's a lull in conversation. "Like you said, she's talented and our voices blend well together, but I think she's also a strong enough performer to hold her own as a solo act."

"Do you have any released songs or demos that you could send over?" the director of the A&R department asks.

Valerie nods. "Yes, and I'd be happy to send some samples of my work."

"That would be great. It'll be nice to have, even if you're the winner. Helps us prepare for Dusty's forthcoming album."

When we leave the label, Valerie has a bright smile on her face, excitement pouring off her in waves, and I'm confident that regardless of what happens at the end of this week, she'll be just fine.

40
baylor

The Road Not Taken

TENSIONS HAVE BEEN high since the concert in Atlanta, yet somehow Dusty chose me to go through to the final week. He's hardly spoken to me, but he still wants me here for some reason.

After Katherine was eliminated, we traveled back to Nashville. Valerie had her final date with Dusty yesterday, so today is my final date. I have no idea what's in store, but I'm hoping it's something that allows us to talk and work things out—at least end things amicably as friends. The secret of my identity is out, and I can't change that—the show can't change that—but I would hate to lose Dusty at the end of this because of it. I can only hope the song I worked on with Charlie was enough to show how devoted I am to this process now.

When I head down to the lobby of the hotel room, the producers are already waiting for me.

"Morning, Baylor." Alex is the producer on site today, which is odd, because it's normally someone else. I don't miss the slight discrepancy in his tone. I'm not sure if that's because he's figured out my relationship with Dusty was more than just emotional or if there's something else going on.

"Hi, Alex."

"You're going to meet Dusty at BNA," he says.

"The airport?" I ask, confused. We were just in Knoxville, so I'm unsure why we're traveling again when the last concert is here in Nashville.

Maybe you're finally getting sent home.

That would certainly make the show more dramatic. End it with a real bang by blindsiding me. It's my own fault for getting tangled up in this web of emotions. I wasn't *supposed* to fall for him, I know that. I was supposed to fade into the background after the first couple weeks then get eliminated.

"Yes. I can't explain much more, Bay. Your car is waiting outside." Alex practically pushes me out the hotel doors.

When we arrive at the airport, I'm not taken to the main terminal like I expected. And my bags aren't there waiting for me either. Instead, we pull right up on the tarmac where Dusty—and a private jet—is waiting.

"What are we doing?" I shield my eyes from the sun.

"Thought we'd take a little day trip. It's a surprise, but I think you'll like it." He takes my hand to lead me over to the stairs to board the plane, and it's as if any hostility he may have felt for me before has melted away. Even if it's a temporary relief, my shoulders relax, and I follow him onboard.

I've never been on a private plane before, so I have nothing to compare it to, but Dusty's is *nice*. It lives up to the expectations and pictures that movies have painted in my mind. The cream interior is complete with a couch, dining table, lounge chairs, and a flat screen television.

"I know you're famous, but I guess I didn't realize *how* famous you are to have your own plane," I murmur as I carefully walk on the carpet as if I'll accidentally ruin something.

He laughs, and I give him a quizzical look.

"It's not *mine*. I don't own it. We usually charter planes for touring, and the company we work with let me book last-minute for today," he explains, visibly amused.

"What do you mean last-minute? I ask. "Where are the cameras?"

"This wasn't in the original plan for today's solo date, but it's arguably the most important one. No cameras today. Just us."

I narrow my eyes. "Why are you being so cryptic?"

"You ask a lot of questions, sweetheart. The original plan was to meet with the label."

"Oh." If we aren't doing that anymore, it probably means I'm not making it to the end. I try my best to hide my disappointment, but my heart is sinking like it weighs a thousand pounds.

Dusty smiles in this knowing way, his lips twitching with amusement. "Trust me, this is going to be so much better than sitting in a conference room with Rob Acerra."

"But you're not going to tell me what it is?"

He shakes his head. "Nope. Can't ruin the surprise."

When the plane takes off, neither of us says a word. Then Dusty breaks the silence. "That song you played in Knoxville…"

I bite the inside of my cheek, waiting for him to continue.

"Charlie told me everything after the show. How you went to him. Did you mean what you said?"

"Every word," I murmur. "I never meant to hurt you. I

should have told you the truth from the beginning, but I was scared. Before I joined the show, my job with SSP was my only ticket to something bigger. I never thought I'd actually…" My voice trails off, even though what I wanted to say was *I never thought I'd fall in love.* "I was selfish, and I'm sorry."

"That means a lot. I care about you so much, Baylor. I don't want to lose you." He takes my hand and presses his lips to it.

"You won't. I'm in this for real."

"By the way, I knew I recognized you." He raises his eyebrows. "You were filming me that first day. During the interviews."

I snort. "Daniella wanted to strangle you. For some reason, she let me off the hook and told me to do social media."

"Believe me, I know. I thought you were a fan. Then I was convinced I'd made you up in my head." He tilts his chin down, shaking his head with a stupid grin on his face. "I'm glad she took on the interviews, though."

A laugh falls from my lips as I think about the fact that I wouldn't be here if it weren't for Daniella. "Me too."

About an hour and a half later, we touch down at our destination.

The middle of nowhere.

I shield my eyes from the sun and frown as I step out of the plane. There's nothing within a three-mile radius except farmland.

"Where are we going?" I ask again, swiveling my head to take in our surroundings.

He shakes his head, pressing his lips together as if suppressing a laugh. "I told you, I can't say because it would ruin the surprise. We're not there yet."

"You're going to murder me, aren't you? You're going to murder me and then dump me in an irrigation ditch," I grumble as I follow him to a car.

"Yes, Baylor. I'm going to murder you then go back to Nashville alone. Not suspicious at all." He opens my car door for me, and even though I roll my eyes, I duck my head under the roof rail and slide onto the leather seats.

"Can you at least give me a hint as to where we're going?" I press, hoping he'll give me something.

"Such a stubborn woman." He playfully nudges me with his elbow before dropping his hand on my thigh and giving it a light squeeze. "I promise I'm not going to murder you, or kidnap you, or do anything illegal. And we're not that far away. Pinky swear." He closes his other hand into a fist and extends his pinky.

"I'm sorry, I guess I'm just not spontaneous." I pull on my jacket. "And I wasn't sure if you were upset with me after what happened in Atlanta." I whisper the last part.

His eyes soften as he lets out a deep sigh. "I'm not upset with you. It was a lot to process at the time, but I'm not upset. Do I wish you hadn't lied? Yes, but I can understand why you did."

We maintain steady eye contact. The kind that's comforting, not invasive.

"I meant what I said that night. It's not a game to me. It may not have been the case in the beginning, but after getting to know you I realized what I want and that's this. Us. And I understand if you don't feel the same, but—"

Dusty cups my jaw as he leans in, softly pressing his lips against mine. My stomach flutters when he pulls back for a moment before our mouths meld together again, this time with an aching passion. He kisses me like he's deprived and craving my touch.

"I believe you," he murmurs against my mouth while cradling the back of my head, slowly stroking my hair.

A few minutes later, we pull off the main highway onto a long gravel road. In the near distance is a white farmhouse with a wraparound porch and a manicured lawn. When we pull up to the house, a golden retriever runs up to the car, tongue lolling.

My eyebrows pinch together. "Is this…?"

"My childhood home? Yes. Come on, you've got some very important people to meet." He opens the door only to get attacked by the dog. And by attacked, I mean with kisses. Dusty beams as he lightly pushes the dog off him. "Hi, girl. Yeah, I missed you, too."

I exit the car and walk over to where Dusty is still wrestling with his dog. My shoes crunch on the gravel, and the dog's ears perk up.

"This is Cola. She won't bite."

I slowly walk up to the dog, letting her sniff my hand. She deems me acceptable and flops her head into my hand at the same time the front door opens.

"Dusty, what are you doing here? And who is this?" an older woman who I assume is Dusty's mother walks down the steps then pulls Dusty into a hug.

"Mom, this is Baylor. Baylor, this is my mom."

I reach out my arm to shake her hand. "It's so nice to meet you, Mrs. Wilder."

Instead of taking my hand, she pulls me into a hug. "I'm a hugger, sweetie. You can call me Gen, and it's lovely to meet you as well. Come on in, you two. Mitchell is in the back, and you're just in time for lunch." Gen walks back up the stairs and opens the front door as Cola races back inside the house.

Dusty and I exchange smiles as we follow. The Wilder home is bright and welcoming, and I move to take off my shoes when I get in the door.

"Baylor, sweetie, don't worry about the shoes. Cola tracks in dirt all the time, not to mention how much she sheds. You'll want to keep them on for that alone, or you'll be taking home a souvenir in the form of dog hair." Gen lets out a hearty laugh.

We follow her through the house until we get to a sliding glass door leading out to a back porch and an expansive fenced yard.

"Mitch! Dusty's home!"

A taller, older version of Dusty spins around from a grill. "Well, I'll be damned. It's good to see you, son."

"Dad, this is Baylor. I wanted y'all to meet her." Dusty's accent comes out even more here than it does in Nashville.

"Baylor, it is a pleasure to meet you. Anyone who can put up with my son here is special." He shakes my hand with a mischievous glint in his eyes.

"He's not as bad as I originally thought," I admit. "When I first met him, I thought he was just another self-centered superstar. But I was wrong."

"He definitely has a way of surprising people," Mitch grunts. "Son, help me carry some things out here?"

Dusty nods, and they disappear back into the house, leaving us out in the sunshine.

"So, when did you first realize you were in love with my son?" Gen asks, completely catching me off guard.

I almost choke on my drink, and I cough to clear my throat. "Pardon?"

"How long have you been in love with Dusty?"

"I—"

"I've been watching the show, you know. You look at him like he put the stars in the sky. And I know my son. He's head over boots for you. If he wasn't, he would have sent you home after the concert in Atlanta." She pauses for a moment then continues in a soft tone. "When us Wilders fall in love, we fall hard, and I can see it in his eyes. He's all in. So, if you don't feel the same way, you need to tell him."

I nod. "I feel the same way. I've been falling for him for a while now."

She reaches out to place her hand over mine. "Thank you for taking care of my son." There's both acknowledgment and approval in her voice.

The sliding door opens to Dusty and Mitchell before I can respond. Dusty kisses his mom on the cheek before taking a seat next to me.

"You didn't scare her off, did you now, Mom?" he teases.

"Oh, my son. If you haven't already scared her off, nothing will."

They banter back and forth, and, for once, my heart isn't heavy seeing this type of family dynamic. It's full.

"Come on, let me give you the tour." Dusty pulls me up from my chair.

I'm able to catch a quick glimpse of Gen exchanging a bemused smile with Mitch before Dusty pulls me into the living room and slides the screen door shut.

"I like your parents," I whisper as he tugs me along to a staircase on the other side of the house.

"They like you, too."

"So, where's this tour I was promised?" I wink as he

presses my back against the wall and undresses me with his eyes.

"Well"—he peppers my neck with kisses—"these are the stairs. Conveniently out of view of the backyard."

"Tell me more," I moan when he nips my ear.

"Up the stairs to the right is a bathroom, and down the hall is my childhood bedroom. Wanna see?"

"Mhm."

He stops kissing me, but only so he can scoop me up in his arms bridal style, and walks up the stairs. When we reach the end of the hall, he puts me down. The door in front of us has a decal that says *Dusty's Room* on it.

"Cute." I snicker, and he rolls his eyes.

"I was an angsty teenager, all right? And it won't come off. I tried," he mutters before opening the door.

The inside of his room is small, but it matches Dusty's personality to a T. Guitars hang on the wall with posters of classic country singers, and a gray comforter lies on the perfectly made full-size bed.

"Like it?" He wraps his arm around my waist, his hand splayed out across my stomach.

"It's almost exactly how I pictured it." I lean into his chest. "You're so lucky."

"Yes, yes I am," he agrees. Flipping me around so I face him, he tucks my hair behind my ear. His eyes trace lines from my eyes down to my lips and back up.

"Are you going to kiss me, or not?"

Dusty yanks me close to him, crashing our lips together. His back is turned toward the wall this time, so I push him against it, pressing my body against his. With a gentle stroke of his tongue, he deepens the kiss, tangling it with mine. His hands roam across my body, through my hair, across my breasts, down my stomach to my hips.

I grind my hips against his front, eliciting a groan from his lips. His length hardens against me, stretching against the fabric of his jeans.

"Baby, I want you so bad, but you're going to have to be quiet," he rasps. "Can you do that for me?"

I nod, because I want him, too. He flips me around so my back is flush against the wall. For a moment everything pauses, our hushed pants the only audible sound. Until he slips a finger beneath the waistband of my jeans with one hand and tugs the zipper with the other. Dragging the fabric down my thighs, he slowly strips my clothing off.

"Arms up," he instructs.

I raise them, and he pulls my shirt over my head. Before he unclasps my bra, he pushes my breasts together, deepening my cleavage.

"Perfect tits, perfect ass, perfect pussy, perfect woman," he purrs, his voice turning my legs into Jell-O. All it takes for me to arch my back, pushing my chest toward him, is grazing my nipple with his knuckles. "So sensitive. I'd bet you're fucking soaked for me and I've barely even touched you."

"Please," I whimper. My body tingles, an aching sensation moving up from my toes to my core. When he slides a finger between my legs, the pleasure intensifies, blazing through me like an inferno. My body writhes against his hand, begging for more. He adds another finger, curling them inside me. I can't help the moan that escapes my lips.

Dusty clamps his palm against my mouth, withdrawing his fingers. "Only good girls get fucked. I'm going to ask again. Can you be a good girl and be quiet?"

His palm is still pressed against my lips, so I nod, warmth pooling between my legs. He flicks my clit then glides a finger down my slit, only to bring it back up to circle my clit again, using my arousal as lube. I squeeze my eyes shut, willing myself not to make a sound, even when he thrusts two fingers inside me, creating unbearable pressure and making my legs quiver underneath me as he brings me closer and closer to release.

"That's my girl."

I throw my head back at his words, the praise sending me unraveling, panting, heart racing.

"I'm going to fuck you now, baby. I need you to stay quiet, okay?" He kisses me then pulls his fingers out, popping them in his mouth and sucking me off them. Then he flips me around, holding my hands then placing my palms against the wall.

From behind, I can hear the pull of a zipper and the thud of his jeans and shirt hitting the floor. Before I know what's happening, his palm is in front of my mouth.

"Spit."

Oh, fucking hell.

I spit in his hand then turn my head as he strokes his cock, my spit dripping down his shaft. Dusty drags the head of his cock across my pussy then pushes inside me until he's fully seated in me. His hands find my waist, and he starts thrusting inside me at a torturously slow pace. I wiggle my hips against him, trying to get more.

"Dusty," I growl. "Fuck me like you mean it."

I don't need to tell him twice as he piles into me over and over. I move my hips with him, our bodies moving together in sync. I slide my hand down to my clit, drawing circles around it, only adding to the shockwaves that ripple up and down my spine.

"Oh, God, you're so deep, Dusty. I'm so close," I moan. My body is putty beneath his fingertips. He's the sculptor, and I'm the clay. He's claiming me, and I'm claiming him.

"Fuck. Fuck, Baylor. Baby," are his last string of words before his cock twitches inside me and I shatter.

Warm lips leave wet prints against my shoulder, and Dusty pulls out of me, his hot cum dripping down the inside of my thigh.

I bend down to pick up my clothes, but he's already beat me to it, tucking away my underwear.

"For safekeeping." He winks.

41
dusty

One Last Time

WE SAY goodbye to my parents—my dad giving Baylor a firm handshake, and my mom pulling her in for a long hug, all the while mouthing to me *she's a keeper*—and head back to Nashville. In a few short days, the finale will air and I'll make my final choice between Valerie and Baylor.

Baylor lies across my lap on the plane ride home, and as I trace the words "I love you" on her thigh, a vision of what life could be like with her flashes through my mind. Tour bus rides and flights to new cities, trips to see my parents—and hers, if she wants to take that step—writing songs together on lazy Sundays.

She's who I want. But a small, nagging part of me tells me it's wrong, that I should go with the safer option. That all of this is just an illusion, a fantasy that will never manifest itself.

I have so much respect and admiration for Valerie, and I know she'll be successful with anything she decides to pursue. But with Baylor, it goes much deeper.

I've done my best not to lead any of the women on, I just pray I haven't planted any false hope.

"Dusty?" she mumbles, her speech coming out lazily from sleep.

"Yeah, baby?"

"Thank you for introducing me to your parents. I loved them." Her eyes flutter shut, and soon she's drifting off to sleep again.

"They loved you, too," I whisper.

Once we get back to Nashville, we drop Baylor off at the hotel then drive through the city to go back to the house. A producer gets a call and hands the phone back to me.

"Hello?"

"Where were you today?" Rob snaps on the other line.

I roll my eyes, huffing out a breath. "Had a change of plans."

"What could have been more important than meeting with the label?"

"My future." I hang up. It'll probably get me in trouble later, but I don't care. I'll deal with the consequences, because spending that time with Baylor off camera, without expectations, was worth it.

It'll always be worth it.

The format for the finale concert and final decision is different from the previous ones. Valerie and Baylor will not only get to perform a small set of five songs each, but my set is split in half, allowing them both to perform songs with me at the very end. Songs that the label has proposed for my next album: the one I'm recording with the winner of *Heart Strings*. It's the ultimate test.

The concert and final decision are being held at the

Ryman Auditorium, but the winner will also have the opportunity to perform on the Opry stage with me.

I made my Opry debut when I was twenty-three, and it's been a long-time goal to one day be inducted as a member. I wonder if Baylor and Valerie have dreamed of singing in the circle.

We have a full day of rehearsal, because we have six new songs to learn. The album will be anywhere from twelve to fifteen songs, so the ones we're performing tomorrow are just a small taste. I was able to look them over, and I was impressed—not that my approval of them really matters to Rob. It'll be interesting to see the girls' takes on them.

They've been practicing their own sets with the band for the past couple hours. I wanted to be surprised, so I'm waiting backstage. It's a small blessing, also, being able to reflect on my time here. If someone had asked me a year ago, or even a couple months ago, if I thought I'd be finding love on a reality dating show, I would have laughed in their face. It's unconventional, yes, but it's worked. And in my opinion, it's no different than meeting someone on a dating app or a blind date, other than it being televised for millions of people to watch every week.

"Dusty, we're ready for you, buddy," Charlie chirps in my earpiece.

I head to the stage, nodding to a few of the producers as I pass them.

Valerie and Baylor turn their heads when they see me, Valerie with a beaming grin, and Baylor with a more reserved expression. They're both wearing more casual clothes, yet they each have a distinct style. Baylor's got on a pair of leggings and an Auburn T-shirt, while Valerie's wearing a tennis skirt and tank top.

"Hi, Dusty," Valerie greets me, walking up to pull me into a hug.

"How'd rehearsal go for you two? Feeling good about your sets?"

They both nod.

"I'm excited for you to listen. I think we came up with some really good material," she continues.

"Baylor?" I call her name.

"Yeah, I'm feeling good." A shyness creeps through in her tone, and for a moment, I question where my fiery girl went.

"Glad to hear it. The label gave me six new songs from the upcoming album to try out, and you'll each get to perform three with me. Did the band show you the songs already?"

"They did."

"Great. My thoughts are to have you, Valerie, perform 'Lights Down Low,' 'Make It or Break It,' and 'Stay Here Forever,' with me, and, Baylor, you'll perform the other three," I explain. Neither of them protest, so I nod at the band. "Valerie, we can go over our songs first, so then you can take a break when Baylor and I go over ours. Does that work?"

"That sounds good to me."

Baylor exits the stage, and my eyes follow her as she leaves.

Practicing the songs with Valerie goes extremely well, without any bumps or issues. Even though she's never performed the songs before, the melodies and harmonies come natural to her, like she has perfect pitch.

"What did you think?" She places her hands on her hips as she looks up at me, sweat gleaming across her forehead.

"It was perfect," I confess. "How did you feel? Do you want to run through them again or do you feel good for tomorrow?"

She shrugs nonchalantly. "I feel pretty good. Besides, we'll have to do a short run-through tomorrow during soundcheck, and I think that'll be enough for me."

"Good to hear. You're good, then, I think. If you want to go get Baylor, we can run through her songs, and then I'm sure the producers will have something for you guys."

"Sure thing." She bounces around the corner to go backstage.

Baylor replaces her and walks over to me gingerly. I pull her into my arms, kissing the top of her head.

"What's going on? You okay?" I whisper.

She cranes her neck to look up at me. "Just nervous, I guess. There's a lot riding on this performance."

"You'll do amazing. I know you will."

She nods, but I'm not sure she believes me. All I want to do is reassure her, validate her, ease her nerves. Because she is amazing. I don't need perfection, I just need someone who will stand by me and fight for us.

We sing through the songs a few times, but I sense her confidence coming back after each one.

"How did that last one feel?"

She bounces on her heels. "A lot better. If I'm honest, I think continuing to run through them will be beating this to death. I'll be fine tomorrow, and if not, there's nothing I can do about it."

I cup her cheeks. "You'll be just fine. It's just a bout of nerves. It's natural."

Chatter from the crowd fills the auditorium as more and more people file in for the concert.

This is it. After tonight, everything will change. The future of my career lies in my hands.

Craig sits on the plush couch in my dressing room, scrolling on his phone. I exhale a little bit louder than anticipated, and his eyes snap up.

"Are you all right?" His gaze fills with concern.

I nod, but my chin's tucked, eyes focused on the ground.

He sets down his phone. "Be real with me, Dusty."

"I'm just worried I'll be making the wrong decision at the end of all this. That's been my concern since the beginning." I put air quotes around *wrong decision*, because although I've never been more sure of who *I* want to pick, I know the label and I don't see eye-to-eye.

"As long as you're confident, does it really matter what anyone else thinks?"

I suck my bottom lip between my teeth. "I guess not. But what happens if Rob doesn't approve? What if I lose my career over this?"

"Let me ask you this. Not as your manager, but Craig to Dusty. What's more important to you? Continuing to make music even if it's with someone you're not happy with, or being with the person you care about even if it means you have to shift? The music will always be there, Dusty."

I let his words sink in for a moment. He's right, the music isn't going anywhere, but what I have with Baylor may be a once in a lifetime opportunity. You don't just let go of lightning in a bottle.

"You have time, but just remember that. There'll be other opportunities out there if that's what we have to do. I know I'm probably supposed to tell you to do what the label wants, but I know you, and there's a ninety percent chance you wouldn't listen to me anyway." He shoots me a crooked grin. "You know yourself better than anyone. Those girls out there?" He points to the TV screen displaying Valerie's performance. "They're both talented. Incredibly so. But you're the only one who can speak on your connection with them. Listen to what this is telling you." He gets up, poking me in the chest.

"My sternum?" I tease.

"No, you idiot." He lets out a bellowing laugh. "Your heart, Dusty. It'll never let you down."

I listen to the rest of Valerie's performance and Baylor's. The band must have worked with her on another song, because at the end of her set, she plays an original that has the crowd on their feet.

Then I go out, and I perform the concert of my life.

Valerie exits the stage, her dress flowing behind her as she waves to the audience and blows them kisses.

Our performance blew the fans away. Even Rob praised me in my earpiece.

But now it's Baylor's turn. She lifts her head high when she walks out, but I can see her hands shaking, even if the audience can't.

When she stands next to me, I take her hand, giving it an encouraging squeeze. A little reminder that says, *I'm here with you.*

The band starts to play the first song. I take the first verse, singing the lyrics with my entire heart and every ounce of emotion in my body. Baylor looks at me with adoration in her eyes as we sing the chorus together, her harmonies mixing perfectly with my melodies.

But then the unthinkable happens—Baylor freezes, the words of the second verse catching in her throat.

Whispers float around in the crowd, none of them understanding what's going on. The band wraps up the song, and she runs off the stage, a look of devastation painted across her features. I want to run after her, but I can't. Not on live television.

I finish the show alone.

the confessionals

Dusty: I know what I have to do. It's not going to be an easy choice, and I know that. I'm going to break peoples' hearts tonight. And I don't know how to feel about that.

Valerie: I'm nervous, I can't deny that. But I'm confident in what we have.

Rob Acerra: If Dusty doesn't choose Valerie tonight after that performance, we're going to have an issue.

Baylor: As much as I want it to be me, I know it's not

going to be. It can't be. From a career standpoint, it has to be Valerie. Tonight's performance was proof of that. I know it, the viewers know it, his label knows it, Dusty knows it.

42
dusty

You and I, Together

"YOU NEED TO CHOOSE VALERIE. The musical connection you have with her is undeniable, Dusty. This is the best decision for you and for the label," Rob barks at me backstage in the dressing room as I pace the floor.

It seems like that's what everyone wants me to do. Even the producers are telling me that Valerie is the one.

"I trust you'll make the right decision here, Dusty. That other girl completely froze on stage. What happens if she does that on tour? It's unacceptable," he chides, shaking his head while cracking his knuckles.

Mistakes happen. We all know that in this industry. There was a lot of pressure riding on tonight.

But I don't say any of that.

"Don't worry, Rob. I've got it all under control. I know the decision that I have to make," I reply with finality in hopes that he'll let it go and let me do what I need.

From the corner, Craig just dips his chin, a look in his eyes that says, *Remember what we talked about.*

We file out of the dressing room, down the hallway to the stage where my future awaits.

I close my eyes, taking a deep breath, before stepping out into the spotlights.

Baylor and Valerie wait on the left side of the stage, and Jarrod stands on the right.

"Ladies and gentlemen, please welcome back to the stage, your lead this season of *Heart Strings*, Dusty Wilder!"

Cheers echo off the walls, and fans hold various signs ranging from *We Love Dusty* to photos of my face.

"Well, my friend, this has been a wild ride of a season, hasn't it?" Jarrod pats my shoulder.

I nod, clamping my lips together thinking about the drama that unfolded in the past ten weeks. "Sure has, Jarrod."

"We've reached the end of the journey. You have two incredible women, two outstanding performers in front of you tonight. One of them will get to record an album and go on tour with you as a new country music duo. Not to mention, you'll also perform on the legendary Grand Ole Opry stage."

He pauses for dramatic effect, the audience clinging to every word. I look over to Valerie and Baylor. Valerie looks confident, as she should. Her performance tonight was electric and well deserving of a spot at Ace High Entertainment. I can tell Baylor is trying to hold in her emotions.

"The time has come, Dusty. Take a moment, because this is about to be the biggest decision of your career."

Images of the last ten weeks flicker through my mind like a film reel. The first time I heard Valerie's voice during the auditions. Our date at the farmers market and cooking together. Performing with her and realizing our musical capabilities complement each other perfectly. Introducing her to the label.

But then Baylor walking down the steps and matching my attitude during our first conversation flashes in my brain. The record store. Kissing her, exploring every inch of her body, learning how to make her fall apart under my fingertips. Aspen revealing her identity to the world, and Baylor making it up to me by writing a song with my band.

I know what I have to do.

"I've made my decision, Jarrod." I take a deep breath, knowing what the label expects of me. What the production company expects of me. Hell, even what America expects of me.

"Who do you want to make music with, Dusty? Which of these ladies are you going to take on tour with you? Who did *you* form a connection with over the past couple months?" Jarrod asks, no doubt to raise tension and anticipation in the audience and anyone who is watching on TV, but what he doesn't realize, is at the end of the day, it *is* about me.

Everyone expects me to do the right thing. To choose the girl that production has set up as a winner the past few weeks. The expectation has been made crystal clear.

The thing is, what Craig said is right. And I've hardly ever been one to follow other peoples' expectations.

"I'm choosing..." I trail off to look at Valerie and Baylor.

Baylor is looking at the ground as if she knows it's not her. Valerie's looking at me. She's classy. Kind. Confident.

A powerhouse of a performer. The perfect choice.

"Baylor."

Gasps spread across the auditorium. I turn my head to the right wing of the stage, where Rob Acerra throws down his clipboard before stomping on it and snapping it in two.

But the world around me freezes when Baylor opens her mouth.

"What are you doing?" She rushes over to me as the producers lead Valerie off the stage. "Valerie, she was *right there*. You need—"

I lift a finger up to her lips. "As much as I tried last week, I can't stop thinking about you. I haven't stopped thinking about you since that first day of interviews when I couldn't get my shit together and you were watching the whole thing. You've completely captured my attention, and there's no one else, Baylor. You're it for me."

"But…why? Why would you choose me when the girl your label wants for you is right there?"

I grab her hands and look into her eyes. "Someone once told me she's only ever done what others expected of her. What she thought *other people* wanted. She thought she had to prove herself to be worthy. Until she realized what she actually wanted and she went for it. Head first, no fear.

"*You* helped me see the light, Baylor. Hell, I came on this show because the label wanted me to, you know that. But coming here, to *Heart Strings*, led me to you. And now I'm taking matters into my own hands, and I'm doing what *I* want. Not what Rob Acerra or Ace High Entertainment or America wants. What *I* want. And what I want—who I want—is you.

"I never thought I'd find someone on this show who matches me so perfectly. You see me for who I am. Not the persona that I put on. Not the famous country singer. You don't see Dusty Wilder, you just see *Dusty*. And I've fallen head over heels for you because of it. None of this matters if you're not here by my side. They could take this all away tomorrow, and I wouldn't care. Because it's you. It's always been you."

"Dusty…"

"Let's make this official, Baylor. You and I, together."

Before I can say another word, she wraps her hands around my neck and crashes her lips to mine. I don't care about the cameras, or Jarrod Stone, or anyone else at this moment. It's just me and the girl I've somehow managed to fall madly in love with in ten weeks on a reality dating show.

When we finally break apart, she whispers, "I love you, Dusty Wilder."

"I love you, too, Baylor. Let's take on the world."

On one of the biggest stages in country music, with the woman I know I'm meant to create music and start a life with, I can say with confidence that I've made it.

epilogue

Forever After All

baylor

one year later

"NASHVILLE, YOU LOOK GORGEOUS TONIGHT!" Dusty greets the crowd when we walk on stage. "Thank you so much for coming out for the final night of the Playing With My Heart Strings tour. We couldn't be more thankful to be ending our first tour in the city where it all began." He looks at me with stars in his eyes.

It took us about four months to record our first album, by the same name as our tour. The first month with Ace High Entertainment was challenging, to say the least. Eventually, I won over many of the executives, even if Rob Acerra and I are still working on things. But I get the impression that he's working on things with many of his artists, Dusty included. We've talked about leaving Ace High to start our own label with Craig, but that won't happen until the tour ends.

Valerie was extended a record deal by both Ace High Entertainment and Six-String Entertainment after the show concluded. She ended up accepting the deal from the latter and is preparing to release her first album after her EP took the world by storm. We still get coffee sometimes when it matches up with our schedules.

Katherine went back home and is still a pediatric nurse, and Sage is in law school here in Nashville. Her goal is to break into music entertainment law so she can represent artists like Dusty who are mistreated by their labels. I'm not sure where Aspen is these days. They say that if someone isn't meant to be in your life, you won't see them around, and that's proven to be true.

Colette was let go from her position as executive producer for Sparks Studio Productions—something about blackmail—and Alex got promoted. The first thing he did, of no shock to anyone, was abolish the no fraternization policy so he could officially announce his relationship with Daniella.

After the release of our album, Dusty and I took a trip to Denver. I sat down with my parents, and we had a long conversation about my feelings toward them and how I believed I was being treated. My mom cried. She didn't realize I felt that way, and they reassured me they're proud of whatever I choose to do in life. We've worked on repairing our relationship, and they've come to several of our shows. I can confidently say they're my biggest fans.

The band begins to play our next song, breaking me out of my thoughts. It's one that Dusty and I wrote together shortly after the finale aired, and I may be biased, but it's one of my favorites on the new album.

He struts over to me, strumming his guitar in between verses, and when the second verse starts, he's right there next to me, singing into the same microphone, our mouths mere breaths away from each other.

We feed off each other's energy, working the stage with the band and getting the crowd invested. But during the last song of the night, our most upbeat song, Dusty falls to the ground, his back turned to me.

The band stops playing and I rush over to him as the crowd goes silent.

"Dusty, Dusty, are you okay?" I grab his shoulder.

"Mhm. Give me one second, okay?" he mumbles.

I back up to give him some space, but none of the other band members seem to be concerned. Dusty stirs, but instead of standing, he turns around on one knee, a blue velvet box in his hand.

"What are you—" I step toward him.

"Baylor, there are a lot of things in my life that I've been unsure about, but the one thing I've never had doubts about is you. Even when my brain was telling me to let you go, my heart was tugging me toward you. You make me a better man in every sense of the word. You push me, remind me who I am when I lose sight of myself, and you love me for me. You're my greatest inspiration, my muse, and the love of my life. Will you, Baylor Leigh Sommerfeld, do me the greatest honor and marry me?"

Tears flood my eyes as he opens the box, revealing a diamond ring. I nod, kneeling on the ground with him as the word, "Yes," falls from my lips. I cup his face in my hands and kiss him, even as the crowd starts cheering.

We stand, and he places the ring on my finger.

"She said yes, everybody!" he cries out, a laugh on the tip of his tongue.

After the concert, we stumble through the front door of our home, Dusty's mouth on mine and our hands roaming each other's bodies.

He pulls back for a moment dragging his gaze up and down my body. "Hi, fiancée."

"Hey, fiancé." I smile. "Baylor Wilder has a nice ring to it."

"It does, doesn't it?" He kisses my neck, walking us further into the house. "You were incredible tonight, but the only thing I want to hear you sing now is my name."

A soft sigh escapes my lips, and my stomach flutters. "Make me yours, Dusty."

His hands snake through my hair, tugging me closer to him as his tongue darts out, swiping across my lip. When I open my mouth to take a breath he deepens the kiss, our tongues tangling with one another.

"Where do you want to go, darlin'?"

"Anywhere. I'll go anywhere with you." I know it's not the answer he wants, but it's not a lie either.

Deciding for me, he lifts me up and my legs straddle his waist. He walks us up the stairs to our bedroom and gently sets me on the edge of the bed.

Dusty wastes no time removing my clothes, stripping me down to my bra and underwear. He touches my cheek with the back of his hand and drags it down. "I love you."

"I love you, too," I whisper.

He leans in to brush his lips over mine before slowly moving them down my body—down the front of my throat, across my collarbone, the top of my breasts. He unclasps my bra, letting it fall to the floor with the soft thud.

My head falls back when he swipes his tongue over my nipple before gently pinching it between his teeth, and heat pools between my legs.

"I need you," I start to whimper, but I suck in a sharp breath when his fingers slip into my waistband and tease my clit. When he drags a finger down my center, he hums in approval then inserts one, curling it inside me. Pressure immediately builds in my core, and my breaths come out ragged and raw.

"I've hardly touched you, baby." He grins.

"Yes, and I need you to fix that," I huff.

In response, he pulls my underwear down to my ankles then lowers himself to his knees. Wetting his lips with his tongue, he adds a second finger, using his thumb to rub circles on my clit.

My hips buck up, flames licking at my toes, and I try to squeeze my legs together. Using his free hand, he spreads my legs and then latches his mouth to me. Dusty swirls his tongue over my clit then in one broad stroke, glides his tongue over my entrance. His fingers spread my pussy as he devours me.

My skin prickles at his touch, and my eyes roll back until I'm seeing stars.

After I come down from my high, I sit up.

"My turn. Get on the bed," I order but then quickly stop him when he stands. "Wait. Clothes off first. This isn't fair."

"As you wish." He laughs, tugging his shirt off in a fluid motion then dropping his jeans and briefs.

I push him onto the bed, crawling up to him. His cock is rock hard, and I reach for it, tugging on it a few times before lowering my mouth over the tip. My tongue flits over his head, over the salty drops of pre-cum. I sink down further, hollowing out my cheeks to take more of him.

He brushes my hair out of my face, holding it behind my ear as he watches me, soft groans escaping his lips every time his cock hits the back of my throat.

"Baylor, baby, I'm not going to last if you keep going," he rasps, and for some reason, it only makes me want to do this more, to have his cum shoot down my throat.

I bob my head up and down faster, using my hands to pump his length in tandem with my mouth. When I look up, his eyes are shut, one hand clutching the bedsheets, the other on the back of my head to control the pace and push my head down further.

His dick pulses in my mouth, and I can tell he's close so I keep going, letting him fuck my throat. Dusty's breathing quickens and his body shudders as he comes. Swallowing his release, I sit up on my knees.

"How was that?" I ask.

"Amazing. Incredible. I can't believe I get to have you for the rest of my life." He grips his dick, stroking it to keep it hard. "I want to see you ride it, baby."

I straddle his hips and, using my hand to guide him toward my entrance, sink down on him. We both inhale a breath as I adjust to his size, but then I start rocking my hips, creating friction between us. His hands find my waist and his hips buck up as I start to move up and down on him, skin slapping against skin in a steady rhythm.

Each time our bodies connect, it's like I'm giving him a piece of my soul and gaining a part of his.

"Come for me, Bay," he moans.

After a few more thrusts, an orgasm washes over me,

my vision fading to black as I splinter around him, my pussy throbbing and his cock pulsing.

When we finish, he pulls me close to him, planting a kiss on my forehead as I lay my head on his chest.

Heart Strings brought me so many things. It gave me the confidence to go after what I've always wanted, some of the best friends in the world, and it gave me Dusty.

Never in a million years did I think I would compete on a reality dating show, let alone find love on one. I was a skeptic. But now I know that while many things don't last, the right person will stand by your side no matter what.

That's what I see in Dusty. As I stare at the diamond ring on my finger and the man lying next to me, I laugh to myself.

I guess *Heart Strings* found me forever, after all.

closed-door modifications

For those who want a reading experience without explicit sexual content (or for those who want to easily find the spice), here are the chapters that include open-door scenes. Please note that each of these chapters include explicit sexual content that is fully consensual.

If you would like to skip the spice, please note the starting points in parentheses that will provide you with the best reading experience. Fully skipping the chapters with spice starting points will cause you to miss out on important scenes and plot points.

- Chapter 21
- Chapter 24
- Chapter 28 (until scene break)
- Chapter 31 (after scene break)
- Chapter 33
- Chapter 40 (starting on page 339)
- Epilogue (after scene break)

acknowledgments

Playing With My Heart Strings started as a passion project in February 2024 to get my creativity flowing during a writing slump. This book is a love letter to country music, the city of Nashville, and of course, reality TV. But somewhere between coming up with the idea of a country music star whose label forced him to star as a lead on a dating show and an ambitious publicist just looking to advance her career, and typing "The End," it turned into so much more. It became a story of female friendship in a competitive environment, of realizing your dreams are worthwhile and that, even in the darkest hour, no one has the power to take them away from you, and a testament to the power of love. Even though this story made me want to rip my hair out several times, and I was convinced I'd never actually finish writing, I believe so strongly in it. I hope that passion has shone through these pages.

None of my books would be possible without the army of people I have supporting me behind the scenes. I'm so lucky to have such amazing people standing in my corner.

To my fiancé, even though I've involved you in the writing process less and less, you've always supported my dreams and pushed me to continue when I've wanted to give up. You're my peace in the chaos, my lighthouse, and my anchor. You've helped me gain the confidence to share my stories with the world, and for that I'm eternally grateful. I hope you know how proud I am of you, too.

To my family for always being a phone call away and supporting me through all the ups and downs that life throws at me. We don't always get to choose our family, but I'm so glad you're mine.

Xandy, I would love to say that our writing calls helped me finish this book, but I think they actually *prevented* me from writing it. Nevertheless, I know I wouldn't be where I am today without you, our friendship, and our daily conversations. Everyone says you shouldn't talk to strangers on the Internet, much less get on a plane or drive over 600 miles to meet them, but I'm glad we did. You've been such a blessing in my life and writing career.

Nat, for not batting an eye when I asked if you could read a *very* rough version of this draft, jumping in head first to give me ideas to make this book the best it can be, and listening to all my chaotic voice notes. Dusty and Baylor's relationship would not be the same without you and some of my favorite scenes in the book would not exist. Thank you for making such incredible edits and helping me behind the scenes.

Keona—for taking the weight off my shoulders that I didn't know I needed help carrying. Kait and Tiffani—for being my life rafts when I'm about to crash out and always having my back. Delaney—my soul sister who matches me in chaos. And Ciara—my book mom, voice of reason, and cheerleader. Publishing—especially in an industry where women tend to be pitted against each other—can be lonely and isolating, so meeting such incredible women through social media has been one of the greatest gifts of my twenties. Thank you for lifting me up and reminding me who I am as a writer when I start to lose sight of it.

Sam, at Ink & Laurel, for the gorgeous illustrated cover. Working with you was such a joy. You took my vision and turned it into a masterpiece. I can't wait for it to be displayed on shelves everywhere.

Delaney, Erin, Kait, Keona, Shaylene, SJ, and Tiffani, thank you so much for beta reading! Your reactions gave me life and had me giggling, kicking my feet, and your feedback is invaluable to me.

Andrea, thank you for sticking with me since my debut (even though I'm hiring you, you still choose to continue dealing with me). The expertise and care that you put into editing only scratches the surface of your impact on my writing. I've learned so much from you, and I'm so glad we finally got to meet in person in Canada a couple months ago, even though traveling there was only slightly traumatic for both of us.

To my content team, thank you again for everything you've done for this book release. I'm so incredibly lucky to have people like you reading and sharing my books with the world.

A HUGE thank you to the thousands of readers who expressed their interest in receiving an ARC and/or reading the book after pub day and everyone who shared about the book leading up to release.

To TikTok for introducing me to Swedish candy, to Swedish candy for sustaining me during late-night writing sessions, Ella Embers for enabling my Swedish candy addiction, and to my Cirkul and Hydrojug water bottles for finally giving me a reason to actually be hydrated. I owe it all to you.

To all my favorite reality TV shows—specifically *Farmer Wants a Wife* and *The Bachelor*—for sparking the idea for this book. You will forever be my not-so-secret love and guilty pleasure.

And finally to you, dear reader. Whether you're an

ARC reader, diving in after release day, this is the first time you've read one of my books, or you've been here from the beginning, thank you. Everyday, you allow me to chase after my dreams. I'm my biggest critic, so thank you for allowing me to prove that my goals are worthwhile.

thanks for reading

If you enjoyed *Playing With My Heart Strings,* I would greatly appreciate if you left a review on Amazon, Goodreads, or any other platform!

For more updates on the H.K. Green Universe, subscribe to my newsletter.

about the author

H.K. Green is a contemporary romance author based out of Montana, writing raw, emotional stories that will break your heart then put it back together.

Inspired by real-life, relatable challenges, her books feature found families, a healthy dose of sarcastic banter and emotional angst, strong female leads, and the men who'll do anything to give them the world.

When she's not writing, she can be found curling up with all kinds of books, hanging out with her rescue animals, going to rodeos or her family's farm and ranch, and spending time with her real-life book boyfriend.

You can connect with H.K. Green on Instagram and TikTok @authorhkgreen and learn more on her website at www.authorhkgreen.com.